Bound By Passion

Makayla Smyles

Dedication

I dedicate this novel to the special woman who raised and cared for me, my ninety-six-year-old grandmother, Willie Mae, or Mama as I call her. There were times that I thought you were pretty tough on me, but as I grew older, matured, and had my own family, I began to understand that you were only preparing me for life and some of its challenges. Your encouraging words of wisdom gave me strength on the days they were needed most. When I told you what I was writing, you never condemned me. Instead, you reminded me that I was not the creator of romance or sex and it was just another part of life and living. I even found out you like Zane! We laughed a lot that afternoon, especially when you told me about how some of the church women and men were cheating on their spouses back in the days. The secrets you shared meant a lot, and they created a bond that I'll always cherish. You made sure I had a strong, spiritual background and the strength to stand up for what I believe in. Mama, you told me to write well and to do my best because anything can be beautiful if presented the right way. You're right, there is much beauty in romance, passion, and erotica. Mama, I love you and I thank you for supporting, sacrificing, praying for, and being the greatest part in molding me into the woman that I am today.

Acknowledgements

To my family and friends who stood with me, offered unconditional support, patience, and words of encouragement, thank you. I'll always remember and be thankful for you traveling on this journey with me. Yes, it has been a long road but a worthwhile one filled with lessons, trials, and detours. I love you all!

Lakisha Wheeler@KeeKee360, no words will never express my gratitude for what you've helped me accomplish through my journey. Your professionalism, friendship, and crazy laughter will always be treasured.

Just writing or throwing some words or sentences on paper isn't all it takes to produce a novel; it takes a great editor to help make it smooth and standout. Oasis, thank you for the coaching, the time you made for my work and the expertise you shared.

For you that were obstacle and headaches, I thank you as well. You may have slowed my progress down, but you didn't stop me. There were times when I wanted to give up, but being a strong will person, I couldn't see myself doing that. I kept pushing along no matter how slow or how long it has taken. In life, we all will go through things that will make us stronger or break us. Thanks for making me an even stronger person.

I will never say I did it by myself because it has taken a team in order for my words to be shared with readers. Please know, each of you played an intricate part in me getting this far with Bound By Passion and I'm very thankful.

Chapter One

As Charles slowly took off Breanna's clothes, the candlelight reflected off their bare bodies. No words were being spoken between the two of them, but a mutual understanding of the emotions present was palpable.

Standing, touching, and embracing each other, the passion became overwhelming. With the back of his hand, Charles stroked the side of Breanna's face. Looking into his eyes, she placed her hand in his and let out a soft sigh, her body trembling.

"It's okay. I'm going to love you with gentle care and make you feel as special as you are."

After speaking, Charles embraced her, and then led her to the bed. Sensual smells, candlelight, the sound of falling water from the fountain, romantic music, and warm oil awaited her. Charles had turned her bedroom into a romantic haven for the night.

"Come on," he whispered as he kissed her full lips.

He placed Breanna on the bed the way he wanted her. Laying on her stomach, her body was aligned with her arms close to her sides. Once she was comfortable in her position, he massaged her with a special oil blend he'd created just for her. With his large hands, he gently caressed her luscious curves. Charles noticed her becoming more relaxed as the tension left her body.

When he reached her buttocks, he kissed each one of them, while continuing his journey. He then patted her ass and directed her to roll over on her back. Charles took a deep breath and stared. Bre's caramel-colored breasts stood firm and held his attention. Charles sucked on her nipples, and as he placed his hand between her legs, he discovered the wetness he'd created.

Overcome by the intensity of his longing, Charles closed his eyes while soft words escaped his lips. "Ahh, Breanna."

He wiped the sweat forming across his forehead and stood up; however, he quickly bent back down to taste the juices pooling between her legs and calling him. Bre pulled her legs closer to her body so her pussy was completely exposed. After Charles played with and sucked on her clitoris, helping her achieve an intense orgasm that rocked her entire body, he backed away to recover his strength.

Pouring more oil into his hands, he massaged the front of her body, stroking one breast at a time as he stared at her naked shape with hunger in his eyes. Bre lay completely focused on Charles and how he was making her feel. They both knew this moment was about more than sex; the time he was taking to touch, soothe, and relax her body required a deeper level of intimacy.

When he finished massaging Bre, Charles pulled her body against his and gently touched her all over. A desire of passion overtook them; it wasn't long before they made love. Much more meaning was present now than ever before, and a passion unlike any they'd ever experienced had built. Tears and sweat flowed from their bodies. No matter how tight they held each other, it seemed as if it weren't close enough. Their souls engulfed in insurmountable desire. Kissing, loving, and touching her all over, Charles' deep passionate expressions were intense. Their lovemaking was phenomenal. It was a reality they shared, and it was beautiful.

Without warning, a stream of tears rolled down Bre's face. Charles understood her emotions, and he held her body even closer as he continued to make love to her. His manhood moved back and forth as its shaft stroked her clitoris with soothing stimulation. As the thrusting became stronger and harder, their bodies moved the bed. Bre wrapped her legs around Charles' body. As the intensity grew, they held each other even tighter. Charles pounded harder and harder. His thick cock swelled with excitement as their moans grew louder and louder. A long, hard growl erupted from Charles. As his dick exited Bre's warm pussy, he released his seed, completely covering her sweaty breasts. Even being left without strength and energy, it was a good feeling for her.

Just as Bre fell into a comfortable sleep, the phone rang. She pulled herself together for a moment before realizing the origin of the sound. She slowly rolled over and saw the big red numbers: 7:16 am. "Who's calling me so early on a Saturday morning?" she said.

She carefully lifted Charles' arm, which was wrapped around her, and reached over to pick up the phone. Before she had a chance to speak, Breanna heard loud fussing and the sound of children talking and moving about. "Oh, Lord, why did it have to be this morning?" she asked herself and rolled her eyes.

Shaking her head, she got out of the bed and walked into the living room. Those noises reminded her of why she'd moved so far away from her family. Every day there seemed to be some crisis paired with the recurring fussing and fighting. Before the words "hello" or "good morning" left her lips, a frantic voice shouted into her ear.

"Girl, I need a break! These kids and that damn man are getting on my last nerve, and I'm about to lose my mind!" Betty shrieked before bursting into tears and breaking out in hysterics.

Bre quickly became fully alerted. Something terrible was happening, and she knew her sister needed her complete attention. A real crisis was going on and she needed to find out what was going on. "What's wrong, Betty? Try to take a deep breath and calm down so you can tell me what's going on."

"I'm just tired of it all!" she said. "Dealing with a cheating husband, trying to take care of these kids, and working two jobs is killing me."

Breanna understood her pain. Here she was in Savannah, Georgia, and Betty was all the way in the Bronx, New York, which seemed worlds away. She knew Tony, Betty's husband, always had been a disappointment. He completely lacked ambition, and Betty never had much of it herself. As long as he was out on the town, smoking, drinking, sleeping with different women, and doing whatever he thought was a good time, he was happy. He was a man with no job, no class, no respect for anyone, and no common sense. Bre always thought Betty needed to get rid of him.

They talked for almost an hour; it seemed to calm Betty down. After the call ended, Betty's situation continued to bother Bre. Something terrible was going on because she'd never known her sister to breakdown like that. One thing was certain: Bre had seen her go through crap with that asshole of a husband for far too long. Breanna was able to visualize Betty's light skin now. Her pale and her warm brown eyes tainted with red. She imagined her sister's narrow face soaked with tears. Bre's heart ached for Betty.

Thinking about what Tony might be putting her sister through pissed Bre off. She wanted to go there and kick his ass. Why Betty continued to stay with him was a mystery. Bre understood Betty was compelled to marry Tony because she was pregnant, but he always did her wrong, even when she did her very best attempting to please him.

Bre was startled by a cool sensation on the back of her neck.

"Hey, it's just me, Breanna," Charles said as he made his way in front of her. He knew she was preoccupied with deep thought by the look of distress displayed on her face. "Is everything okay?" he said, pulling her into his arms.

"Everything's fine," she said, avoiding all eye contact.

He looked at her with disbelief and exhaled a soft sigh. After a few moments of silence, he offered a suggestion. "Let's go down by the creek this afternoon. It's where I go to clear my mind of life's stresses and worries." He knew something was troubling Breanna, even though she chose not to tell him.

She offered a half smile and nodded her head in agreement. The lingering thoughts and worry of her sister's disturbing call made

Bre wonder if she'd be good company, but she knew Charles's concern for her was genuine.

"Babe, I'm gonna go home and take care of some things, but I'll be back soon," he said. He gave her a kiss on the forehead and a tight squeeze before leaving.

Since she was awake, Bre thought she might as well do something aside from sitting around and worrying. When she thought about how upset Betty was, she was unable to avoid hurting for her. Though Breanna was younger than Betty, she was stronger. Betty was always a bit quiet and didn't mind being walked over at times, but Breanna always had a voice and the inner strength to support herself.

Despite Bre's pleas, Betty married Tony. It wasn't fair for Breanna to deal with the problems Tony caused for her sister and their kids; however, she realized she wasn't able to shut Betty out because of who she'd married. They were sisters. Still, Bre would not let the day go to waste. She had to keep busy, so she wouldn't spend the day worrying.

She stepped into the shower and allowed the warm water to rush down her skin. As she lathered herself, the soft, relaxing fragrance from her body wash quieted her troubling thoughts about Betty. Just as she finished rinsing the lather from her body, she heard a faint knock at her door.

"What else is there to happen this morning?" she said, grabbing her towel and wrapped it around her wet body. She yelled, "Who is it?"

"Breanna…it's me, Charles."

"Wait just a minute." Breanna made sure the towel was secure and covering her body as she opened the front door for Charles. "Come on in."

After Charles's tall, muscular frame walked through the door, Bre closed it behind him. She took note of his well-defined back muscles as he walked past her. Charles was a very attractive black man who would probably please any woman.

"I thought you were coming a little later?" she said as the water dripped from her body.

Turning to Bre and unable to say a word, he gazed at her with his mouth slightly open. Charles was admiring her small, wet body that the towel outlined. He longed to make love to her again. With a grin, he said, "Were you expecting someone else?" Big dimples formed in his cheeks as he smiled.

She didn't find his question amusing at first.

"Come on, girl. I'm just kidding around with you. Loosen up a little."

After that, she had to laugh along with him.

"Go put on some clothes so we can get out and relax."

As she walked back to her bedroom, he patted her butt with lust displayed on his face. She dressed in thin, light clothing for the hot day and took extra time on her long, thick hair. When she finished getting herself ready for the day, Bre went back into the living room where Charles stood admiring the pictures of her and her son, Alex, hanging on the walls.

"I'm ready, Charlie."

"Breanna, I was thinking about a few things," he said, turning to her in a quick motion.

"What things?" she said, frowning.

Charles walked directly in front of her and placed his hands on her shoulders. "Girl, relax and loosen up. You get too serious and cause unnecessary tension on yourself. You stay in defense mode. Stop being so uptight," he said, frustrated.

There was nothing for Bre to do besides apologize for snapping at him.

"Come on. You've had a rough day so far, but I'm gonna help make it better," he said, smiling and extending his hand to lead the way out.

When she placed her hand in his, he pulled her into him and gave her a kiss before they walked out the door.

Charles and Breanna were quiet during their drive to the creek.

Every once in a while, they each would glance in the other's direction and smile, but the silence remained. When they arrived, Bre was able to smell the freshness of the nearby water. She'd never seen this area before; it was beautiful. Tranquillity flowed throughout her body, thanks to the calm, quiet air. Breanna was completely taken by the beauty surrounding her, and Charles watched as she took a deep breath and smiled.

"Thanks, Charles."

"Everything is gonna be okay, Breanna."

Somehow, she believed he was right.

Charles grabbed the basket, blanket, towel, and a bottle of giant bubbles from the back seat and began walking. She wondered what the bubbles were for, but she didn't ask. The suspense was intriguing.

"Come on, slowpoke!" he said.

His movements were languid and soothing. Charles never missed a beat in his steps. He spread the blanket a few yards from the bank of the creek and set the picnic basket down by the roots of a dogwood tree. He then put the bubbles down on the blanket.

Nestled in perfect positions near the flowing water, the dogwood trees—with their soft pink and white blossoms—painted a beautiful picture. It was a perfect visual for a magazine, portraying a secluded romantic weekend getaway. It seemed as though all Bre's troubles dissipated into the air and evaporated in the rays of the hot sun.

"Friends are scarce, Bre. You're a beautiful black woman who needs and deserves a loving, caring friend like me. Don't think I'm only calling myself your friend because of last night. This is much more than sex. You don't have to be so tough and defensive all the time."

"I didn't close you out," Bre said. Her voice was faint voice; she lowered her head.

"No, you didn't close me out completely, but you tried. You keep up this tough act to keep people out of your business, but people aren't all the same. There are some good people who actually care." Charles paused for a moment then shook his head and laughed. "You're something else, Breanna. I saw a side of you this morning I've never seen before; it was the emotional side of you." He moved closer to Bre as he gently rubbed her arm. The tone of his voice became serious. "What I'm trying to say is that I want to be there for it all, the good and the bad. Bre, I want to be the man who's always there for you."

Breanna knew Charles was genuine in what he was saying, and it meant a lot. Perhaps he was the breath of fresh air she needed in her life. She was discovering a new part of herself, and she liked it. Still, she remained silent.

Charles got up, stood over her, and told her that if she still needed a hug, it was available. Her eyes filled with tears as emotion overcame her. She wanted it desperately, but she wasn't completely comfortable letting her shield down.

"Come on, Breanna."

Charles pulled her into his arms and held her tight, but in a gentle manner. She took a shallow breath and then moaned a low sigh of relief as more of her tension dissipated. He continued to hold her as he slowly stroked her hair. For the first time in a very long time, she sensed a level of security from a man. He slowly stepped away from their embrace, then led her onto the blanket, leaned over, and grabbed the bottle of bubbles.

"I want to show you the kid in me," he said with a grin. He pulled the wand out of the bottle and dipped it back in to make sure it was soaked with the bubbly liquid. "Watch this." He gently blew on the wand.

Bubbles flew everywhere as the sunlight glistened on them, making rainbows. Bre and Charles jumped around in them and laughed light heartedly like children. After playing with the bubbles, they ate the sandwiches he'd packed, talked, and laughed. It seemed as if all Bre's worries were long gone. They were learning more about each other, and she even became comfortable enough to tell him a little about her past, which was another reason she'd moved from

New York to Savannah. She was now laughing and talking with Charles while having no thoughts of Betty and her troubles. Charles's efforts to help her relax had succeeded. He'd touched a part of her that was silent for years. Before Bre realized it, hours had passed. She wasn't certain if she was ready for this to end. She hadn't been this relaxed in a long time.

Charles got up. "Come let me show you something, Bre."

Without hesitation, she got up and followed him until it appeared they were unable to travel any farther. He paused as he looked from left to right. She looked in the direction he was looking, wondering where he was leading her.

Charles reached for her hand and led her forward again. "Careful, I don't want you falling. It's already taken me more than a year just to get you to trust me this much, so I sure as hell don't want you to fall and blame me. You'd never speak to me again."

They both laughed.

"Oh, stop it. I'm not that bad," she said.

"Well, that's the thing. You think you're not, but you are."

Breanna was silent while thoughts dashed through her mind. Once again, Charles burst out with a loud laugh as he shook his head.

He looked down at her and whispered, "I'm still gonna be your friend."

"Well, I may not want to be your friend, Mr. Charles," she said, joking.

They kept walking until they reached a spot where they were able to sit and dangle their feet in the crisp water. She was overwhelmed by the beauty and tranquillity of the creek; it was perfect. Though the morning had given her no positive indicators, the day turned out to be better than she'd expected.

Charles always appeared to be caring and loving, but today Bre learned more about him. During this peaceful time, she thought about many things. She realized she'd cut herself off from people, and it had been her intention to do so. She hadn't realized how much of a wall she'd built around herself. To Breanna, just saying a friendly "hello" in passing was enough interaction.

Bre remembered when she first arrived in this town. It seemed as if everyone wanted to get involved in her business, but she put their nosiness to a quick halt. She was young and believed the only thing she'd ever known was fatigue and anger. Breanna wasn't about to take the least bit of crap from anyone. After growing up in a community where everyone knew everything about everyone, she didn't want that kind of life anymore. Privacy and calmness were all this young woman wanted.

"Hey, what are you thinking about over there?" Charles said.

"Nothing. I'm just enjoying the peace and beauty of this place."

"Come on, you can tell me what you were thinking. Go ahead…tell me you were thinking about jumping on me," Charles said in a playful manner.

"Why would I want to fight you?" Bre gave him a look.

"Who said anything about fighting? I was thinking about something else," Charles said, grinning.

Once again, he let out a loud short laugh. She knew he was giving her a hard time purposely, so she'd relax, let loose, and enjoyed herself. Breanna found herself laughing along with him.

When they both stopped laughing, they found themselves gazing into each other's eyes. There was no exchange of words, and there were no sounds, aside from the calm breeze and the water flowing through the creek.

As Charles continued to gaze into her eyes, he lifted his hand and stroked her face. "Breanna, you are so beautiful."

Attempting to calm her emotions she remained silent, but gave him a slight smile and touched his hand as it stroked her skin.

After an hour or so more, they agreed they should be leaving. Bre took one last view at the beauty, making sure she'd always remember it. She frames the moment in her mind forever. As they headed back, they walked close together and held hands. The blanket was still where they left it, along with the remaining bits of sandwiches they hadn't finished. Together, they packed everything and headed to the car. On the ride back home, they were quiet, but thoughts rushed through both of their heads.

When they arrived back at Breanna's home, Charles made sure she was inside and safe before he turned and walked away. Bre stood at the window and watched him drive off. Once he was out of sight, she walked back outside and stood on the porch to take in another breath and reflect on the day.

Chapter Two

As Breanna passed by the telephone, she saw the red message light blinking. She hesitated, wondering who had called. The only thing she knew was that she wanted no one or anything to bother her. She'd had a wonderful day, and wanted no one to ruin it.

The phone rang.

Bre assumed it was Betty and debated whether she should answer it. Overcome with guilt, she answered, although she didn't want to hear how upset Betty was again. Tony kept Betty's life filled with drama, and Bre knew it would not be any different if her sister continued to stay with him.

"Hello?" she said hesitantly.

"It's me, Bre," came the familiar, panicked voice.

"What's wrong now, Betty?"

As Betty sobbed, she attempted to speak, but Bre couldn't understand a word.

"Betty, I can't understand you. You need to get control of yourself. Take a deep breath and start over with what you're trying to say."

"Tony is leaving me and the kids! He's been seeing this bitch, and they have a baby! What am I supposed to do now? I busted my ass keeping this family together and making sure my kids had a father around. I can't believe he's doing this. What the hell am I supposed to do?"

Breanna took in a deep breath, trying to figure out what to say. With caution, she said, "Betty, I realize this must be hard, but you have to pull yourself together for your children's sake. They're your first responsibility. I can understand the pain you're going through, but life goes on. It'll be okay. I don't mean to sound insensitive, but let's be honest: don't you think you deserve better treatment than what you've received from Tony?"

Bre was amazed at how Betty was so worked up over Tony. He was such a loser! Although Breanna felt this way, she didn't want to come out and say it to Betty.

"Yeah, I know. I've worked and paid all the bills by myself, made sure the kids had everything they needed, kept a roof over our head and everyone fed. I did everything without any help from him. He didn't even work most of the time. It was me that took care of him. I've been good to Tony," Betty said with tears staining her voice.

"Listen to what you keep saying. You keep telling me what you've done, but what in the hell has he done besides beat your ass and sit around watching the damn TV all fucking day long? He's not worth a damn. He's a sorry-ass dad and husband. Let him go if he believes he's gonna be happier with another woman. You should shout for joy knowing he's leaving and becoming someone else's problem."

Bre sighed aloud in disgust so Betty would now realize she didn't give one damn about Tony. She was shaking her head, after realizing she ended up doing the exact thing she was trying to avoid.

"Why are you being so nasty, Breanna? I think you're still angry with men, or maybe you're jealous 'because I kept mine." Betty stopped sobbing.

There was a moment of silence before she continued speaking in a firm tone to Bre.

"Mama said you always thought only of yourself and never tried to understand anyone else. Don't you think I love my husband?"

Before Bre answered, Betty continued her rampage. "Well, I do. Why do you think I've kept this marriage together for fourteen years?"

"Okay, Betty, just stop. If you want to have a pity party, you're on your own." Bre took a deep breath and let it out slow before letting Betty have it. "Never tell me any shit about being angry because you kept such a sorry-ass man. Have you taken a look at the price you've paid for keeping him? You've gotten black eyes and been on a whole list of antidepressants while working multiple jobs at the same time. Even after all that, you still continued to deal with a marriage to a man who screwed anything with a pussy."

Breanna stopped for a moment and reminded herself that Betty wasn't the bad guy, and she was under a lot of stress. Bre was angry, but she tried to keep her composure. "And don't tell me some stupid shit about me being jealous of you keeping such a man. What woman in her right state of mind wants a piece of shit like Tony? Girl, you got life all messed up. Those babies are the ones who are suffering, and it's not because of his ass leaving. I bet they're glad to see his sorry ass go. The only thing he does is lay on the couch screaming for a remote control and yelling at those kids."

Breanna was now pacing back and forth as she shouted at Betty. She kept her composure, but she no longer cared about Betty's feelings. The only thing she knew was that she was reaching out to show love and concern for her sister, but Betty was making her out as the villain. There was no way she'd allow Betty to attack her, regardless of the situation.

Betty was silent and knew she'd struck a nerve with Breanna. As Breanna shouted, Betty wept in silence.

"You need to get your priorities in line, Betty. And as for you and mama's thoughts about me, I couldn't care less. I guess the two of you need to sit back and reflect on what I had to sacrifice for you all, especially you. I moved to get away from all the drama y'all keep creating. It was always one thing after another. Your problem is that mama always wanted to place you on some damn pedestal because of your yellow-ass complexion, and it kept you from seeing what life is all about."

Breanna heard Betty whimpering, so she stopped. Bre was aghast by what Betty had the nerve to say to her. Bre knew she had to end the call before she said anything else that she would regret later. They didn't need to keep fighting with each other because of Tony.

"Betty, my bath is waiting, and I need to go so I can get things done. You need to think about what your life has been like with your husband, so you'll be able to make good, solid choices for you and those kids' future."

Betty was no longer sobbing. Bre was certain she'd said things her sister didn't want to hear, but she felt Betty needed to hear what she had to say. There was a slight pause before Betty asked Bre a question.

"How can I do it by myself, Bre?"

Before answering her, Bre wiped her eyes and smiled. With that question, Bre knew her sister had taken in what she'd said. A tear rolled down her cheek as she empathized with the pain her sister felt. Before answering, Bre took in a deep breath and then released it.

"You'll be fine. Focus on what you need to do, be prayerful and everything will work out."

Breanna would always be there for Betty and the kids. Betty needed to realize things would get better once she found the strength to move on. Bre knew her sister deserved so much more.

"You need to try and get some rest and I'll call you tomorrow," Breanna said. "Don't worry too much about this, because it'll all work out for the better. You need to have faith and strength, but most of all you need God back in your life. You can't make it without Him, and you know this already."

"I do," Betty said in a soft tone.

The call ended much better than Bre thought it would have at one point. She knew Betty's pain wasn't about losing a man she was in love with, but rather about her business being the impending fresh gossip of the day. Unbeknownst to her, she'd been the subject of gossip for years. Everyone already knew Tony had always cheated on her while she worked herself almost to death. The only thing people would talk about now was that she'd finally be free of that animal.

After a hot bath, Bre sat with her soft towel wrapped around her body, thinking about what she'd said, and her sister's pain.

Even being exhausted, Breanna tossed and turned for what seemed like hours before falling asleep. When she awoke in the morning, she heard rain pounding on the roof. Lightning lit up the dark sky as thunder roared. Rain hit the windows as if someone were emptying buckets of water onto them.

The electricity was out due to the storm. There was nothing but falling rain for hours, and the howling winds slammed the lower tree branches against the house. The rocking chairs on the porch swung violently back and forth. The harder the wind blew in the rain, the faster they rocked. It was near the end of the summer, and the storms were becoming more intense and violent. The worst part of the storm was coming to an end, but Bre could still see sharp flashes of lightning periodically and hear distant thunder rumbling across the sky. Still, she was happy to have her electricity on again. It was only ten o'clock, but it seemed much later because of the dreary weather and dark skies. In a trance-like state, Bre sat on the couch with her knees pulled into her chest as she watched the falling rain.

A loud knock at the door startled Breanna. Her heart raced as she jumped to her feet.

"Open the door, Breanna, before I drown out here."

She rushed over to the door and let Charles in. He put his umbrella in the corner, looked at her with a big smile, and removed his raincoat while keeping his eyes connected with hers.

"For you to come out in this weather, I must have been on your mind," she said with a slight smile on her face.

"I had to come over to make sure the storm didn't blow you away, Ms. Breanna Lee."

"Oh, really?" She touched the raindrops on his face.

The wet, rainy weather set the mood for romance. They sat on the leather couch and made small talk and laughed. Her eyes watched each movement of his lips; her mouth thirsted for their sweetness. In the midst of their conversation, their words ended. In Charles's eyes, Bre saw the passion that filled them. They kissed passionately while his hand rubbed her ass.

He took her by the hand and led the way. Before completely entering Breanna's bedroom, Charles looked down and kissed her full lips. Kisses followed each other at shorter intervals as he rubbed her breasts. Abruptly, he stopped and hugged her, as if to say she belonged to him.

Bre backed away and walked over to the window where she gazed at the falling rain. Charles walked up behind her and kissed her neck, and her anticipation for what she knew was coming aroused her. She felt his hard dick press against her through his pants; she felt his desire. In a gentle manner, he turned her around and gave her a long delicate kiss. It was soft, long, and slow. It wasn't long before she was rubbing his manhood, and craving it with great desire. Her pussy was wet, burning with need. She was ready to have Charles to melt in her warmth from deep inside.

With Charles leading her away from the window, she was more than happy to follow, knowing what was about to happen. Charles removed his clothes and undressed her as if he were opening a gift. Each intentional touch against Bre's skin drove her wild. Her breasts became exposed, and they longed for his lips. Her nipples were hard, pointed and so inviting. He caressed them with his fingers and then wrapped his mouth around one at a time. From the left one and then to the right one, he enjoyed every pleasurable moment. His mouth was on her nipples, and the head of his stiff harden muscle pressed against stimulated her clit as he pumped his lower body in slow motion. Fill with desire and passion, her pussy was wet. Touching herself, she collected the wet juices on her fingers and rubbed the sweet nectar over Charles' body.

He whispered, "You're so wet."

She nodded her head as she pushed him back onto the bed and

gave his cock a nice, long, sensual lick. Bre then placed her mouth over the head of his dick and sucked. He was losing control, but Bre wasn't ready for that to happen, so she worked toward the upper part of his body. Charles rolled over and began fingering the inside of her soft, pink pussy. Bre rode his fingers like a dick with slow steady strokes. Shit! She became lost in the intensity of good feeling and was about to cum. She let out a loud moan as she reached her orgasm. Charles's journey didn't end there. Dipping his tongue in and enjoying the abundant juices that gathered between her legs, she came again. In his mouth this time. She felt as if she were in heaven and didn't want him to stop. Her legs trembled, but she opened them wider and wider as an open invitation for him to quench his hungry thirst.

Charles came up and gave her a deep kiss. The sweet aroma of Bre's pussy was all over his face. It was overwhelming, but such a wonderful feeling. Words alone couldn't describe her feelings.

While looking into her eyes, he said, "I'm gonna make love to you like never before."

Slowly, he entered her pussy. They made love to each other. Their bodies were moving along to an unheard beat, but they were in complete harmony. Still, Charles's entire dick wasn't in her, so she continued to open her legs wider and pulled him in further as they moved back and forth and around and around. Bre's emotions had taken over. She was in another world with this man, and she was loving the way he was making her feel. Nothing around them mattered because they were making love.

Charles's entire dick was inside her now. He was trying to keep control, but the sweetness of her pussy was stealing it away. She felt his cock continuing to grow even more and more inside her. Her pussy remained wet, and a hunger was being satisfied. She felt herself having another orgasm. Still, she wanted more. They held the other tight and fucked as if it would be their last time. He pushed his dick in deeper and harder, moving faster with quicker strokes. Bre was on fire and Charles was grunting. She was cumming again, and so was

Charles.

"Bre…baby…I'm cumming."

"Oh, Charles," she said. Her eyes rolled back, and the tips of her fingers pressed into his muscular back.

"C'mon, Bre…fuck me, baby."

"Oh, Charles…fuck me harder, babe."

Together, they shared one hell of an orgasm.

While holding each other in silence, they both realized what they'd shared seemed magical. Charles held her in his arms and gave her a soft kiss on the shoulder as he pulled her even closer into his body.

"Are you okay, babe?"

Bre turned to him, smiled, and said, "Why wouldn't I be after all that?"

He smiled and kissed her again, and then everything started over. Their energy levels were high, and there was a continuous hunger for each other. As Charles continued making love to Bre, he spoke words to express his love.

It wasn't long before both Charles and Bre were sleeping sound; their lovemaking session had depleted all their energy. The rain had almost come to a complete stop, and the sun was trying to peer through the dark clouds.

"Good afternoon, sleepyhead," Charles said as he kissed her on the head.

"Good afternoon to you, too, Mr. Charlie," she said while stretching. Even though she was still sleepy, she was awake and smiling. She'd had a fantastic morning. "Babe, I have to get a shower, so I can get some things done before I pick Alex up."

Alex was Bre's four-year-old son, and he was her heart. His smile and bright eyes could melt anyone. Despite the disappointment and heartbreak his father had caused her, she'd never regretted having her son. He was her joy and life.

Charles whispered in her ear, "Why don't we get in the shower together and get a quickie in?"

"A quickie?" she said with a devilish look on her face. "It's been a long time since I had a quickie." Bre lifted her eyelids and chuckled while staring at Charles.

"Wait no longer. Let's get up and get in the shower."

He patted her on her ass, hopped up, did a little dance to make his oversized dick twirl, and headed to the bathroom. Once Bre heard the water, she couldn't resist joining him.

Charles guided her in a position that allowed the warm water to flow down her back and between her butt cheeks. It wet her pussy enough for him to plunge his dick inside and pound. Every stroke was met with lubricated warm water. The sound of water, dick, and pussy was music to their ears, a sensual musical. Bre was hot and Charles was hard. Morning sex used to be one of Bre's favorites, quick and fast. It gave her a horny high all throughout the day.

Moving faster and deeper, Charles grabbed her hips and left no room in between. All they could hear was the splash of balls, grunts and moans, and water until his hot cum shot all over her butt and he let out a strong growl.

It was time for him to go, but it took all he had to leave Bre.

"Okay, honey, you need to get going so I can go get my baby," she said.

Charles picked up his keys and headed to the door. She followed behind him to make sure he left with a little love.

"I'll see you later," he said as he squeezed her ass and gave her a nice, long goodbye kiss.

After Charles left, Bre sat for a moment to reminisce about her time with him. One thing was certain: she was enjoying every moment she had with him. Walking over to her nightstand, Bre picked up the phone and called her girlfriend, Deloris, with whom Alex had spent the weekend.

"Hey, Dee, how's everything going?"

"You know Alex is fine; he's in good hands. Is everything okay with you?"

"Yeah." There was a slight pause. "Yeah, everything's fine, just fine."

"Um, huh, I hear you. Bre, it sounds like you had an interesting weekend. Don't think I'm blind. I know something's going on between you and Charlie, so don't even try to lie."

"Dee, you think you know everything. And if you must know, I spent some time with him. I like him a lot, but there's still a lot I need to get to know about him. You know they all start out good and all that, but they always show their asses later."

As Bre was talking to Dee, she was also changing the linens on her bed. Even though he was no longer around, she could still smell Charles. She held the pillowcase to her nose, closed her eyes, and inhaled as she listened to her friend.

"That could be true, Bre, but give him the benefit of the doubt. I think he's a decent man, but you have to remember none of us are perfect, not even your funky butt. You took time and got to know him before you slept with him, so you have to stop always second guessing yourself. Don't convict that man of another man's crime. Hell, I'm surprised he could get some from you."

They both laughed. Dee knew Bre was hard on men because of Alex's father, Munda.

"Whatever! Let me speak to my little man," Bre said, still laughing because Dee was telling the truth.

"Don took the kids out for a walk, and you know Natches is tagging right alongside him."

Breanna had to laugh because she knew exactly what Dee meant. With every step Alex took, Natches was close by.

"That's his little buddy, and in a way, it makes me feel better. Natches doesn't allow strangers to get too close to him before he barks and growl," Breanna said.

They both laughed while reflecting on times with Alex and Natches.

"Let him know I'll be there to pick him up soon."

"Um-huh, girl. You better enjoy getting your pussy taken care of while you can because I don't know if your little man will be keen on Charles getting too close to his mommy."

They laughed and said their goodbyes. Dee's statement made Bre think. Even though Charles and Alex got along very well, it would still be a challenge for him. She let go of the thought quickly because it wasn't as if she and Charles were making plans for a lifetime commitment. She didn't want to think too far in advance cause nothing in life was a guarantee.

Chapter Three

Breanna's co-worker and friend, Deb, observed her and knew something was up. She leaned her long body against an empty desk and cleared her throat in an audible tone to get Breanna's attention.

"Girl, what are you thinking about?" Deb said, tapping her foot as she stared at Bre and waited for her to respond.

With a slight grin on her face, Bre looked at Deb for a few seconds without speaking. She knew Deb was dying to find out what was going on with her.

"Tell me who's put a smile like that on your face?" Folding her hands and leaning forward, she gave Bre a look that relayed her determination and undeniable persistence.

"Go away, Deb," Breanna said in a joking manner as she smiled. After a short pause and readjusting herself in the chair, Bre said, "I was just thinking about a conversation I had with my sister."

"I sure don't have a smile like that on my face when I think about a conversation I've had with my sister or any other woman, as a matter of fact." Deb walked around to Bre and whispered in her ear, "I don't know who you think you're fooling, but it's not me. What did you do this weekend, anyway? That storm put everyone in the mood to make love. Is that what you did? Did you get you some ding-a-ling, girl?" After that, Deb stood up, placed her hands on her hips, and nodded knowingly as she looked at Bre.

"I did nothing, girl. I stayed home and talked to my sister while getting some cleaning done. Anyway, why are you hounding me? Shouldn't you be leaving, or did you not see the time? It's 5:03," Bre said, nudging Deb as she stood up and walked to her printer.

"I guess you're just trying to brush me off now, but that's fine." Deb rolled her eyes and sucked her teeth as she walked to her own desk. "I need to get out of this hellhole, anyway." Deb stopped in the middle of her step, turned to Bre while pointing her finger, and said, "You know, I'm a fellow counselor, and we should be able to help each other. Never say I didn't try offering you a free courtesy service. Hell, being a social worker is a professional courtesy, since the state doesn't pay us worth a damn." After saying that, Deb turned and quickly walked away.

Breanna couldn't do anything except laugh. Deb Wilson was a streetwise person, and you couldn't get too much past her. Though she was slim and seemed almost weightless, she was tough. She kept her hair cut short and always trimmed neatly. Her deep, dark skin was smooth and flawless.

Deb grabbed her purse out of her bottom desk drawer and told Bre to hurry up so they could leave. Walking to the parking garage, they talked about this and that and laughed a lot. Without any particular reason, Deb asked Bre about one of her acquaintance she wasn't too fond of, and the tone of the conversation changed.

"Bre, when was the last time you spoke to Renee?"

"I spoke to her a few days ago," she said. "You know her man has been keeping her busy."

"What man?" Deb frowned as if she'd seen something gross.

"Where have you been, Deb? She's been seeing this guy for a few months, and they seem to be hitting it off well."

"Well, damn!" Deb said with a look of disgust on her face. "Breanna, I'm not talking about anyone, but Renee is such an ugly woman. She's the spitting image of Flavor Flav on one of his worst days, and you know it." Before Deb got all her words out, she laughed.

The two of them were in hysterics. Bre managed to stop

laughing for a few minutes to agree with Deb.

"Yes, yes, she looks a mess. I don't know why she won't do something to her hair."

"Bre, if she has her own man, then I should have ten. I know every woman deserves a good man, but it shouldn't be someone else's husband. Now, that's something I have a problem with. I heard her ass was messing around with some married man at one time."

The two women then became serious. They could act silly and even get a bit wild at times, but when it came to the issue of interfering with family, neither of them was laughing.

"Why in the hell do women like that shit?" Breanna said. "I can't understand that for the life of me. It's not like men will leave their wives for a piece of pussy."

"Bre, if you let her tell it, she has a completely different opinion. These women need to learn how to have a bit more respect and love for themselves."

"I kind of feel sorry for her. Everyone has some good in them, including Renee. We all have our faults."

After reaching their cars, Deb still knew no more about Bre's rainy Sunday than before.

She said, "Breanna, don't think you're off the hook, because I don't buy that 'thinking about the conversation my sister and I had' shit. I know you have to pick up the little man from daycare, but don't think you don't have to answer my question."

"Deb, go home, and have a good evening."

They both laughed good-naturedly as they parted to head to their cars.

As Breanna and Alex were arriving home, they saw Bernice, their neighbor, sitting on her front porch. It was almost as though she was waiting for Breanna. While Breanna and her son were getting out of the car, Bernice stood and walked to the edge of her front porch. She was the nosy newswoman of the neighborhood. Bre acknowledged her by waving her hand but didn't bother to offer any verbal conversation.

"Hey there, Alex."

With a smile on his little, brown, round face, Alex said, "Hi, Ms. Bernice."

But Bre knew it wasn't Alex Bernice was interested in; it was his mother's business.

How are you doing, Breanna?"

"I'm fine, Ms. Bernice. How are you doing?" she said obligatorily.

"That was some storm we had yesterday, wasn't it?"

"Yes, it sure was. We hadn't had one that bad for some time," Breanna said while trying to unlock the door.

"I wondered if you had enough candles, but by the time the rain slowed up, I saw Charles pulling up in your driveway. I figured he'd probably got some for you since he was out."

Breanna quickly opened her front door and directed Alex to go inside. Ms. Bernice had picked the wrong day to be meddlesome, but Bre had something for her nosy ass.

She said, "My electricity was restored by that time. Wasn't yours, too?" Bre turned her back before bursting out laughing. "You have a good evening, Bernice," she said, disappearing into her home and leaving a stunned Bernice behind her.

Bernice was just being her nosy-ass self and Bre refused to buy into any of her little games. She thrived on getting fresh gossip started.

Alex dropped his backpack off in the middle of his bedroom floor and took off to grab his afternoon snack before he and Bre took Natches for his walk. While changing her clothes, Bre turned toward her nightstand, where she saw the red light flashing on the answering machine. Bre pushed the play button to listen to the messages.

The voice was one she was all too familiar with, and one she didn't want to hear again for the rest of her life. Bre became paralyzed and unable to do anything for a moment. She couldn't believe *he* was calling. Anger and pain rushed through her body. After all the time that had passed, she could only wonder what would compel him to call.

In her state of shock, she hadn't heard the message, so she rewound and played it again.

"Hi, Breanna, this is Munda, and I'd like to talk to you. Please call me at 912-555-1235."

Every horrible word he'd ever spoken rushed through her mind. She could remember praying and begging God to give her some understanding as to why this man had turned into such a cold and heartless human being.

Breanna sat down on her bed to pull herself together. Munda had put her through a living hell. She could never forget what he did and the things he'd said to her. There'd been many times that she had to choose between buying diapers, formula, and paying for childcare instead of having a meal for herself. It was never a question or second thought to sacrifice for her child. With God's grace and love, she and Alex made it. He'd never gone hungry, nor without a roof over his head. Even though there'd been some close calls, they remained only that: close calls.

Munda's message seemed to have placed Bre in a state of shock. She stood, staring into space for the next few minutes as thoughts rushed through her mind.

"This can't be happening," she said while bringing her shaking hands to her face and pacing back and forth.

"Mommy, c'mon!" Alex was yelling. Before she could say anything, he burst into her room. "What's taking so long?" He was impatient.

Bre turned, smiled at him, gave him a tight hug, and told him she loved him. "Give me a minute, and I'll be ready." She gave him a pat on his butt and sent him out of the room.

She listened as he and Natches ran through the house. Without listening to the next message, Bre quickly changed and headed out for their evening walk.

***

After being gone with Natches for about forty-five minutes, they were back at the house. Bre prepared Alex's bath water, making sure there were lots of bubbles. While he played in the tub, she thought about the troubling message she'd received as she moved about the kitchen getting their meal together. By the time the food was ready, and their plates were prepared, Alex was running through the house naked.

"Boy, why are you running in here without your clothes on? And I haven't bathed you yet."

Alex stood with his arms in the air and told his mother he was a big boy and he'd bathed himself. Bre placed her hands on her hips, but before she could say anything, Alex told her to smell him. She grabbed the towel, dried his wet body, and helped him get into his sleepers.

After dinner, Bre read him a story and got him to bed. As he dozed off, she gave him a kiss and made sure he was tucked in tight. Minutes slipped by as she remained sitting on the edge of Alex's bed, watching him sleep. Munda's unexpected call caused a lot of memories to rush back through her head.

Startled by the ringing of her phone, Bre thoughts were interrupted as she quickly jerked around. She stood staring at it for a moment with her hands on her chest. Attempting to disguise her voice, she said, "Hello?"

"Are you okay, Bre?" Charles said, detecting the slight trembling in her voice.

"I'm fine." She giggled. She explained to him that she'd been in deep thought and the phone startled her when it rang.

"Deep thought?" he said as his tone became lower and more serious.

"Yes, deep thoughts."

There was a hesitant tone in Bre's voice as she spoke. It was obvious to her that Munda's earlier call had upset her even more than she realized. She was on edge and nervous not knowing why he'd called or what he wanted. Bre wasn't ready to tell Charles about her phone call from Munda. There was a long pause after she made that statement, but Charles soon broke the silence.

"Babe, I don't know what you've gone through, but I know there's more to you than you've shared so far. You should know by now that it's really okay to trust and talk to me about anything. I'll never do anything to harm you. Do you understand me?"

Breanna acknowledged that she did, and Charles could hear the tone of her voice change. Their conversation continued with small talk, but one thing was certain: they both knew something special was developing between them. Talking to Charles was very easy for Bre. Most of all, he made her laugh. And for a moment she forgot about the things that troubled her. The longer she listened to his sexy voice on the phone, the hornier she became.

At one point she felt her pussy pulsating. Her mind wandered. Bre was longing for Charles. She wanted to feel every inch of him inside her; she wanted to be next to him making love and feeling safe.

That call was what she needed. Charles soothed a part of her that longed for comforting. It had been a long time since she felt such comfort from a man. With all the bad experiences and misfortunes, she'd gone through in her life, she knew there would be an inner struggle to let her guard down and trust Charles.

Charles was right to guess that she was hurt badly in the past, but it wasn't just by a man. She was hurt by many people, including her family. Bre often looked back at her life and reminded herself that she was a good woman and deserved the best. She didn't want to get caught up in the things that took place in her past. Perhaps she'd need to go back to settle some things someday, but it wasn't a priority for her right now.

Getting away from her family and other people who were directly involved in her life was the best thing Bre could have done for herself. It was always the same old bullshit, day in and day out. Family members were always talking about and disrespecting one another. Most times, watching her family, neighbors, and associates interact was like watching an unfunny sitcom filled with dysfunction. She was at the point where she didn't want to think about the past and allow it to take away from the enjoyable conversation she was sharing with Charles.

It hadn't been easy, but trust in the Lord had carried Breanna a long way. She knew Alex needed a man in his life. She also knew she wasn't going to allow just anyone around him. Breanna worried a lot about him not having a father in his life, and there were times it caused her deep sadness. All she knew was that she would make every possible effort to make sure her little man lacked nothing because of his father's absence.

As Bre and Charles talked on the phone, she peeped out the window to make sure Bernice wasn't outside. She then poured a glass of wine and made her way out onto the porch. It was a beautiful, quiet night with the moon sitting high and casting its light down below. The calm, fresh breeze was soothing. Her mind journeyed many miles away while she laughed and talked.

Having been on the phone for over an hour, Charles assumed Bre needed her rest before having to get up for work the next day. Though they both hated to end the conversation, they eventually did, after saying goodnight to each other a few times.

Breanna took a few sips of wine and laid her head back as she marveled at the stars resting in the dark sky. She thought about what she was feeling for Charles. She'd been carrying a lot of baggage, but she was ready to dump it. There was no denying the strong emotions she was developing for Charles, but she was scared of caring for another man, getting hurt, and suffering the painful emotions that would follow. The heartbreak would be unbearable for her. Thinking back on her past, tears flowed.

It was getting late, and she needed to call Betty before heading to bed. God knew she didn't want to give her sister too much space to think about her broken marriage; another chance for those two could mean twenty more years of hell.

Breanna got comfortable and made the call, only to hear a small voice come through the phone.

"Hello, who is this?"

"Hi Angel, it's Aunt Breanna. How are you doing?"

"I'm fine."

"Where's your mommy?"

"She had to go to the store for some stuff."

Breanna looked at the time: 10:15 p.m. It wasn't like Betty to go to the store at this time of night. She began to wonder how to get to the truth as to her sister's whereabouts. Bre was worried that Betty may have been out trying to salvage things with Tony. After many thoughts rushed through her mind, Bre asked Angel to tell her big brother to come to the phone. She heard her screaming for Jamar in the background.

"Who is it?" he snapped.

"It's Auntie Breanna."

"Mama told you not to answer the phone, girl. Go sit down before you get us in more trouble."

Bre listened to the background conversation and knew Betty must have given the children her infamous "tell them I ran to the store" instructions. Betty lived in her own world with her own rules and ways. She had the kids trained not to answer the phone when she wasn't around and not to give out any personal information as to what transpired on the inside of their home. Whatever happened on inside of their home stayed there, or there were consequences. She heard Jamar getting closer to the phone. The closer he got, the quieter his fussing at Angel became.

"Hi, Auntie," he said.

"How are you doing, honey?"

"I'm okay," he said. He didn't sound too sure, though.

"Jamar, tell your mom I said to call me."

"Okay. I'll tell her."

"Goodbye, sweetie."

"Bye, Auntie."

Bre had taken care of everything she needed to. Now she could now get some rest. With the stress of work, being a single mom, and worrying about her sister, she was exhausted. The only thing she had the energy to do was grab a quick shower and call it a night. Afterwards, she couldn't remember anything more than her head hitting the pillow. It had been a long day.

Chapter Four

The next day at work was dragging. Bre was still a bit tired and all she wanted was to get home, have some personal time, and do something to help her unwind. She knew what she wanted, and she would make sure she took the time to get it.

Breanna was horny all morning. As the day continued, the feeling increased more and more. She could only think about being sexually satisfied. On her drive home, she decided she would pamper herself. In tune with her body, Bre knew she needed some personal attention—the kind many women would ever admit they need or indulge in. She needed to satisfy her own sexual needs.

After getting Alex situated for the night, Bre could finally settle down after her long day and busy night. The phone rang. Breanna tried to answer it, grab a CD, and keep her drink within the glass all at once. It was Betty. She needed a listening ear and a shoulder to cry on. While trying to get things adjusted around her on the couch, the cold glass touched Bre's naked pussy that her short nightie didn't do a good job of hiding. She wanted to tell Betty she needed to call her back, but she knew her sister needed her support. The cool sensation of the glass touching her hot pussy could have brought her an instant orgasm, but she put those thoughts out of her mind by reassuring herself she'd get the much-needed attention later. She wanted to masturbate and reach an orgasm by herself, but it would have to wait.

After Betty's call, Breanna lit scented candles throughout the bathroom and bedroom and loaded songs from her playlist by two of her favorite artists: Gerald Levert and Luther Vandross. Those men seemed to wet her panties every time she listened to their sensual voices. She wanted the fragrance to fill the room, so she delayed running her bathwater for half an hour. During that time, she gathered all the essentials she'd need before and after her bath.

Bre was well in tune with what she was feeling and what she needed. Her mind was open to taking charge and satisfying her own sexual needs. There was tension that needed releasing, and she was mature and comfortable enough to do so. Sitting on the side of her bathtub, she started her bathwater and placed her hand through its running stream, making sure it wasn't too hot or too cold. The water's temperature was perfect. Bre entered the tub of water and slowly submerged her body. She laid her head back, took in a deep breath, and exhaled.

Breanna could feel what seemed to be every tight muscle loosening. With gentle strokes, she rubbed her beautiful, smooth, even-toned skin. As the candles flickered, their reflection on the water danced across it like little stars in the sky.

After soaking, relaxing, and pampering herself for some time, the water turned cool. Reluctantly, she decided it was time get out and rinsed the last bit of suds off her body. The crisp air chilled her wet body, so she moved closer to the burning candles hoping to find a little warmth while drying her body. With only the candles burning and the soft music playing, Bre climbed into her bed and snuggled into a pillow. Smelling the cleanliness from her bath brought back the longing sexual gratification.

While touching herself, she could feel the wetness developing between her legs. She reached down, and within an instant, a pool of wetness appeared. Bre pulled one leg up while the other one remained extended, she spread the lips of her pussy and massaged her clit; the feeling caused her to moan with great satisfaction. Bre soon reached over and grabbed a piece of ice out of the glass on her nightstand. She lifted her other leg and spread them both as wide as she could. With the ice in one hand, she rubbed her sultry pussy. Though the ice was cold and made her take in a deep breath, she found it thrilling and fulfilling.

Continuing to rub the ice inside the corridors of her wet pussy, Bre's imagination ran wild. Her hips thrust slowly to the sensation. The more she thrust, the wider her legs opened. Recalling her recent sexual escapades with Charles, she called out his name as if it was him making her feel so good. The thought of him being there depositing small pieces of cold ice into her hot pussy and then warming it up again with his tongue caused her to open her legs even wider and thrust harder. That thought thrilled her. Her body was moving in a circular motion, and then up and down. Thrusting and touching every part of her pussy, she could feel herself reaching her climax.

Not wanting the moment to end, Bre tried to hold on as long as she could to the pleasurable moment. She parted the lips of her pussy; her exposed clitoris begged for more. Everything was wetness and sensation. She'd reached her weakest point; she knew it was only a matter of time before her eruption. The closer she came to climaxing, her moans grew louder and louder, and the thrusting became harder and harder. As she let out a scream from her orgasm, the bed filled with her wetness and her body became weak and limp. Having satisfied her need completely, Bre rolled over on her pillow and fell into a peaceful sleep.

The next morning, Bre was able to focus and take care of some things without distraction. She could also have some quiet time to process some of her many thoughts. Deloris had picked Alex up early so he could spend the day at the zoo with her and Zack. When the doorbell rang, Bre was certain it was Charles. She quickly took a glance at herself in the mirror as she rushed to open the door.

It wasn't Charles.

It wasn't anyone she wanted to see.

"Why in the hell are you at my house? How did you find me?" Bre said through clenched teeth. She had an urge to kick the asshole in the balls, sending him crashing to the ground. Fear, bitterness, and hatred were taking over all at the same time.

"Breanna, I tried calling you several times, but you wouldn't return my calls. We need to talk."

She watched Munda as a million thoughts rushed through her mind. Bre knew she had every reason to be angry and resentful toward him.

Before responding, she looked up at him with a frown and began screaming. "Not answering your phone calls and messages should have been enough to let you know I didn't want to see or talk to you. What the hell do you want?" There was no second-guessing it; Bre was still bitter.

"How's the boy?" Munda said as his voice cracked.

She could tell he was a bit nervous. His hands were making odd jerky movements as if he wanted to reach out and touch Bre. He knew that wouldn't be appropriate. After not getting an immediate response from her, he repeated the question in a much lower tone. He placed one of his hands in his pockets and rubbed his bald head with the other. Munda gazed at Bre as he waited for her to respond.

"What!" she screamed in disbelief. She took a few steps closer to him as she placed her hands on her hips and furrowed her eyebrows. "After almost four fucking years, you have the audacity to ask about my son? Is that all you can ask? You don't even know his name, do you? If I'd known it was you at my damn door, I never would have opened it." She pointed and shook her finger at him, chastising him.

"I'm not here for any trouble, Bre, and I'm sorry about everything."

"Sorry? You're fucking sorry, and you took this long to say it! Sorry my ass. Get away from my house now, and I mean it!"

Anger, hurt, and betrayal seemed to suffocate Breanna as her eyes watered. While screaming, her voice trembled. After a brief pause and trying to regain control, she covered her face with her hands and shook her head in disbelief.

"Please, just give me a couple of minutes. I want to make things right. We've both made mistakes. I want to get to know our son. Can we please go inside? Please."

Bre saw Deloris pulling up in the driveway while Alex sat in the back seat, peering out the window. An anxious feeling came over her; there was no way she wanted her son to discover that Munda was his father, nor did she want Alex to notice how upset she was. She stepped aside and let the asshole in.

***

Seeing the strange car, Deloris told the kids to wait inside the car for a moment while she made sure Breanna was okay. When Bre opened the door, Deloris stood unable to move and at a loss for words. She shook her head in disbelief from the shock of seeing Munda standing in the living room. Deloris looked outside at Alex who was not determined to get inside to his mom. Before she could stop him, he'd already open the door and was headed to his mom. The moment became more intense as Alex jumped into her arms and held her tight. His little face lit up, and the only thing he knew was that he was ready to receive the love his mom gave him so freely. Breanna held him close as if she hadn't seen him in months.

"I missed you, Mommy," he said to her as she embraced him.

Bre was overcome with emotion as Munda stood there looking at the two of them. It had to be obvious to anyone that the love between the mother and her son was deep and natural. Alex talked quickly about his day and never acknowledged Munda. When Bre lowered him back to the floor, she gave him a kiss on the cheek and told him to go in the backyard with Zack and Natches. He took off without giving it a second thought.

"Girl, are you okay?" Deloris said, walking toward Bre and Munda with a look of confusion on her face.

"I'm fine, Dee. It's okay."

She was too angry to look in her direction. All she could do was look at Munda with anger and hatred seething in her eyes. She was ready to punch the man right in the nose.

"Oh, hell no! It doesn't look okay," Deloris said in a nasty tone. "And what damn rock did you crawl out from under, Munda?" Deloris snapped at him, pulling her mid-length hair out of her round face. It was obvious she wanted to hit him as well while clenching her fists and rolling her eyes at him. "Whichever rock it was, you'd better climb your ass back under it before we call the police."

"Good afternoon to you, too, Deloris." Munda frowned at her in annoyance.

Breanna didn't want a scene, so she closed the door and blinds. She already knew Bernice, her nosey neighbor, had noticed the strange car and was peeping out the window. Bre asked Deloris to go check on the kids so she could speak to Munda without Alex walking in on them again.

Walking farther into the room, the pictures of Alex captured Munda's attention. He'd grown quieter, and looking at his expression, she could see his deep regret. His eyes filled with tears, and it took a great effort for him to get his words out. She could see that Alex and the pictures of him had a profound effect on Munda. She watched as his eyes went from one picture to another. His head hung low with sadness. She felt certain he wasn't prepared for the emotions that he was now facing.

There was silence for a few minutes as she paced back and forth. She didn't know what else to say. After some time, she heard Deloris make her way back into the room.

"Is his sorry ass gone?" Deloris said before knowing that Munda was still there. She didn't care about how emotional he was. Dee felt it was time for him to deal with the consequences of his actions and the pain he'd caused her friend. Mumbling underneath her breath, she walked back out the room.

"Wow, he's a big boy," Munda said as he nodded his head.

She rolled her eyes. "If you'd stuck around and not run off like some foolish irresponsible schoolboy, you wouldn't be so shocked. Did you ever think about doing that? Did you think about anything besides your ridiculous theory of me cheating and Alex being someone else's baby?"

Munda stood speechless. His mouth moved but nothing was heard. He was obviously trying to think of a way to respond. He looked confused.

"Don't just stand there, answer the question. Answer it damnit!"

Bre's anger grew. A tightness in her stomach brought back all the pain and hurt Munda had inflicted on her years ago. He reached out to touch her arm, but she pulled away from him. He did not understand the full impact of what he was dealing with.

"I promise to make up everything. Please! Give me a little break." His tone was one of desperation.

Even though his plea seemed sincere, Bre wasn't cutting him any breaks. "Man, you must think I'm stupid," she said. "I trusted you to do the right thing, but you didn't. There's no love in this house for you. None!"

The veins in Breanna's temples were throbbing. She could feel the tears and sweat covering her face. Most of all, her heart felt it was about to jump out of her chest. She paced as she continued speaking. "When did I ever give you a valid reason to believe I was sleeping around? Damn you, Munda! You concluded that I was cheating, and you accepted it as fact." Bre pointed her finger in his face.

"No! The night you left the house after getting a phone call that you were so secretive about, I followed you because you weren't your normal self. I saw you meet a man in the parking lot, and you all were talking, and then you hugged and held him. This is something I saw with my own eyes, Breanna. Things changed more and more. You stopped talking and became very distant. Everything was very secretive with you." He paused hoping she would say something before he continued. "There was another night that your phone rang, and you got out of bed and dashed into the bathroom whispering. Bre, you thought I was asleep, but I wasn't. When you got dressed and left out, I followed you. Again, you met with that same man. The two of you sat in the coffeehouse for almost two hours, talking and touching. A few weeks after that, you tell me we're having a baby."

"And you didn't have the decency to talk to me about what you'd seen? Fuck you, Munda!" Breanna shouted.

Before she could say another word, Dee rushed to the back door, making sure the kids didn't walk in on Breanna and Munda's conversation.

"Breanna, I made a mistake, a horrible mistake. I didn't want to think the worst, but after hearing you were seeing someone else, it all seemed to make sense."

Before Munda could get another word out, Bre interrupted him.

"Just stop it! I would have never cheated on you and you should have known that! I was doing my fucking job. The man you saw me with had been raped! He was going through something terrible and finally trusted me. He needed my help, Munda. That was the only thing going on. It was a sensitive issue that I and a co-worker was handling."

"Oh my God." Munda placed both his hands on his head and let out a loud sigh. He didn't know what to say, so he remained silent with a look of despair on his face.

"Bre, I didn't know...I didn't know."

"Munda, you didn't have to know. The only thing you had to do was trust me. I told you I was helping a client. Instead of trusting me, you listened to some bullshit someone else told you."

"Bre, I always trusted you, but you became secretive, and you weren't acting like your usual self. You became distant and distracted. You weren't talking to me."

"Maybe I should have said something, but I promised that man I wouldn't tell anyone. I was trying to do what was right and keep him from feeling even more alone and broken."

He didn't speak. The look on his face was one she'd never seen before. Beads of sweat covered his forehead and his lips trembled.

Bre was disgusted. "Get the hell out of my house. I can't deal with this shit anymore. Get out now!"

Munda remained speechless. He looked at her as if she'd lost all her senses. She hadn't lost her mind at all. It was the memory of going through a pregnancy alone and knowing how tight things had gotten for her and Alex that caused her to react this way.

Deloris came back into the room and looked at Munda. "Didn't you hear what Bre said, or do you not understand English? You need to leave now. If you have one ounce of decency left, you'll leave."

Munda turned and walked slowly out the door, Breanna burst out crying.

"Bre, Alex can come home with us while you take care of yourself. You know it's his second home anyway," Deloris said.

"No, it's okay," Bre said. "I'm not gonna let him come here and destroy our plans." She was still in tears, but she fought hard to hold them back in front of Deloris, and she definitely didn't want Alex to walk in and see her crying. She felt like her world was falling apart and she was about to lose control.

"Dee, I'll be back in a few minutes," she said and walked down the hallway.

"Take your time, Bre."

Breanna hurried into her bedroom and closed the door. Weeping even more now, she could only wonder why Munda had come back. She sat down on the floor beside her bed so she could cry her heart out without Deloris hearing.

Her stomach felt as if it had been hit with a great force. With one arm wrapped around her waist, she wept from her anger and pain. After about fifteen minutes of hard crying, she settled down.

Outside her bedroom door, Deloris said, "Bre, are you okay?"

Breanna sat straight up and wiped her tears away. "I'm fine."

"Is it okay for me to come in?"

"Yes, Dee, you can come in."

Dee sat down next to Breanna and placed her arms around her. Bre let out a slow breath and leaned her head onto Deloris' shoulder without saying a word. In an attempt to comfort Bre, Dee offered encouraging words of strength. She knew this had to be a difficult time for her friend. For years, Munda had not bothered to contact Bre or even inquire about his child, and all of a sudden out of nowhere he appears.

Dee sat up straight and looked at Bre. "Bre, I can't believe he showed up. That son of a bitch hurt you, and you have every reason for feeling the way you do. You need to talk to him sooner or later to put this behind you."

Breanna looked directly in Dee's eyes and nodded her head. She knew Dee was right but wasn't ready to talk to him yet. She needed time and space.

"Deloris, I know I have to deal with it, but I'm not ready right now."

"I'm gonna take Alex home with us. I'll check on you later."

Deloris gave her a big hug and walked out of the room. Breanna lay on her bed for some time after that, thinking about the love she and Munda once shared; the pain he'd caused her seemed so much greater than the love he'd once given her.

Breanna rested a while before taking a long a hot shower. When she re-entered the living room, she peeped out of the window to ensure there was no sign of Munda. Whether she wanted to or not, she had to deal with the fact that Munda had shown up, and she was certain he wasn't going away.

Alex would be the one with the most to lose or gain in this situation. Her anger wasn't about Munda showing up out of nowhere, asking to see his son; it was how he'd treated her over four years ago. There were many painful memories, but there were also many good ones. None of her emotions made any sense right now.

After some time, Bre decided to retrieve the number he'd left on her answering machine. Talking to him wasn't what she wanted, but she knew there was no getting around it. She feared her life would turn upside down from Munda's sudden appearance. She sat at the table wondering why in the world he showed up now. All she could think about was the scene from earlier that morning.

The phone rang, but she made no effort to answer it. As soon as the answering machine picked up, the caller hung up. Once more, the phone rang. This time she answered it, and she was glad she did. Her ray of sunshine had come through to brighten her gloomy day.

"Whoa, where's that smile that always comes through the phone? Breanna, is everything okay?"

Bre exhaled a sigh of relief. "Charles," she said. "I'm doing okay."

"Are you sure?"

"I'm sure."

Breanna tried to keep from talking about her problem, but Charles insisted. His voice was calm. She wanted to open up and tell him everything that was going on. She didn't want him to think she was a woman who always had some sort of drama going on in her life. Despite what she thought, Breanna shared what happened earlier.

"It's that obvious something's wrong with me, huh?"

"Yes. You seem to have a sadness in your voice, or maybe you're preoccupied with deep thoughts."

"Wow...that obvious, huh?" she said while fighting back her tears.

Charles knew that whatever it was, it was serious. "Bre, give me a few minutes, and I'll be right over."

Charles wanted to offer her the comfort he knew she probably needed. While Breanna waited for Charles's arrival, she washed her face and regained her composure. It was only fifteen minutes later when Bre heard his car in the driveway. Before he could knock, she opened the door. With no exchange of words, Charles pulled her into his arms and gave her a long and tight hug. Her body trembled as her eyes filled with tears.

"Bre, what in the heck is going on?" He had a look of deep concern on his face.

"I don't know where to start," she said, bursting into tears.

"Babe, just begin where you feel comfortable. You can go as slow as you want. I'm free for a few hours, so I'm all yours. Is your sister okay?"

Bre nodded her head. "Yes. Alex's father was here earlier. I wasn't expecting him. I never thought I'd see him again." Bre closed her eyes and shook her head.

"I see." There was silence for a minute. "Bre, when's the last time he was in your life?"

"He left a few weeks after I told him of my pregnancy. I saw him a few months after Alex's birth, but no more after that. Alex is four, and he knows nothing about his father. We're doing fine now, and there's no need for him to show up suddenly."

"Well, since he's appeared for whatever reason, you must be open-minded enough to see where he's coming from or what he has to say."

Even though Charles was trying to offer her some solid advice, he was also a little reluctant. He didn't want to do anything to push her back into Munda's arms, but he offered her the right thing to do. His soothing tone was calming and sincere.

"I know nothing about the relationship the two of you shared, but I have to trust you to do what's best. Whatever it is or will be, know that I'll be here for you."

Breanna knew Charles meant every word. His concern and care were genuine. The gentleness and understanding that he offered meant a lot to her, and she no longer felt as if her life was going to fall apart at any moment.

She said, "Charles, how have I managed without having you in my life all these years?"

"Babe, I was wondering the same thing," he said. "How have you managed without me in your life?"

They both laughed. Charles's timing was always perfect.

"Bre, it's important to me that you're happy. You should find out if this guy's intentions are sincere."

Charles spoke to Bre as she lay in his arms. She remained quiet and listened carefully to every word he spoke while stroking her long, black hair.

"I know it's hard, but you needed this to happen so you can be sure of which direction you're going."

With emphases on his statement, he made sure she understood the importance of facing and dealing with Munda. Bre acknowledged that she was listening to him by nodding her head in a slow motion.

"Perhaps you may need to get away and think things through. This just hit you from out of nowhere, so you need time to process it. What do you think?"

"It makes sense," she said in a soft tone.

A couple of hours passed as they sat chatting and holding each other, soothing both of their souls. Bre was where she wanted to be and loving every moment.

"Bre, I have to be at work at seven, but I want you to get out of the house for a little while. Go get some fresh air. You should go down by the creek since you have a few hours of daylight left. The calmness there will help you think and relax. I want you back to smiling and being your silly sexy self. And I always want to hear that beautiful smile in your voice. Is Alex spending the night with Dee?"

"Yeah, he's there for the night. With everything going on, Deloris took him home with her and Zack."

Charles gave Bre one last, long, firm hug and a sensual kiss before leaving.

***

As she moved along to get out of her house, Bre only thought of Charles and his words. When it came to Munda, she was on an emotional roller coaster. Charles was right about her needing closure in order to move on. There were still so many unanswered questions, and she needed answers.

The creek sounded like an excellent idea; it was peaceful and calming. It was the perfect place to do some serious thinking. With that thought, she grabbed a blanket and packed a few things to nibble on and drink. There would be no ringing phones or anyone stopping by to surprise her.

Chapter Five

Breanna drove to the creek. She let down her windows just before arriving to reacquaint herself with the smell of the fresh water. For a few minutes, she sat in her car thinking about how it was only last Saturday that she and Charles were there.

"Okay, girl, you can't just sit here," she said aloud. She gathered her things from the car and searched for a spot to spread out her blanket and unwind.

The creek was a place where she was able to relax and regain focus. She lay on her back and watched white fluffy clouds move through the clear, blue sky. The sight reminded her of a Bible verse in the King James Version of the *Woman, Thou Art Loosed Edition* she hadn't thought about in a long time. Nahum 1:3 reads, "His way is in the whirlwind and the storm and clouds are the dust of his feet."

She kept thinking how beautiful and amazing God's creations are. The flowing waters that ran through the shallow paths and the sounds of the small creatures along with the many trees made the creek simple but gorgeous. With life being busy and hectic at times, Bre never took the time to appreciate the surrounding beauty. How she wished she'd discovered the place a long time ago since it offered a certain magical, soothing energy.

Last week it had been Betty's drama; this week it's Munda's unexpected return. The thought of what might happen next frighten Bre. Nevertheless, she acknowledged the fact that she'd would have to deal with Munda soon. She'd never imagined having to deal with such a situation. Breanna had always said she didn't want children after having watched family members struggle with raising kids with no father. It was hard for the mothers, but even harder on the children.

Breanna's thoughts became clearer. A part of her was still furious, and she had valid reasons for the anger. She knew she was innocent of all the things he once accused her of doing. There were no words to express the impact of the betrayal Munda caused her.

Thinking aloud, she said, "God, why? Why now?"

Her questions led into a deeper conversation with Him. Bre wasn't an overly religious person, but she had her own intimate relationship with God. Through her trials and tribulations, she learned a long time ago to depend only on Him. When she was facing and going through her rough time with Munda, everyone gossiped. The only thing that kept her moving ahead was her faith. That was the main thing that helped her keep her head lifted and her spirits high through it all.

Bre sat on the blanket with her feet flat while her chin rested on her knees as many thoughts passed through her mind. Her attention drifted to a deer drinking water on the other side of the creek. She watched it become familiar with its surroundings. With a careful watch, it was as if the deer sensed that Breanna wasn't there to cause any threat or harm. Bre was only admiring the beauty of nature.

The magical wonders of the creek amazed her. Time seemed to have rushed by. Regrettably, she knew it was time to leave after a few hours of exploration and observation. She got up, stretched, and packed all her belongings. After loading everything into the car, she inhaled to take in the fresh, clean air. One last time, she looked at the beauty of nature. The sound of the rolling water nearby gave her a sense of freedom.

Breanna realized there was no way she could solve her problems in one afternoon. Through all the anger, her greatest fear was she might still have unresolved feelings for Munda. Ultimately, she would have to sift through all her emotions to get to the core of her feelings, but that was something she needed to do alone.

On her drive back, everything was quiet in the dusk of the evening. She arrived home to see no one in her driveway or an answering machine message awaiting her. She opened a couple of windows, allowing the fresh air to circulate through the house. During the end of the summer, the crisp breeze from outside cooled the inside of her home.

In for the rest of the evening, Bre decided she would enjoy a television show or a good movie. It was one of those evenings where she wanted to kick back in the middle of the bed and do absolutely nothing.

Before settling down, she called Deloris to make sure Alex was okay.

"Hey, Dee," she said.

"How are you doing, Bre?"

"I'm doing much better." With a smile in her voice, she said, "How's my little man?" Even though she knew he was fine, Bre still asked.

Laughing out loud, Dee responded, "Girl, that boy is fine. As long as he's asking a million questions and running around playing, he's happy."

Bre sat on the edge of her bed, twirling the ends of her hair as she continued talking with Dee.

"Have you processed what transpired today, Bre?" Dee asked with concern in her voice.

"I ended up going down by the creek and spending some quiet time with my thoughts. I'm sorry about all this."

"You don't have to be sorry about anything. What matters is that you're okay. And what creek did you go to? Better yet, when did you start going to the creek?"

"Charles took me there last weekend after dealing with Betty's drama and it turned out to be the perfect place for calming me."

"That's right; the two of you had a long weekend together last week. I'm glad he's there for you, girl. Oh, before I forget, Renee called and said she wanted to make sure everything was alright with you. She probably got a hint of gossip from that old lady across from you."

"You should have told her to call me her damn self and ask," Bre said.

"Bre, she was trying to be sneaky and find out what was going on. She loves to feed on negative things that happen to others. I can't find one damn reason why we even deal with her."

"Don't let that bother you. She's always been that way, so we must deal with her carefully. Handle her with a long-handled spoon. We've always had to treat her in that manner, so don't think that after all this time, she's changed," Bre said as she let out a sigh.

"You're right. No one else will deal with her raggedy ass. I don't understand why you still deal with her after what she said behind your back. Did you ever let her know you found out what she was telling people?"

"Naw, she's clueless. I used to get angry when I thought about how she told people my child was from a one-night stand. Now, I pity her."

"Why have any compassion for her sneaky lying ass? She did you wrong."

Breanna said, "Honey, because her child is from a one-night stand. Don't forget, we're not in a huge town, so news travels fast."

"You're kidding! I didn't know that shit. Damn!"

"I kid you not. I thought I told you. She's not the most attractive person in the world, Dee, but somebody planted their seed inside her dirty ass and got her pregnant."

"Not the most attractive? Shit, just call it as you see it. Her ass is ugly as hell, and to top it all off, she has a horrible figure. She's definitely a brown bag case," Deloris said in a serious, but funny tone.

They burst out in laughter because it was the truth. Renee was a person who had to be dealt with from a distance. She couldn't be trusted for a moment. She was always in the middle of some mess because of her mouth.

"How did you ever meet someone like her, Bre?"

"Through Betty."

"Damn! How does Betty meet all these messed up people? Speaking of which, is Betty still with that sorry-ass excuse for a man?"

"Girl, his ass left her and the kids."

"Hell, I know she's shouting with joy and praise."

Bre burst out laughing. "You would think so, but she's taking it pretty bad."

"What's wrong with her ass? That's a relationship I don't understand at all. There was no way she was supposed to end up with that piece of scum."

"That makes two of us."

"He must have found someone else to support his sorry ass."

"Don't get me to lying," Bre said. "All I know is that some girl just had his baby, and he left to go live with them."

"Shut up, girl!" Dee said. Shocked. "I know you're lying, Bre."

"Nope, I'm not. Betty told me herself. She was taking it kinda hard, but I told her she deserves so much better and she should see it as an opportunity to get herself together."

"Breanna, that S.O.B. probably knew that girl would take his sorry ass to court for child support if he didn't take care of the baby. He's just trying to run a game by moving in them and pretending he loves her. He knows he won't have to go through that with Betty."

"Dee, I never thought about that. That's a trifling-ass man if I've ever seen one. And Betty better put his ass on child support, especially with three kids to take care."

"C'mon now, Bre. Think about it. That man only loves and cares for himself. Who's the girl?"

"I don't know, but I'm sure Betty does. I'll ask her if I get the opportunity. We probably know her, too. The girl can't live too far away because he doesn't have a car, and he's too lazy to ride a bicycle.

Then again, I don't know. He could have beat up on Betty and took her car."

"That's a shame," Deloris said. "I hope it all works out for her. We've all been through 'man drama' before."

Everything got quiet. She knew Deloris would shift the subject back to her and Munda.

"Bre, what are you gonna do about Munda?"

"I'll talk to him soon. No one could have told me I'd see him again. I don't even know how he found me."

"Huh. For some reason, I always believed he would show up sooner or later. I figured it would've been sooner." Deloris became very serious and hit Bre a heavy question. "I've got a question for you, girl: do you still love him?"

"Damn, what kind of question is that?" Bre snapped.

"It's one I want an answer to. You should want the answer too if you don't already know it."

Dee was obviously not going to withdraw her question.

"Well, I'm waiting," she said in a harsh tone. "Even if you don't answer the question for me, you eventually must answer it for yourself." In a more sympathetic tone, she continued to speak to Breanna. "I know you loved Munda with all your heart, and I know about the devastation you experienced, but we all need closure to our broken relationships. Girl, you may not want to admit the effect it's had on you, but trust me, it's there."

Bre couldn't see all of Dee's body gestures, but she could imagine Dee looking over her glasses and waving her hand back and forth as if she were standing directly in front of Bre.

"Dee, I'm dealing with all of this the best way I know how. It hit me all at once, and it's gonna take time for me to figure things out."

She chose her words wisely because she knew Dee was right. As the hurt and memories came back again, Breanna cried.

"Bre, I don't care how strong and determined you are. This is something you can never stop thinking about since you have to see

Alex every day. That's like looking at a miniature Munda."

"I already know this," Bre expressed in a firm tone. "That's why I'm so angry. I shared everything with Munda: my love, my body, my deepest hurts, my secrets, and a son. It wasn't supposed to turn out like this." The hurt overcame her as tears fell once more.

"Bre, it's gonna be okay. And remember, I'll always be here for you."

"It's just so much on me at one time, and I need to get control of my emotions and thoughts before talking to Munda and Alex. He has a right to know his dad, but I don't want him to find out by Munda telling him. It's something I need to do."

"Better you than me. I'm gonna let you go so you can get some rest. And when this Munda drama passes, we've got to talk about Charles."

"Goodnight, Deloris."

That was the last person Bre would talk to for the night. She turned the television off and turned the radio on; she loved to disappear into jazz music. With her window half open, the curtains moved in and out with the breeze. She closed her eyes and took a deep breath. Thoughts of Munda and what happened between them didn't leave her mind that night.

Breanna thought about how Alex could benefit from having his father around. She didn't doubt her parenting skills, but something told her there could be great advantages to Alex getting to know his dad. Maybe they would have a wonderful relationship.

Breanna questioned the sincerity of Munda wanting to be an integral part of Alex's life. A son was all he ever wanted before everything exploded. Rampant thoughts about Munda's reason for showing up rushed through her mind.

Restless, Bre walked into Alex's room, picked up one of his stuffed friends, and walked over to his bed. A slight smile appeared on her face as she rubbed her hand across the soft fur. The bear held lots of history and memories. She bought it for him the night before his birth. Breanna curled up in Alex's small bed and drifted off to sleep.

Bre jumped up thinking that it was a workday and that she'd overslept. It didn't take long for her to come to her senses and remember it wasn't. Making her way into the bathroom and looking in the mirror, she decided to work on her eyes first. It was one of those mornings where she was glad nobody could see her face.

The birds sang loudly. Bre could tell from the bright sun and the way the soft white clouds slowly moved across the light blue sky that it was going to be a beautiful day. She started a pot of coffee and proceeded to the front porch to grab the Sunday morning paper. Bre checked out the headlines and proceeded to the employment section. She kept her eyes on the job market and paid close attention to paralegal openings for Betty. There were plenty. She supposed even ambulance chasers needed paralegals, even if there was a recession going on.

Breanna knew she needed to go to church to gain some perspective. She needed a spiritual experience to give her the strength to get through the turmoil and chaos. She was no stranger to the power of prayer. Having grown up in the church gave her a strong foundation in acknowledging the spiritual part of herself. It was times like these she needed to go back to her foundation, be around fellow believers, and heal in peace.

When Bre arrived, things were just beginning. The choir was singing "Take Me to The King." Breanna found the words to be incredibly powerful. The song made her realize just how much God loved her. The sermon held an even more powerful message. Both the song and sermon seemed as if they were a custom design for her. After leaving the church, she had a new attitude and enough strength and courage to face her past.

***

After settling down at home, she walked to the porch and sat in her rocking chair. Even though it was the end of summer, it was still hot from noon until early evening. Today was a bit cooler, which made her more aware that the seasons were changing. The once shiny green leaves were now brown and lifeless as they fell to the ground, a sign of cooler days ahead. The changes that occur in nature was always an amazement to her.

The sermon stuck with Bre and persuaded her to make the call to Munda. It was something she had to do while she still had the strength and mindset. Nervously, Breanna dialed Munda's number. She let out a sigh of relief after it went directly to his voicemail. Her hands were sweaty. She told herself to calm down as she hit the redial button a couple of minutes later.

"Hello?"

From the time Munda answered, he didn't have a chance to say another word. Bre couldn't hold back what she'd had kept deep within herself for years. Even though her closest friends thought they understood how bad she hurt, the magnitude of her pain was much greater. For Munda to have walked away from Bre the way he did was the ultimate betrayal. She'd loved that man; he was a part of her soul. Munda now had the chance to understand the great torment he'd inflicted upon her.

"How could you walk off and leave me? Did you actually think I would have done anything to hurt you in any way? We were a family, Munda, and we had plans for our future. Instead of talking to me about what was going on, you walked away." Bre was breathing hard; her heart was pounding. "What kind of man does shit like that? If you really loved me, you wouldn't have left. That's not what real men do. You were happy that we were having a baby and were wishing for the son you'd always wanted. Anyone would have thought you'd hit the lottery. Within a week you had the future of that baby already planned. You called your friends and family sharing the joyous news. Out of the blue and without warning or explanation you left. My whole world turned upside down and inside out. Fuck you, Munda!"

There was silence on the other end of the phone, and the only thing she could hear was her own heavy breathing. She was trying to hold back tears.

"Say something, Munda! I'm sure you must have something to say because your ass has been quiet for four years!"

"You're right," he said.

Aside from her huffing and puffing, the only thing Bre could hear was her racing heart. It was as if she were listening to it through a stethoscope. As it pounded faster and faster, she lost the ability to speak.

"Bre, I can't tell you how sorry I am. If I could do things over, I would do them completely differently."

Weeping and slowly shaking her head, Bre kept asking *why* over and over. Tears rushed down her cheeks, and her shoulders shook as she waited for an answer. Munda listened as she cried. There was no hiding from the pain he'd caused. She remembered the many times she'd prayed to God for peace, strength, and understanding. She curled her body in an upright fetal position and swayed.

"Breanna, I'll make up for everything I've done. I promise," he said.

Bre could hear the regret and sorrow in his voice.

Those words meant nothing to her. With all the time that had passed, the memories and pain still lingered. The only question she could ask was, "Why did you allow it to happen?"

She could hear his voice cracking as he cleared his throat. Maybe for the first time, he realized the magnitude of the damage he'd caused.

As he asked her if he could call her back in a few minutes, his voice shook. Even though she couldn't see his tears, she knew they were present. She told him goodbye and immediately hung up the phone without waiting for him to respond. Anger arose in her because she couldn't understand what was more important than talking and trying to get the problem worked out. No matter how much she fussed, cussed, and asked questions, it didn't make her feel any better. She still didn't get all the answers she needed for closure. She paced back and forth through her house, trying to regroup.

Breanna told herself, "No, I'm not gonna keep doing this to myself. This is it." Bre snatched a tissue from the box and dried her face as she pulled herself together. Taking note of her possessions and what she'd accomplished alone, she had a lot to be thankful for. There wasn't one person who could honestly say they'd given her something. No matter how hard times were, she survived. She was ready to let go completely and move along, but instead, she got a bomb—Munda's return.

Breanna gave Deloris a call to let her know she was on her way to pick up Alex. They spoke about the conversation she'd had with Munda. It didn't take much for Dee to realize Bre was still upset and in pain from the sadness and hurt. She heard in her voice. She offered to have Alex stay over, but Bre wasn't going without her little one another night, no matter how badly she was hurting or what she was facing. By the time she arrived at Dee's, Alex was already asleep.

"He must have had a long day," Bre said, looking down at him smiling.

Dee realized Alex gave his mother great strength.

"You know how it goes when he and Zack are together. To top things off, we went over to my brother's house, and he has a couple of pups there. Alex really took to one of them, and they played together for hours."

Bre didn't respond but continued looking down at Alex with a smile as he slept in peace.

Even when she put Alex in his car seat, he still didn't wake up. Bre and Dee hugged each other and said their goodbyes. Upon arriving home, Alex opened his eyes only enough to give his mom a slight smile and wrap his arms around her neck tight as she carried him to his bedroom.

There was a noise outside. Bre's first instinct was to ignore it. She assumed it to be a stray cat that had climbed on her front porch. When the sound returned, she went to check what was going on outside. Carefully, she eased to the door and stood up on her toes to peek out the peephole. Someone was out there. Her heart pounded.

Never taking her eyes off what appeared to be a man, she reached for the light switch with her left hand. Startled by the bright light, the man turned around with the quickness. She unlocked the door and snatched it open.

"What are you doing here?" she snapped at him. She didn't want to yell too loud and wake up Alex or any neighbors, Bernice in particular.

Standing with his hands half-extended, as if he were ready to beg, Munda pleaded, "Can I come in, please? Please...I need for us to talk."

A million thoughts rushed through Bre's mind. She stood stagnant with disbelief and looked at him angrily. She couldn't believe Munda had shown up at her door again without being invited. Her head tilted to one side as she continued to gaze at him without saying one word.

"Please, Bre, we need to talk."

"Why should I talk to you? When I talked to you on the phone, you ended the conversation."

In a humble tone, he said, "You don't understand. It wasn't that I didn't want to talk. You think I don't have feelings?"

"I'm not really concerned with your feelings." Bre's anger was palpable in her cool indifference to Munda.

"Bre, please, let's go inside."

After much begging and pleading, Bre let him in. Looking around, he immediately took notice of Alex's pictures again. She didn't say a word. His swollen, bloodshot eyes let her know he'd probably done his own share of shedding tears. Tears formed as his hands met together like he was about to pray. Munda choked on his words as he attempted to speak. As much as she hated to, she almost felt sorry for him. His pain was visible as he attempted to make eye contact with her.

"I'm sorry...I really am," Munda said in a faint tone.

At that point, Bre didn't know what to say. Both of them were hurting, but most of all, she was furious about the way Munda had treated her.

"We should have been able to talk," she said, "but instead, we ended up fighting and hating each other. Why did I deserve such treatment? I did nothing to hurt you."

"I'm sorry, Breanna."

He walked up to her and wiped away the tears that were rolling down her pretty face. She slung his hand away from her face. Even though his compassion and regrets were sincere, Bre was not in the state of mind to accept them. Munda stood there, obviously not knowing what to say or do.

Her heart was beating fast, and she didn't know what to say or even think at that point. She looked down to break the eye contact. When she looked up again, tears were streaming down his face. What was she to say? She didn't know how to respond to him. She didn't know what he expected. Turning to the couch, she signaled with her head for him to take a seat. Before they sat down, she took the tissue that she'd used to wipe her own tears earlier and wiped his face. As she did so, he placed his hand on top of hers and allowed it to follow the motions of her gentle strokes. Still, they said nothing. While turning to get up and walk away, he gently grabbed her arm.

"Thank you for taking care of my son."

Breanna still said nothing because she needed no one thanking her for taking care of the child she'd brought into this world.

"Munda, what do you want? Tell me why you're actually here."

"Breanna, I'd like to get to know my son. I want him to get to know me, his father."

"Oh, so out of the clear blue sky you decided this is what you want?"

Bre formed a fist with her right hand, pounded it in her left hand, and momentarily turned away from Munda; his assumption that he could walk back into her life infuriated her again.

With her teeth clinched together and in a firm snappy tone, she asked question after question. "How could you walk away and not contact us for so long? Did you ever wonder if we were okay?"

"He's my son, too, Bre. You think I'm not gonna love someone who's a part of me?" He paused and then continued. "I love that little boy, and there hasn't been one day I didn't regret walking away. Pride and shame consumed me, but my heart condemned me. Bre, I didn't know how to come back. I wish I could go back and do things over again, but I know life doesn't work that way. I've prayed and cried many tears. I'm simply trying to correct my wrong."

She listened to every heartfelt word he spoke, so she'd be able to process them later.

"Please, may I see him for a little while?"

Munda waited for a response, but Bre rolled her eyes at his audacity to ask such a question. Munda waited in silence, hoping she'd eventually say something. Bre knew Munda accepted the fact that it would be tough getting through to her. She wouldn't go through any more pain for him and didn't care what their feelings might have been for each other before because an innocent child was involved. Breanna guarded Alex closely to keep him out of harm's way and safe, just as a mother should. Munda hadn't made it to the "safe list" with her yet, and to do so would take a long time. They reached a point where they could talk about what went wrong. There were so many twists and turns. Things weren't making sense. She talked with Munda for almost an hour before she decided she needed some rest.

"I have to get up early in the morning, so I need to go get some sleep," she said, yawning.

"Okay."

After searching around for his keys and locating them between the cushions on the couch, he stood up and placed his hands in his pockets. Before walking out, he gave Breanna a slight smile and thanked her for speaking with him. Breanna quickly returned inside her house and then made her way back to the door and saw that Munda hadn't got into his car. She called out to him. He turned around and proceeded back, extending his hand to accept what she was handing to him. He looked at it, smiled, and nodded his head. It was a recent picture of Alex. Even though things weren't good between the two, Bre was considerate enough to share Alex's picture with him. Maybe it was a way for Bre to torment and remind him what he walked away from or perhaps she wanted him to see what he'd helped create.

"Don't come here again without calling," she said firmly.

"I understand."

Before getting into his car, he stood gloating at Alex's picture once again, then turned back to Bre. "I'll do what's right from now on with you and our son."

Breanna said nothing as she stood with her arms folded. Even after starting his car, he continued smiling at the picture.

Perhaps Munda did a lot of soul searching, and perhaps his heart had been heavy with the burden of guilt. Strange enough, Bre sensed that everything would be okay between him and Alex. Time was essential. There would be some rough moments ahead, but the healing process was underway.

Chapter Six

It was quiet at work, but steady. Breanna had time to sort through her thoughts. Charles had been on her mind just as much as Munda. Things were going well between her and Charles. He seemed like a good man and someone she could build a strong relationship with. He was the first man in over four years to capture her attention. Bre was a bit unsettled that he had some of the similar gentle qualities Munda had once displayed; she wondered if that was what attracted her to him. Too many contradicting emotions were beginning to muddle her mind.

Three days had passed since she'd spoken to Munda. Though he'd called and left messages, she hadn't responded to any of them. Bre was emotionally drained and didn't want to become overwhelmed with pressure. It had taken Munda years to find his way back, so she didn't see any harm in him waiting a few days. Bre had her own thoughts to process as well as worrying about Alex and the emotional changes he might face.

No matter how bad she wanted to hold animosity toward Munda, she couldn't. The bottom line was that sharing a son bounded Munda to her for as long as Alex lived. There was no need to relive the same old thoughts. There was no more time for tears. They offered no answers and life had to move forward.

As Bre lay alone, sleepless, and tossing and turning in bed, thoughts of Munda rushed through her mind. Bre wondered what the nature of his relationship with her would be if he were to remain in her and Alex's lives. The presence of emotional intimacy she once shared with him was resurfacing. She couldn't understand why, which made things even more confusing for her. He'd given her every reason to hate him. The most difficult thing for her to come to terms with was the sexual attraction that was arising. Breanna struggled to admit this, even to herself. The energy between them had always been magnetic. Sex and life with Munda had been like heaven. He had just about everything most women wanted: a great job, great sex and he was easy on the eyes. Before all the mess and complications, Munda had always proven to be a real man in every way possible.

Breanna reflected on the times they'd made love. Munda took her to a level she'd never gone to before. He gave Bre her first orgasm; the memory sent chills up her spine. She missed that. She missed what they'd once shared. Bre closed her eyes, breathed deep, and opened her legs as if she were about to receive great pleasure. She remembered the experiences and satisfaction that Munda had once provided on a regular basis. Her clothes came off, allowing full access to her own body. How could she not think about indulging? Her clitoris was stimulated by gentle strokes while her back formed a small arch from the intense sensation. The flowing wetness took over, and her body contracting with pleasure and even more anticipation.

There was a knock on the door.

She decided to ignore it, but it sounded again. Certain that it was Bernice from across the street, Breanna became annoyed and angry at the same time.

"Breanna! Breanna!" she called as she continued to knock. Frustrated and mumbling to herself, Bernice attempted to peep inside the living room window, but she had no luck seeing anything. In a barely audible voice, Bernice mumbled, "I know that little bitch hears me knocking at this damn door." She looked around like she was searching for another means to see into Bre's house.

Bre watched Bernice fuss to herself and pace around on the

porch like an insane woman after having no luck getting Breanna to answer the door or finding a way to peep inside. Bre covered her mouth as she stood peering and giggling at Bernice with her pink hair rollers scattered over her head. Bernice looked into the peephole to see if she could see anything that way, but still no luck. When that failed, she gave up and went back across the street to her house.

Before returning to her bed, Bre checked on Alex, making sure the knocking hadn't awakened him. Within the next ten minutes, the knocking started again.

"Damn, I'm tired of this aggravating old witch!"

Bre was ready to go off on Bernice at this point. Enough was enough. She leaped from her bed, and with only a couple of buttons on her sheer sleeping shirt done and the matching bottoms open and hanging from her waist, she flung the door open with a massive attitude.

"Is this a bad time?"

Bre let out a loud sigh of disbelief. "No, and what the hell are you doing here?"

After leaning around Bre and into the house to see if anyone else was there, he gazed at her with an odd stare.

"Are you sure?"

"Munda, why are you here?" She frowned and buttoned her shirt to keep his eyes off her body. "Didn't I tell you not to come here without calling?"

"You left a message saying you wanted to talk."

If he only knew what was going on before he appeared, he wouldn't be giving her such a hard time. She continued to complain about him showing up unannounced. Munda bent his knees to lower himself so he was able to see directly into her eyes and apologized.

It wasn't that Munda was trying to intrude or disrespect her wishes of not coming there without calling. He explained after receiving her message, he thought it would be okay to come back and talk. A thin layer of ice broke as Munda took her by the hand, guided her inside the house, and closed the door behind him.

"For a moment, I thought someone was here with you. I hoped that wasn't the case," Munda said.

Bre looked at him in disbelief. Uncertain if he should finish his statement, Munda cleared his throat and stood there looking at her.

"Bre, it would hurt if I found out you were seeing someone. I may not have the right to say this, but it's how I feel."

Bre was awestruck and furious.

"Hell no, you don't have a right to say that."

Both anger and desire overwhelmed Breanna. Munda was unable to focus on her snappy tone because of what he saw, because of his growing lust. Through her thin white top, Bre's nipples stood firm, and her pussy was hot. Her thin bottoms were damp from the wetness of desiring Munda as he stood close to her.

"Bre, what's really wrong with you? You open up a little, and then you shut back down. I know I hurt you in a way I never should have. I can't take away the past, but I can admit my mistakes and try to be a better man, and a good father to my son."

Breanna's eyes remained fixated on Munda until she decided to turn and walk away. He gently grabbed her and wrapped his arms around her. She attempted to pull away from his grip, but Munda held her even tighter so she couldn't break away. Not wanting the conversation to turn sour, he turned her around to face him. They glared into each other's eyes without blinking. Both their hearts were beating. Neither knew what to say or do. Their looks were intense, and their emotions were all over the place. The tension was broken when he gave her a short kiss followed by a more passionate one. His heart pounded even faster and harder. His hands became sweaty as he backed her up against the wall. Their emotions were raw and at a heighten level.

"It's gonna be okay," Munda whispered in her ear.

It was clear that Bre was a bit discombobulated by many feelings that were going on, so he let go. He was still longing to be with her but didn't want to take any chances of upsetting her. Neither one still didn't know what to do or say; the kiss was something neither of them had expected.

Confused by the many unexplainable emotions that were rushing through her mind and soul, Bre became upset. "Get out right now!" Bre walked toward the door. Remembering Alex was only a short distance from them, she lowered her tone and growled, "You need to leave here and don't come back."

Munda tried to defend himself; Bre slapped him.

"What is wrong with you?" Bre said. "Do you think this is how it works?"

"Bre, please, you have it all wrong."

She stood speechless, but her eyes were saying many things. Munda waited for her to speak, but she didn't. The room was full tension, and neither of them knew what to do next. Bre's body was trembling as if she were freezing. With her arms folded she rubbed them with her hands, attempting to warm herself. Although her eyes filled with water, no tears fell. For the first time tonight, she avoided making direct eye contact with Munda. He walked over to her and held her tight in his muscular arms. With reluctance, she slowly placed her arms around him. Once the trembling stopped, he let go of her.

"Where's Alex?" he said.

Bre pointed toward his room and demanded that he not be awakened. Munda walked to the door and opened it see Alex. A smile stained with sadness appeared on his face while he stood staring at his son. Munda closed the door and walked near Breanna.

They stared at each other with many mixed emotions. Munda walked over even closer to her without saying one word. As his hand clutched her shoulders, her body almost went limp and a lump formed in her throat.

Munda let go, took a few steps backwards, and said with deep sincerity, "How did I allow things to go wrong?"

Breanna shrugged her shoulders. A saddened look took over her face as a single tear trickled down her cheek. Munda took both of his hands and held her face while using his thumb to wipe away her tear. His expression was one of compassion and regret. Her hand slowly made it to his strong arm and gave it a gentle touch. She wanted him bad, and his longing for her was just as great if not greater.

"How can I make things right, Bre?"

With her head hanging down, she shook her head as if to say she didn't know. When their eyes met again, he pulled her close to his body and held her. He rocked from side to side as his tight embrace gave each of them comfort. Munda's lips met hers, and a lot of tension disappeared. He could feel her heart pounding heavily. Even though she wanted to fight every emotion she was experiencing, she couldn't. He slowly unbuttoned her shirt and completely exposed her breasts. Stepping back, he looked as if he were trying to sketch the memory of them into his brain. Mesmerized by the beauty that filled his vision, he was unable to move or say anything for a few seconds.

It didn't take long before they were entering her bedroom and securing the door. Munda removed all his clothing as he kissed and caressed her. Standing naked in front of her, there was nothing she could do aside from admiring the beauty of his body. His dark, smooth body was tight and perfectly sculpted. Bre watched in anticipation as his biceps contract with his slightest movement. Kneeling on the bed, he pulled her down next to him and helped her lay down. He lay on his side next to her with one of his hands propped on his head and the other one slowly rubbing her body all over. When she spoke, he leaned his muscular body over and kissed her. From there, their journey began.

On his knees, he made his way down to her feet and spread her legs apart. She could feel the warm juices between her legs. She took in a deep breath as his tongue moved in a circular motion all over and within the walls of her pussy. Bre let out a soft gasp as his tongue caressed her clitoris. His slow intense sucking was sweet. It made her whole body curl up and tremble.

The more he ate her pussy, the wider her legs opened, and the more juices flowed. He worked every corner that she forgot existed.

She could only grab his head and rub it harder and harder.

In a sensual tone, Munda said, "Come on, Bre. Let it all go."

It took all her willpower not to climax. Despite all her efforts, she was about to cum—and he welcomed it. Even though she tried hard to hold on, the thrilling sensation overpowered her. An eruption was taking place. She had no more energy, but she didn't want him to stop. Without saying much, Bre looked at Munda and pointed to her nightstand drawer. Looking at her, then back at the drawer, he opened it to find the condom she was directing him to use.

Slowly, he slid it over his dick and gave her a long, slow, and passionate kiss. It wasn't long before she felt his big dick entering her. With a gentleness, he worked his way in her warmth and made love to her. He breathed a sigh of relief and held her. Munda looked deeply into Breanna's eyes while he made passionate love to her. They held on to each other as if they were holding on for their lives. Slow and steady, he pounded her pussy. Munda made certain he was giving the best of himself to her. They made love for what seemed like hours before they reached an orgasm together. No matter how much time had passed, they undoubtedly had an undying attraction to each other. Breanna fell asleep in Munda's arms and didn't wake up until the very early morning.

Bre rushed to get Munda out before Alex found him there. Before he left the bedroom, he walked over and gave her a soft kiss on her lips. She could no longer deny that she still had a lot of feelings for Munda. That, perhaps, was why she still was so hurt by his past actions.

It was the start of another day with the same routine. Flashbacks of what she and Munda shared ran through her mind. The thoughts alone of what they'd shared made her tremble. She thought about Charles and knew this would hurt him. Bre realized it would be best if she made plans to see him. She would do her best not to allow Munda to complicate her relationship with Charles.

Sitting on the edge of her bed, Bre said to herself, "Girl, what in the hell are you doing?"

Startled, she jumped as the phone rang; it was Charles. Bre looked at the phone for a moment before answering. It had been a couple of days since they'd spoken to each other. With everything going on, she assumed he was giving her room to think and get some things sorted out.

"How's everything going, babe?"

"Hi, Charles. Everything's going fine. How are you?"

"I'm fine, but missing you. I knew you needed some space with everything going on with Alex's dad."

She felt guilty. Breath-taking visions of her night with Munda ran through her mind. "Hold on, Charles. I need to turn off my shower." Bre moved the phone from her lips so she could regain her composure. She took a deep breath. "Okay, I'm back."

"I know it's been hard for you these past few weeks," he said. "Have you taken the time to talk to your son's father?"

"Yes, we've talked."

There was a pause as if he were waiting for her to say something else. Bre was becoming really nervous when it came to Charles. Under no circumstances did she want Charles to become suspicious of anything.

"I guess it's safe to assume it's going okay?" Charles said, trying to encourage her to give him more information.

Though he was being completely reasonable, Bre felt interrogated. "It was really hard at one point, but it's getting a little easier to deal with the anger and resentment."

"I'm sure it's difficult, but something will eventually give."

There had been a lot of giving, but Bre wasn't about to tell him that. She became more confused than ever. Her situation was now a bit more complicated than she could have ever imagined. Here she was with feelings for one man while emotions were being rekindled with another.

"It'll be okay," she said. "I'm trying to keep an open mind and remember that this is all about Alex."

"You'll be fine. I want you to have caution with this man. It's strange that he shows up suddenly. Then again, he may have had some hard thinking to do, and his conscience may have gotten the best of him."

Charles sounded concerned, and Bre knew he thought Munda might want something more with her.

"He said he only wants to be a father to his son." Bre was trying to keep control of Charles' thoughts and not allow him to read anything more into the situation.

"Are you certain that's all he wants? Make sure you tell him you have someone who loves and appreciates you."

Breanna was now overcome with guilt and was at a loss for words. In a very serious voice, she said, "He already knows." She didn't know what else to say to Charles, nor could she have predicted how bad she would feel after sleeping with Munda.

They talked for a few minutes and made tentative plans to see each other.

"Bre, I know you're getting ready for work, but I wanted to let you know I was thinking about you. Remember that I love you, okay?"

"I will," she said. Guilt was riding her hard, but there was no way she wanted Charles to find out about the intimacy she'd shared with Munda. They finalized her travel plans to spend the weekend with him then hung up.

"What the hell am I getting into with these men?" She didn't want to think about it because her life was becoming very complicated, so she focused on taking a warm shower and getting ready for her day.

Breanna was exhausted from not getting enough sleep the night before, due to her and Munda's lovemaking. All she wanted was for her day to pass quickly so she could get back home and rest.

Chapter Seven

During the next few days, Breanna considered allowing Munda to meet Alex. It wasn't an easy decision, but it was one she felt would benefit her son. Munda's phone rang several times before he answered; it was obvious to Bre he was still sleeping.

"Hello?" he said, still half asleep.

"Munda?" Bre said.

Hearing Bre's voice so early caused him to sit straight up in bed and became alert. "Bre, is everything okay? Is Alex okay?"

"Everything's fine." Bre closed her eyes, paused, and took a deep breath. "I've been thinking the past few days, and if you're free this Sunday afternoon, I'll allow you to meet Alex and—"

Before she could finish her statement, Munda blurted out, "Yes, yes, I'm free." It was as if Munda knew what Bre was about to say and was overly eager to hear her next words.

"Meet me at my house on Sunday, around four. Munda, I want to keep this as simple as possible for Alex. We'll take things from there after we see how he accepts or rejects this meeting. Don't you dare make me regret making this decision."

After everything was confirmed, Bre ended the call, exchanging no other words. It appeared that things were beginning to get a little better for Munda. It didn't take long for Breanna's busy day to rush by. On the drive to pick Alex up from daycare, thoughts cluttered her mind concerning Alex and Munda's meeting. On the drive home, she was quiet and nearly non-responsive to Alex's chatting about going to meet up with his buddy, Zack. Pulling into her driveway, Bre turned the car off and stared at Alex.

"What's wrong, Mommy?" Alex said, looking at her and twisting his finger in his nose.

"Get your finger out of your nose, boy," she chided.

Alex giggled as Bre reached over and gave him a kiss and squeezed his face. "Nothing's wrong, love. Come on. Natches is ready to relieve himself."

Hyped, Alex was ready to do whatever, so he could hurry up and spend Friday night hanging out with his pal Zack.

Once Bre got changed and settled, she called for Alex. "Come here, sweetie. Mommy wants to talk to you."

"Okay." He ran to her. He wasn't too interested in what his mom had to say; he only wanted to play with Natches for the moment.

"I have a special person you will meet."

"Who is it?"

"His name is Munda."

"Okay, but why do I have to meet him, Mommy?" Alex raised a brow.

"Well, he's someone you'll probably be seeing for a long time." Bre rubbed Alex's nose and he giggled. "Come on, little man, and let's do what we need to so we can meet up with Zack and Dee."

When they arrived at Chuck E. Cheese, Zack and Dee were already waiting with a cup of tokens. While the two boys ran around and played, Bre and Dee sat and talked. Dee was happy that Bre was allowing Alex to meet Munda and get to know him as his dad.

***

It wasn't long before Sunday arrived, and Bre was nervous as hell. She reminded Alex that Munda would come over soon. Just as she looked up at the clock, she heard the closing of a car door. Munda had made his way over to the house. When he rang the doorbell, Natches began barking and Alex ran to peep out of the curtains. Munda's emotions took over as he watched his son looking at him, waving. Upon opening the door and letting Munda in, Breanna could tell he was fighting back tears, because he kept wiping his eyes and clearing his throat.

"Good to see you, Alex," Munda said. He stood there with a huge smile on his face while looking at his son.

Fidgeting with his little fingers, Alex looked at Munda without saying a word. His little face had an expression of confusion as if he was unsure how to react. Moving closer to his mom, he continued to watch Munda with caution and uncertainty, but a slight grin remained on his face. Alex remained quiet, which was rare.

"Alex, do you remember me saying you'd be meeting your dad?" Bre knelt in front of him.

Alex nodded his head. As Munda extended his hand to introduce himself, Alex looked up at Bre with a half-smile on his face. She nodded her head at him to let him know it was okay to talk to him.

"You're tall," Alex said.

Munda smiled. "Is that right? Well, I think you will be pretty tall yourself when you're all grown up."

"Me too," Alex said.

"Do you mind if I pick you up and give you a hug?"

Again, Alex looked to see if it was okay with his mom. She nodded. Bre knew Munda's heart melted as he lifted Alex and held him tight with his eyes closed. One tear dripped from his cheek, and Bre knew from that moment on everything would be okay. Munda was holding his son for the first time and it was very emotional for him. Lowering Alex back down to the floor, Munda gave him another hug. He looked at Alex from head to toe, noting every small detail. He rubbed his head and then held his little hands; it was a powerful moment Bre would never forget.

Alex stared at Munda. "Are you really my daddy?"

The question caught both his parents off guard. Bre didn't know what to say. Munda lifted Alex up in his arms again and gave him a big nod.

Alex's little arms wrapped around his neck. "I've always wanted a daddy."

"You two stay here, and I'm gonna let Natches out back," Bre said.

Breanna used Natches as a way to get away and process what had just happened. This was having a great emotional impact on her. Ten minutes later, she walked back with Natches. Alex and his dog took off running towards the back door. The atmosphere felt different. Everything and everyone seemed at peace. There was no tension between Munda and Bre. For the first time, Alex had both his mom and dad.

"Are you okay?" Breanna stared at Munda.

He looked at her for a moment and then wrapped his arms around her. "Thank you, Bre. This is the best day of my life. That little boy is special." He gave her a hug and a kiss and looked her in her eyes. "Bre, you will never regret this."

"You better make sure you never walk out on him again."

Munda went into the backyard where Natches and Alex ran wild. It wasn't long before Bre discreetly stood at the door, listening to them talk. Alex asked his dad question after question. With patience, Munda answered each one to Alex's satisfaction. Each time she heard Alex address Munda as "Daddy," she smiled. Bre could only imagine how it made Munda feel. Just as she was about to join Alex and Munda, the phone rang.

"Hello?"

"Hey, babe. How's everything going?"

Alex ran in and said, "Can daddy take me and Natches to the park?"

Munda was behind him, explaining that it would only be for a little while so Natches could run. He assured her he'd take good care of both Natches and Alex. Bre was silent for a moment before she agreed with a bit of reluctance.

"I'm sorry, honey. You have my full attention now," Bre said as she walked near the window, watching Munda and Alex leave together.

"It seems like you have a lot going on."

Bre sighed. "Munda and Alex finally met."

"Now I see why you're so preoccupied." Charles became silent, and the only thing Bre heard was his fingernails tapping on something. "How did that go, Bre? I hope he'll be a real man this time and not run out on his kid."

"I'll give him the benefit of doubt for now. He knows he has only one chance."

"You seem to be very confident in what he'll do, considering his prior behavior."

Breanna knew Charles was bothered by Munda's presence, but he avoided voicing his direct opinion. That was fine since she didn't want to get into that conversation. Instead of getting into an uncomfortable topic, she reminded Charles of their Saturday evening plans. Charles told Bre about his erotic plans for her when she heard Alex and Natches running on the porch. She told Charles she needed to get Alex settled and take some time to calm herself down. By the time Alex made it into her bedroom, she was hanging up the phone.

"We had fun, Mommy."

"Is that right? Where's your dad?"

"He's coming."

By the time Alex got those words out, Munda was peeping into her bedroom. She looked at him and smiled, pleased that the two of them were getting along so well.

"Are you okay, Bre? You seem a little flushed."

"I'm okay."

"OK, but something seems to be wrong," he said with a bit of concern in his voice.

Breanna could tell Munda was trying to figure out what was going on. He kept staring at her, but he didn't say anything more. Alex went over to Munda and stood next to him, then held on to his daddy's hand.

Kneeling, Munda gave Alex a hug and said, "I love you, son."

It seemed to confirm what Bre had already concluded: Munda would be around for a long time. While looking at the two them together, tears of joy ran down her face.

"Mommy, what's wrong?"

"Nothing's wrong, sweetie."

"Well, why are you crying?" he said in an innocent but confused tone.

"Sometimes people cry when they're happy."

"Are you happy, Mommy?"

Bre bent down and gave him. "Yes, little man...I'm very happy."

Breanna picked him up and gave him a tight hug.

When Alex saw Munda looking, he said, "Daddy needs a hug, too."

Munda agreed with him and extended his arms. Bre rolled her eyes at Munda, knowing he was taking full advantage of the moment. Still, she gave him a hug to appease Alex. The three of them played around, laughed, and talked. It was like they'd always been together as a family. Even though it was getting late, Munda hated for his time with Bre and Alex to end.

"I guess I'd better give you guys some time to rest." Munda was disappointed.

They all walked Munda to the door and said their goodbyes. It had been a long day, and she needed to give Alex a snack so he could get a bath and head to bed.

After a full afternoon with his dad and dog, Alex was worn out. By the time he ate his evening snack and got a bath, he fell fast asleep. For a couple of hours, Bre sat up thinking and reliving the first moment Munda got to meet and interact with his son. It was a joyous moment she'd never imagined seeing. The instant bond of love that Munda displayed while holding Alex for the first time was unforgettable. Though he'd missed a lot of time with Alex, she believed he would always try to make it up to him.

Her eyes grew tired, and she caught herself dozing off. It was time for her to head to bed. Upon entering her bedroom, she saw Alex curled up in her bed. Breanna wasn't certain when he got out of his bed and came into hers. When she gently crawled in next to Alex, she placed her arms around him and kissed him on the cheek.

"I love you, Mommy," he mumbled.

Chapter Eight

Betty would finally arrive within the next couple of weeks. Breanna understood it was a hard decision for her, but they both knew it was a good decision. There was nothing keeping her in Brooklyn anymore. All she had left there were a few so-called friends who gossiped about her whenever she faced hard times.

Breanna had planned for her sister, nieces, and nephews for weeks. Now their arrival was only a short time away. She didn't know how long she would have to share space with them, but somehow, they'd manage. It probably would be some time before she and Alex would have the house to themselves after her sister's arrival, so she tried to take full advantage of every peaceful and private moment. Bre explained to Alex that they would be sharing their home with Aunt Betty and his cousins. He didn't seem to mind; however, she already knew he'd have to make some adjustments since he wasn't used to sharing his space and belongings. Bre felt this would be his greatest challenge.

Bre sat in the quiet darkness and thought about many things. Soon her thoughts drifted to Charles. Intimate thoughts of him made her miss her privacy already. She realized there would be no more heated conversations over the telephone at night to get her all worked up or their late-night rendezvous. Bre started gently stroking herself. With such intense thought, so intense that she grabbed the phone and began dialing.

"Hello?" Charles' sensual voice came through the phone.

"Hi, babe. You were on my mind, and I wanted to hear your voice."

He let out a chuckle. "Is that right, Bre?"

"Would you like to know what I was thinking?"

"Yes, tell me." Charles repositioned himself on the couch where he was sitting, giving Bre his undivided attention.

"I was thinking how worked up I get when you're not around. Like now, I'm lying here thinking about you with my legs wide open and massaging my clit." Bre sighed then closed her eyes and moaned.

"Damn, babe!"

Now, Bre really had Charles' attention.

"I wish I was there in person to do that for you. I wish I was eating up all your sweetness and making you scream my name. Girl, you got my dick hard as a rock."

"It's too bad you're working tonight because I could give you some good loving."

"Shit, girl, I hate that I have to go, too."

The two continued talking and teasing each other until Bre detected a change in Charles's voice.

"What's wrong, Charles?"

"Bre, the issue with Alex's dad bothers me a little. It makes me a little nervous."

Breanna wasn't shocked by Charles' statement. She knew it was only a matter of time before he revealed his concerns about Munda. It was always obvious that Charles suspected Munda was interested in more than Alex.

"Why would that bother you? He's only my son's father and nothing more."

"The two of you have a strong, close history and a son together. How are your emotions when you're around him? When two people love each other as much as you two did and then have a child, you share a special bond."

"But it's not like that, Charles." No matter what words came from Bre's mouth, she knew Charles was right. Things were already happening between her and Munda.

"Yes, I understand what you're saying, but I have a question for you," he said.

Bre became a bit nervous and braced herself for Charles's question. "You can ask me anything."

"Okay." Charles hesitated for a moment. "If Alex's father proves he's changed, would you give him a second chance for the sake of your son?"

There was an intense tone in his voice. Bre could feel all of Charles's attention focus on her as he waited for her to answer.

In a very sincere tone, Bre said, "It doesn't matter that Munda is around. Nothing has changed between us. We're fine." Bre didn't know if she was attempting to convince herself or Charles. One thing was for sure: she knew the conversation needed to end. For the time being, Charles seemed satisfied with her response, and Bre ended the call on a sweet note.

***

Bre's day at work was a little hectic, and it seemed as if everything that could go wrong went wrong, but she would not let the chaos get to her. The week seemed to drag by slow, but the weekend was finally close by.

"Girl, you still have that glow," Deb said with a grin on her face.

"What do you mean, Deb?" Bre looked at her.

"You know how we girls gleam when we've gotten our kitty taken care of really good."

They both laughed.

"Deb, you are so damn silly."

"You can call it what you want, but I know there's something big going on with you, and a man is somewhere in the picture, Bre."

"You think you have everything all figured out, don't you, Deb?"

"I know I do. No woman walks around with a glow like that on her face unless she's being laid really good or using a damn good vibrator. If it's a vibrator, I wanna know what kind, the manufacturer, and where you got it from!"

They both burst out laughing. Deb was a happy free-spirited person and always seemed to have an abundance of energy. She kept everyone laughing, even when things seemed grim. Despite her lively personality, she didn't take much shit from anyone. One thing for certain, she was fair with everyone and most people had a lot of respect for her.

"Go back to work, Bre. I'm gonna get it out of you sooner or later," Deb said, turning away with a sassy grin on her face.

"I'll tell you about him at lunch." Bre waved to Deb as she was walked back to her desk.

Bre continued working on a few things so she could at least see some progress by the end of the day. She loved her career, but there were challenges. Each day, she would encounter people who really needed help. Much too often she witnessed people getting denied by the system while others abused it and took it for granted. Her reward was being able to at least make life a bit easier for someone that needed help.

She often saw mothers dealing with adult children who had come back home with little ones who hadn't been getting the proper care. There were also those who'd become victims of the economic crisis and needed a little help to get back on their feet. Everyone had a story.

An hour later Deb walked up and said, "Come on, girl. Aren't we having lunch together?"

"Deb, let me wrap up a few things." Breanna locked down her computer, put some papers away, and met Deb in front of the elevator.

"Where do you wanna go for lunch, Bre?"

"Let's go where we can sit and talk."

"Why don't we grab a salad or something from the deli and sit outside?"

"That sounds good. It's a beautiful day."

"You can start talking any time," Deb said with excitement in her voice. She couldn't wait to find out what was going on.

All Bre could do was laugh at her friend. "You were right: I have been seeing someone."

"I already knew that much. I wanna know the hot details about him. Quit stalling, girl, and get to talking."

"It's Charles."

"Charles?" Deb's eyes grew big as she made a keen, high-pitched scream. "I knew it!"

"Yep, it's Charles." Bre blushed.

"C'mon, give me the details. No wonder that rumor started that he was at your house during all that rain."

Breanna almost choked. They both laughed hysterically as they always did. People in the deli looked at them in annoyance, but the stares didn't make them stop laughing. Bre didn't even have to ask how she knew because Bernice never wasted time spreading the latest gossip or rumor. That woman was a real piece of work. The two ladies got their salads and headed outside.

"Deb, now you know that was so wrong of Bernice. When I got home from work that Monday evening, she made a smart comment. Before she could really get started, I cut the conversation short. The next time, I'll let her see something she'll be too embarrassed to tell anyone about."

They laughed again and came up with wild things for Bernice to see.

Deb cleared her throat and regained her composure. "We also know she saw him coming out of your house on that Saturday morning."

Deb was obviously enjoying the whole thing. She already knew Charles was the man who was causing Bre to smile.

"Girl, it's good to see you smiling and happy. We, women, deserve to find happiness with a good man."

"How do you know he's a good man, Deb?"

"He's making my friend smile." She reached over and gave Bre a firm hug. "Breanna, you have been glowing. What took you so long to figure out he was really into you?"

"What do you mean?"

"I know y'all would talk from time to time when you were around each other, but he asked more personal questions. He talked to me about you at the community picnic months ago."

"Really? That was almost a year ago." Breanna was truly surprised.

"Yeah. He was watching you and Alex running around playing, and he wanted to know things about you. When I saw him at the hospital, where he works as a nurse, he asked about you again. I told him you had a bad attitude and he probably should stay clear of you." Deb shrugged her shoulders and took a bite of her salad.

"Why would you tell him that? You wouldn't have told him anything as crazy as that, would you?"

"Nope, but I wanted to. I figured since y'all talked from time to time, he already figured out you're a crazy person." Deb looked at her and laughed. "Bre, I'm just kidding with you. I could tell he'd been watching and admiring you. He was trying hard to get information about you without being so obvious. Didn't Renee tell you?"

"Tell me what?"

"Charles intended to give me his number so I could give it to you, but Renee took it and said she would do it since she would see you later that day."

"Renee never gave me anything."

Bre frowned. She was trying to figure out why Renee never gave her the number, but it wasn't surprising since this was not the first time Renee did something underhanded.

"I know for a fact that I gave her that damn number. At one point, Charles even told Renee that was okay, because he'd run into you again sooner or later. Now that I'm thinking back, it was as if he didn't trust her with his number."

"Are you sure?" Bre said, still looking confused

"I'm damn sure. The more I think about it, I'm sure something strange was going on between the two of them. I don't know what was going on or what went on, but there was something wrong with that picture. Renee kept that number from you on purpose."

"Maybe she forgot to give me the number." Bre paused for a moment to process her thoughts. "That bitch kept the number on purpose. She didn't forget shit!"

Deb's demeanor changed quickly because she knew without any doubt Renee had been up to something conniving and underhanded. "Um-huh. I say there's something more to the story, too, Bre. There's something about Renee that simply doesn't set right with me. If I was a betting woman, I'd say she wanted Charles for herself."

"We ended up getting together regardless, so whatever her intentions were, they failed."

"Girl, I wanna know about the good stuff…you know, the sex."

"Why? So you can get all worked up and go home to play with your own kitty?"

"You're not right, Bre."

"I'm trying to spare you. I don't want you to lie up in your bed, trying to imagine how Charles was eating my pussy so good, I begged him to stop. You don't need to be sitting around wondering what it feels like having multiple orgasms with a partner that can keep a hard-on as long as you want him to. It wouldn't be right for me to tell you I got banged so hard and so freaking good to the point I almost forgot what day of the week it was. What kind of friend would do such a thing?"

Breanna could almost see Deb's mind trying to imagine everything she was telling her. Deb could only gape at her in astonishment.

"You lucky, bitch," Deb said, rolling her eyes and sucking her teeth in a teasing manner.

"Whatever." Bre crossed her legs, trying to stop her kitty from getting over excited.

They both laughed. Deb continued asking questions, and Bre tortured her with details that were sure to send her mind on a wild adventure.

"So, you got the best fuck of your life, huh?"

"He was running a close tie."

"Well, damn! Who had first?"

"Alex's dad. Munda almost drove me mad the first time he made love to me."

"How in the hell did you get so lucky? I always end up with some sorry ass that can't last five minutes. All these men want to do was hop on top, do some old quick up and down bullshit, and fall asleep."

Bre laughed so hard her stomach ached. She doubled over with laughter. She always found herself in uncontrollable fits of laughter when she was with Deb. "Deb, bring your silly butt on, and let's get back to work."

Bre enjoyed having a friend like Deb around to talk about things with and to share things with. Deb talked a lot of shit, but she had a husband she loved. For the past few days, Munda had been taking Natches and Alex to the park for about an hour in the evenings. That helped Bre out a lot since she'd been busy preparing things for Betty and her kids, but the lack of sleep was catching up with her. No matter what time restraints she was under, she had to find time to spend with Charles. She also knew he still had concerns about Munda. Bre was just as worried as Charles, but there was no way she would tell him that.

Each day, Deloris would call to check on her and see if there were any new developments. She was a fan of Munda's until he walked out on Bre. Even after he left, Dee searched for understanding because it was out of his character to do such a thing.

The evening went smoothly. Munda took Alex out for dinner so Bre could get some rest. He even offered to bring her a plate to bed, but she was too tired to eat. She didn't know what time he left. The next thing she knew, her alarm was going off and Natches stood near her bed with his leash in his mouth. He was like a second child. As soon as he saw her eyes open, he'd bark and wagging his tail, as if he were saying "Good morning." He knew her routine. He watched as she walked into Alex's room to make sure he was okay and then into the bathroom.

After Bre emerged from the bathroom and headed to the kitchen to start her morning coffee, Natches knew it was now time for her to take him outside. Even though she thought Natches's morning walks was a hassle when she first got him, but now it was an opportunity to have some personal time with God, to inhale the fresh morning air, and to hear the sweet sounds of nature. There were never many people outside during this time of the morning, but she knew Bernice was somewhere peeping out of her window.

It was the start of a new day, and Bre felt rejuvenated. Even being torn between Munda and Charles, having Alex's father around seemed to make life much easier for both her and Alex. She was glad everything was working out for the best. For the first time, she was feeling as if she weren't completely alone in raising Alex.

When Bre reached work, Deb was also arriving. Bre waited for her to get out of her car so they could walk into the office together. She was smiling and in a good mood.

"You sure seem happy this morning, Deb," she said.

"Perhaps I got a little some of what you've been getting."

"I know one thing for certain: if you got some of what I had, it wasn't a little something." Bre winked.

"Bre, you are such a nasty bitch!" Deb could only shake her head and laugh. "How's everything going with your busy life?"

"It's going okay. Munda and Alex are getting along fine, and Charles is hanging in there."

"Is he jealous of Munda being around?"

"Yes, but I don't know why." She knew but didn't want to admit it.

"So, you get to have both your cake and ice cream, too, huh?"

"What do you mean?"

"I mean both Munda and Charles. You can't tell me sparks haven't been flying at home with Munda."

Bre stopped, rolled her eyes, and pointed her finger at Deb. "You're wrong, Deb."

"Okay, we shall see."

Deb knew as well as Bre did that she was right. Bre might wasn't willing to admit this to her, but she had to face the truth herself. Bre refused to think about Munda and their relationship too much. How could she tell anyone what was going on when she didn't know herself?

She was preoccupied with thoughts of Charles and Munda. Her emotions were going crazy. The time spent with both men was special and meaningful.

Chapter Nine

Breanna began making babysitting plans for Alex so he could be cared for while she spent some very intimate, uninterrupted time with Charles. The thought of asking Munda came to mind, but that was out of the question. She knew he would have a thousand questions that she didn't want to answer. With Charles having been away with his ailing father in Florida for the past couple of months, he and Bre had a lot of catching up to do.

She also didn't want to ask Munda because of who she was spending time with, and obviously what they'd be doing. The fact was she'd given herself to Munda in an intimate way, and now she would be with Charles. A part of her didn't want Munda to know she was so closely involved with someone. Deloris and Bre were pretty good about taking care of each other's kids, so she'd be the one to watch Alex.

Strange as it sounded, she didn't want to hurt Munda, but there was no way she would give up the opportunity to have a secure relationship with a man willing to love and stand by her during both the good and bad. Even though Munda had come back to be in Alex's life, it didn't mean everything else would be fine. Breanna was sure it wouldn't be a problem for Deloris, but she had to make sure. She picked up the phone to call her.

"Hello?"

"Hi, Deloris."

"Hey, Bre! What's going on?"

"I need a huge favor."

"Okay, what's going on?"

"I need someone to look after Alex next weekend."

"Let me pull out my little black book and see if I can fit him into my schedule." They laughed. "Bre, Alex will be fine here. He and Zack can entertain each other. Where are you going?"

"Florida. I need to spend some time with Charles."

"Good Lord. Does Munda know?"

"Munda isn't my husband or father. What am I supposed to do? Stop whatever's going on in my life because he suddenly showed up? I don't think so."

"You're right, but haven't you two been getting it on?"

"Deloris! Why would you ask such a question?"

"Well, I'm not stupid. I saw how the two of you were looking at each other, so I knew something was up."

"It's not like that. It happened once and I felt terrible. I got caught up in the moment. It wasn't planned, Dee. Sleeping with Munda was the last thing on my mind. It was a huge mistake."

"Damn, I'm trying to get one dick and you have two. You should be ashamed of yourself."

"C'mon, Dee, I didn't plan to sleep with Munda. If I could go back and undo it, I would."

Bre tried not to let her anguish show, but she knew it was finally time to be honest with her friend. She knew Dee would help her with her struggles by listening and being an objective voice.

"If you need to talk, I'm here. I know this has to be tough. You and Munda have a special bond. You have history. And you share a son."

"You're right, Dee. I don't know what it was between the two of us. When we touched each other sparks flew. He was a part of my happiness. The only thing I know is that I need a fresh start. I want the opportunity to find happiness again."

"We all deserve happiness."

"Girl, let me take myself to bed and get some sleep, because I can go on and on about this. I'll talk to you later in the week."

"Goodnight, Bre."

Standing at the window, Bre could see the small tree branches swaying from the breeze. The sky was clear and the stars twinkled above. Calm had claimed her place on a peaceful night. Many naughty thoughts of Charles rushed through Bre's head. She couldn't wait to get next to him. It was late. Bre, however, remembered him telling her that she could call him anytime. She wanted him to know she was making plans for a special weekend, so she dialed his number. When Charles answered his phone in a seductive tone, Bre couldn't help herself. "My, my, my, what a strong and sexy voice you have."

"Ms. Bre. This is a much-welcomed call."

She could hear his smile through the phone.

"I debated on whether or not to call you because of the time, but I remembered what you told me."

"I'm glad you did, Baby Cakes, because I'd been thinking about you while driving home from work."

"And what were you thinking?"

"Hmm, I was thinking how nice it would be to come home and hold you in my arms and warm you up."

"Just warm?" she said with a sarcastic tone.

"You don't like warm?"

"Warm is okay, but with you, hot is even better."

She leaned her head back against her headboard as she twirled her hair with her fingers. Bre knew Charles was probably feeling horny too. She knew first-hand what he was capable of doing to her, and she wanted what he had to give.

"Interesting…I was trying to be conservative, but with you, it would be hot all the way."

"Don't get me started. You may start a fire you can't put out."

They laughed and then made small talk. She always found comfort in talking to Charles. He was attentive and always seemed to have the right thing to say.

"Guess what?"

"Let me see...you have everything taken care of for next weekend."

"How did you know?" she asked while blushing.

"I was hoping for that."

"Well, you got your wish."

"Bre, I can't wait for you to get here. I have something special planned for you."

"Such as?"

"You'll see. But one thing is for certain: I'll put the fire out."

"Is that a promise?"

"No, it's a guarantee."

The hum of Charles' sexy voice was making her horny. She became a bit fidgety as wild, lustful thoughts ran through her mind. The longer they continued the conversation, the more she wanted him near her.

"What are you doing at this very moment?" she said.

"Thinking about how horny I am and wishing you were here to give me some relief. You know how hot I get from listening to your voice."

"No, but you can tell me now and show me later."

"You make my dick feel like it might explode into a hundred pieces. I need some relief from you, Bre."

"Babe, you are in for a real treat. I'm gonna eat your pussy and swallow every drip of juice that falls. You'll be begging me to stop."

"Don't think you'll be the only one giving your all. After I wrap my tongue around your dick, you'll get an instant hard-on whenever you think of me."

All this talk made her pussy wet. All she could think about was having Charles's big dick inside of her. She continued to talk and lay there, wishing for something impossible to have at that moment. She knew she had to hurry up and end the call so she could pull out her extended friend, her Mandingo.

"Bre, you are killing me."

"Are you gonna jack off now?"

"No, I'll save everything for you, but I will go take a cold shower. Your ticket is on me. I told you I wanted you here, so I'll do my part in this. I'll purchase your ticket tomorrow and send you the details."

"No, I told you I want to drive there. It is only a few hours, and the scenery will be nice. Okay, love? Enjoy your evening, and we'll talk later."

"How can I when you've ruined me for the night? That's okay, though, because I'm sure you'll make up for it later."

"I will. I promise. Goodnight, honey."

"Goodnight, babe."

Bre slid her fingers back and forth in her wet pussy. She wanted to scream. She knew she needed Mandingo for tonight. Finally, she got up from the bed, reached to the top shelf in her closet, and pulled out her handy little friend. He was nice, firm, and a deep shade of brown. He was seven inches long with a thick circumference.

The first thing Bre did was check Alex to make sure he was sound asleep. She didn't need to get busted with a rubber dick in her. What the hell was she thinking? Why in the world should she be using something that can't rub or lick her breasts, moan back, or hold her close after she had as many orgasms as possible? Why should she subject herself to this when Munda was only a phone call away? She wanted a warm, live body next to her.

She picked up the phone and put it down just as quick. Out loud, she gave herself every reason not to call Munda at this time of night. The more she thought about it, the more she realized it wasn't just about sex. Munda was getting back into her heart. The weeks they'd been sharing time with Alex had led them all to become closer. They were around each other just about every day. Whether Bre wanted to admit it or not, emotions were rebuilding more and more without her putting forth any effort. Just as she shook things off and went to bed, the phone rang; it was Munda, and he sounded a bit strange.

"Is something wrong, Munda?" Bre was concerned; she hadn't heard him like this before.

"There's something I have to take care of, and I'm trying to figure it out but I can't. I need to talk to you, Bre."

There was silence for a moment, and then Munda told her she wasn't obligated to talk to him if she wasn't up to it. Bre knew that whatever was bothering him, it was serious.

"You're quiet, Bre."

"I was just thinking, Munda."

"Sounds like you've been doing some serious thinking, too."

"Yes, I have. There's a lot to think about."

"Why don't you come over and do some thinking with me, Bre? Please, just listen to me. I just need to talk and get all of this stuff sorted out."

Bre explained to Munda that Alex was sleeping and she wasn't about to wake him up and bring him out. Munda understood, but he was disappointed. They finished up the conversation, and Bre told him maybe they could talk another time. Each one of them tossed and turned while they thought about each other.

A light appeared outside. Bre knew it was Munda pulling into the driveway. Before he knocked, she was standing there ready to receive whatever he had to deliver. Even before the door closed all the way, he wasted no time getting down to business. The thick bulge in his pants made her desires grow even more.

"Munda," was the only thing he allowed to come out of her mouth.

He lifted her. She wrapped her legs around his waist and hung onto his body as he sucked her breasts and carried her into the bedroom. The soft aroma of jasmine in her bedroom and the sexy sounds of R&B enhanced the mood. Even before he placed the condom over his dick and entered her, she could see the juices coming from it.

"This is your dick, babe," he said.

Looking into Munda's eyes, Bre saw that he was on a serious mission. Nonstop, he was pumping her to where she thought she would scream. As he worked her over, the sweat was falling from his body; he never missed a beat.

"This is my pussy, Bre...it's mine."

Bre could only moan from the satisfaction she was getting.

Munda rolled over and sat her on top of him. With his strength, he lifted her and moved her up and down on his dick. The passion between them was at its peak. She could see Munda clenching his teeth. The full expression on his face told her he was ready to explode. Tighter and tighter, he held onto her ass as he made it pounce up and down on his huge dick. The veins in his neck and forehead were protruding. All of a sudden it was over. They clinched each other tightly. With no words being exchanged and neither of them having any movement, they appeared lifeless.

The bed was soaked from the sweat and cum released from their bodies; it was as if someone had dumped a gallon of water on the bed.

"Damn," Bre said. Her body was exhausted from the adventure she'd just undergone.

"Did I satisfy your hunger?"

"Yes, and you probably supplied me with a doggy bag for later."

Munda had given her a good fucking she could think about later, which would cause her to have another orgasm just from the thought of it. As she lay with her head resting on his chest, he stroked her hair back. Charles didn't enter her mind again that night. At that moment, it seemed as if it were only she and Munda in this big world. Everything seemed right. Even from the very beginning their emotions connected in a special way. She felt as if her soul was intertwining with his, the same as it had years ago.

Patting her on the ass, Munda got her to roll over on her stomach. With his strong hands he massaged her shoulders as he straddled her back on his knees. Feeling his dick resting on her ass, she closed her eyes and exhaled. From shoulder to shoulder, he kissed her. The escaping juices from her warm pussy lubricated his dick. Munda tried to remain in control as he moved his body up and down in her slippery wetness. The sweet sound that came from him made Bre work her body even harder giving him even more pleasure.

Placing his arms under her body and holding her tighter, Munda said, "Oh, Bre, this is sweetness."

Closing his eyes and taking a deep breath, Munda stopped pumping and leaned his head back for a moment to regain control of himself. Rolling Bre over onto her back, he lifted one of her legs and placed it over his shoulder. He then kissed her inner thigh and slowly removed his hand from it. Looking at her, he guided his thick cock into her tight, wet pussy. She felt her eyes roll back and her mouth open. When she pulled herself off the bed to reach and lick Munda's nipples, it was on. Munda's dick had her name on it; it was hers for the taking. All she wanted to do was give him a piece of pussy he'd remember for a very long time.

Breanna held on to Munda's torso as she rode his dick in a slow steady motion from left to right, up and down, and back to the right and then the left. The rhythm was strong, and she didn't skip a beat. Munda hung on and kept up with everything she had for him. It was too good to let go. She knew he was getting as tired as she was, but she wanted to make sure he was equally satisfied.

They rolled over, and she knew she had the power to take him out. She pushed Munda's hands off her body and rode his dick faster and harder. Even when he wanted to touch her body, she'd only pushed his hands away. Feeling his dick growing bigger and bigger, she slowed her motion almost a complete stop.

"Let me give you something real good," she whispered in his ear.

Her hands pressed against his thick abs as she looked at him, smiling. Wanting to take Munda to another level, Bre separated her pussy from his dick by moving backwards so she'd have room to work while blowing his horn.

"Oh, damn, babe. Ooh, it feels so wonderful…it feels so damn good."

Oblivious, Munda raised his body up, attempting to see the pleasure Bre was having. Even with the great effort of trying to sit up and watch her motions, he could only drop back down on the bed. He pulled at her hair and rubbed her head as he moaned and grunted.

Bre wrapped her tongue around his dick and caressed it. Hearing his moans of pleasure made her want to work even harder at satisfying him. She made it her mission to send him to new sexual heights.

Engulfing the head of his dick into her mouth, she knew she would give him one hell of a treat. As she sucked, she continued to stimulate the head of his dick with her tongue. From the head to the very bottom, she allowed her tongue to work its stimulating magic.

Munda's hands gripped her hair, and his legs began trembling while Breanna continued her mission. She wanted to watch him have a powerful orgasm. Bre's slight pulling of his dick and the caressing of his balls by softly sucking them took Munda to his breaking point. His sounds of the pleasure grew louder and more intense.

"Please don't stop, Bre," was all he could say.

She had no intention of stopping.

Munda let out a strong, powerful eruption as his body subdued itself to an orgasm that took him to another level. His seed shot out of his dick with force, flowing like hot lava from a volcano. He gripped the sheets and his body stiffened and became paralyzed. Her small hands reached out to touch his body so he would know they were taking a journey together. Breanna gave Munda a part of herself that she'd been holding on to for a long time. Everything felt right being with him. Once again, they lay there holding on to the moments of passion they'd shared. The night seemed very still until she heard a little voice.

"Mommy, Mommy!"

Bre jumped straight out of bed. As she made her way to the

door, she threw on the little gold gown that had quickly found its way to the floor.

Alex called out her name again as she was rushing to him. His little face was wet with tears. She wasted no time grabbing him and pulling him into her arms and making him feel safe. She held him tight in her arms to assure him that everything was fine.

"He was mean to me and Zack, Mommy."

"Who was mean to you, love?"

"The monster, Mommy."

She pulled him back into her sweaty body.

"It was just a silly dream. Mommy isn't gonna let anyone or anything hurt you. I promise I'll keep you safe."

Alex held on tight to her arm. With his little voice, he asked if he could come and sleep in her bed. Before she could say anything, Munda was walking toward them.

"Daddy!"

When she turned around, Munda was reaching out to lift Alex up into the safety of his arms.

"Go lay back down, I'll get him settled in," he said.

"Are you certain?"

Munda rubbed Alex's back and looked at him. With a warm smile on his face, he replied, "We can handle this."

Bre slowly backed away with a look of uncertainty on her face.

Thirty minutes or so passed as she waited, but Munda still hadn't returned to the room. Bre didn't want to intrude on his trying to comfort their son, but she needed to make sure everything was okay. After quietly easing her way to the door, she saw her little man and Munda cuddled up sleeping. She watched them and hoped the moment would remain part of her memory forever. The beauty of it brought tears to her eyes. There she stood in silence, appreciating the bond Munda had formed with their child. Bre was completely taken.

For the first time, her home held her entire family. She couldn't imagine wanting anything more. All those good feelings were creeping back. It was still too early to figure out what she wanted, though, or better yet what would be best for everyone.

Bre went back to her bed and held tight on to a couple of pillows. She soon drifted off into a deep sleep. It wasn't long before the alarm was sounding and letting her know it was time to get up and face a new day. Munda was carefully easing his way out of Alex's room while trying not to wake him.

"I wonder who was doing the comforting. And thanks for being there to make him feel safe." Bre gave him a warm sincere smile as she touched his hand.

"Bre, don't thank me for that. That's our son and you don't have to do everything by yourself any longer."

In her mind, she was wondering why it took so long for him to use his brain, but she only smiled while he continued to talk. The love, care, and time Munda was offering his son made it obvious Alex had opened a secret part of Munda's heart. The innocence and love of his child stole his heart. By the time Bre and Munda got back into her bedroom, he swung her around and wrapped his arms around her waist.

"I'm gonna get going so I don't disrupt your routine."

"Huh. Life is funny, isn't it, Munda? Just when you think you have it all figured out, you get thrown for a loop."

The phone rang. She looked at it and then at Munda.

"Aren't you gonna answer your phone?"

She walked over to the phone to take a look. Out of all mornings, Charles was calling bright and early. She decided not to answer and smiled at Munda.

"Looks like a wrong number," she said in her most convincing way.

He stood there for a moment and squinted at her. The phone rang again. Munda walked over to get his shirt, but he continued over to where the phone was sitting. He looked at the Caller ID and asked her if he should answer. "It's a Charles Long. Maybe I should let him know he's calling the wrong number."

As Munda got ready to answer the phone, Bre yelled, "You

don't answer my phone!"

Everything got quiet. Munda stood in complete silence, looking at her. He wasn't slow at all; he knew why she didn't want him to answer. Bre could feel everything shift downhill.

"Bre, what the hell just happened? You're screaming at me, telling me I don't answer your phone."

Munda picked up the pillow that was on the floor and threw it hard onto the bed. He then got dressed and walked out of the house without saying another word. She didn't know what she could say to take away his anger. Watching him drive away made something inside of her ache. Her mind told her he'd be fine and just to let things go, but her heart told her to comfort him. She didn't know what to do. She didn't know what his thoughts were.

"Damn, damn, damn," came out of her mouth as she pounded the mattress with her fists.

She flopped on the edge of her bed and sat with all the good thoughts from last night, and then the terrible one that had ended her beautiful morning. What a night it was, filled with emotions and passion. She slid under her covers while grabbing a pillow and curling herself into the fetal position. Her heart ached. Not only was she hurting, she could also feel Munda's pain and anger. All of her actions had led to major complications.

This was a terrible way for their night to end. For once, Bre could watch Munda step in and really play the role of father to his son. She was hurting just as much as Munda. She knew he wanted his family back and was giving all of himself to her and their son. Despite all this, she had to return Charles's call. Breanna felt like crap behind hurting Munda. She didn't want to hurt anyone else, Charles in particular.

Bre wanted to call Charles back, but she showered first. She needed that time to pull herself together.

"Hello?" the perky voice spoke.

"Good morning. How are you?"

"I'm fine, but I wish I was there making love to you, Bre."

"Really?" Bre could only think about the memories she and Munda had created throughout the night.

"I tried calling you twice this morning, but you didn't answer."

"You probably called when I was in the shower."

"That's what I figured."

"Honey, I don't mean to cut you short, but I'm running late. I promise we'll talk this evening."

It wasn't that Bre was running late; it was that she couldn't focus. She was overwhelmed with worry. At one point, tears formed in her eyes, but she held herself together. Bre didn't know how to fix this one. The only thing she was certain about was that it wasn't just a meaningless screw. What she and Munda had shared last night made her realize their emotions for each other had never died. After sitting and thinking for a few minutes, she moved around. It was time to start her routine of getting ready.

"Alex, it's time to wake up, love." Bre watched him stretching and turning over in his bed. "Come on, baby. It's time to get up and start the day."

"Mommy, where's my daddy?"

"He's at his house."

"He left?"

"Yes. He only stopped by to see you last night then he went back home."

Bre sat on the corner of Alex's bed and gave him a kiss on the forehead.

"Why can't he stay here?"

She looked at Alex and gave him a tight squeeze. Her heart melted from the deeper sorrow of his question.

"Sweetie, we'll have to talk about that later when we have time. Right now, you need to get up so I can get you to school and I can get to work. We don't live and eat for free, you know."

It seemed as if Alex was moving in slow motion and wasn't making any effort to move any faster. Bre watched him waste time. He sat on the toilet, looked around, and talked aloud to himself. He could drive her absolutely crazy doing this, but she figured he was going through a phase.

"Alex! Get moving, boy. You don't have time to be out there in La La Land."

Once Alex finally got through the process of getting dressed and having breakfast, it was about time to leave. He was talking away, but it only seemed like a background conversation because Breanna was consumed by what had transpired between her and his dad. She had an awful lot on her mind.

***

Bre pulled up in the daycare driveway early, so she was happy to have some free time before work. For a Friday, the traffic wasn't bad. The ride to work was quiet, and she could think in peace. Despite her instincts, she dialed Munda's number from her cell phone.

"Hi. I wasn't sure you'd answer."

"Do you think I should have, knowing it was you calling?" Munda snapped.

"I guess you're angry."

"Nah., I was at first, but then I thought, what the heck, at least you got what you wanted for that moment. I was just a substitute fuck for the night." Munda was hard and cold.

"Excuse me?" His remark shocked Bre.

"I'd say we had an even exchange since we both got off. I guess it was a meaningless screw to you, Bre. What, your boyfriend couldn't get to you last night?"

"Why are you talking like that? Why do you have to be so nasty?"

"Am I being nasty, Bre? I think you were being nasty."

Bre had no words to defend herself. She remained silent as she thought of the next thing to say. "I'm almost at work, but I'll call you when I get home this evening. I don't want there to be any hatred between the two of us."

Munda didn't end the call with a goodbye. Instead, he hung up abruptly. This made her feel even worse. She also realized she would face a greater challenge if she didn't figure out some things.

The morning was already going bad, and Bre didn't expect it to get any better. She knew each day at work was filled with new drama, new faces, and new headaches. She also knew she couldn't allow her personal problems to follow her into her workplace, but this would be a tough day for her. Deb was the first person she saw.

"Good morning, Deb."

"Morning, girl. TGIF!"

"Thank goodness. I need a couple of days off."

"They just go by too fast, and that's no lie," Deb said.

They both laughed and made a little more small talk before they started work.

The day that followed was busy and fast-paced. Perhaps, for Bre's sake, that was a good thing. It kept her preoccupied, so she didn't have time to think about what had gone on that morning, but as the time came near for her to leave, she thought about Munda and what thoughts he was possibly having. She became saddened once again.

"What are you doing for the weekend, Bre?" Deb said.

"I'm not certain, but you know I have to get Alex out of the house, or else he'll drive me nuts."

"Let him spend the night with Munda, girl, and have some time to yourself."

"I don't know about that one, Deb," Bre said and shrugged her shoulders.

Within her own mind, Bre thought Munda would probably think she was just trying to get some time to spend with Charles. She didn't want that. Their situation was too delicate already, and she wanted no more misunderstandings.

"Bre, why would you have a problem with that? They get along fine, and they have a very close relationship. Let them have some time alone in Munda's home."

"I think this will be a bad weekend for that."

"Why?"

"Munda spent the night, but he left furious this morning."

"Oooooooh."

"Deb, it was such an awesome night. We made love like never before, and the passion was unbelievable."

Deb lifted her hands in the air with great confusion. "So what's the problem, girl? Bre, no matter what anyone says or thinks, you and this man have some unfinished business." Deb sighed and placed her hands on her hips. "How in the hell can you move on with another man when you need to figure things out with Munda?" She waited for Bre to respond, but when Bre remained silent, Deb talked again. She was pointing her finger at Bre as if she were scolding her. "Bre, what happened in your past was bad, but when it comes to the heart, we really don't have that much control. And knowing people the way I do, and how the mind works, I'll say you need to do an emotional check with yourself. Don't get into a mess because of a past mistake. In this life, we will get hurt, but we must learn to forgive and not keep dwelling on it. Girl…"

Deb stopped because she saw tears in Bre's eyes. Instead of continuing to talk, she gave Bre a much-needed hug.

"Charles called this morning while Munda was still at my house."

"Oh shit! I guess that caused problems."

"Yes, it did. Charles doesn't know Munda was there, but Munda knew it was Charles. I didn't know what to say or do. He left angrily."

"Get your stuff and let's go, because I'm a bit behind on things. Bre, you should have told me you were having such a rough day. Damn, you have a lot on your plate. Matter of fact, it's overflowing."

Deb closed her eyes, and while letting go of her embrace with Bre, she said, "What are you gonna do about Charles?"

"I'm gonna continue spending time with him."

After saying that, a look of sadness appeared in Bre's eyes. Her feelings for Munda were resurfacing once again, and it was a lot for her to face. Deb could see her pain.

Shaking her head, Deb looked at Bre and smiled. "Girl, you got it going on. Take your time and do what you feel is right in your heart. Think things through and make a decision that'll make you happy."

They found a seat at an outside table under a big oak tree.

"So, Munda knows about Charles now." Deb was prying.

"Yup, that's about the size of it. I had no clue Munda would show up last night. Hell, I don't want or need any more complications in my life. I don't understand what's happening between Munda and me. One thing just led to another."

From Bre's inability to make direct eye contact, not to mention Bre was moving around as if she were uncomfortable, Deb knew there was more to the story. She also knew Bre did not want to face the possibility that she and Munda had some strong, unresolved emotional ties. Bre's mind was now focused on picking up Alex and getting home so her weekend could begin. Seldom did she make any big plans for Alex and herself; they would always play it by ear unless there was something major she wanted to do with him. Saturdays never really got started for them until after noon. This was the only day she and Alex could sleep in late.

"It's the weekend, baby."

Yeah!" he screamed.

They gave each other their normal hugs while asking about each other's day. As they drove home, Alex talked and talked and talked. He always had something to tell her that happened at school, and he was good about slipping in questions in-between his stories.

"There's my daddy!"

Pulling into her driveway, Bre could see Munda sitting in the swing on her front porch. Before she turned the engine off, Alex jumped out of the car and was rushing to his dad.

"Hi," Munda said with hesitation.

"Hi," Bre said in a very low tone.

There was tension, and Bre was being very careful. They both made direct eye contact, trying to figure out what each other was thinking.

"Aren't you gonna let Natches out?" Munda pointed to the door.

Bre could hear the dog standing close to the door barking, and she was sure his tail was wagging away. As soon as she opened the door, Natches flew out, jumping around and licking on his little master. They both made it down the steps and claimed the front yard as their playground.

Munda motioned for her to come and sit by him.

"I didn't expect to find you here." Bre sat down in the swing next to him.

"You want me to leave?" He gazed into her eyes while waiting for her to answer.

"That's not what I said, Munda."

"The question remains: do you want me to leave?"

"No," she said as she lowered her head.

Munda pulled her over, gave her a kiss on the forehead, and placed his arms around her. She let out a deep, slow, silent breath in relief that he wasn't upset any longer.

"Bre, I don't know what I'm gonna do or can even do about you seeing someone."

The evening was silent and calm, except for the squeaking of the swing as they rocked back and forth.

"Hey, Breanna. It's a nice evening, isn't it?"

Nosy-ass Bernice.

"How are you, Bernice?"

"It's the weekend and I'm so glad," she said as she walked toward the troubled couple.

Breanna didn't know why she was so glad because she didn't work. The only thing she did was sit home all day, peeping out the window, and trying to figure out everyone's business. To Breanna, every day was a weekend for Bernice.

"Daddy, come here," Alex yelled.

Munda rubbed Bre's thigh as he got up to see what Alex wanted.

"Oh, that's the baby's daddy. I see where little Alex gets those good looks."

Bernice stared off into the distance as if she were looking at Alex, but Bre knew she was checking out Munda's body. He was wearing a pair of jeans that complemented his body well. Even though they were loose fitting, they showed just enough bulge to inspire lust. Both Bre and Bernice checked out Munda's every move as he walked and lifted Alex in his arms. Watching Munda made Bre think about last night and how good he'd made her feel. Bre felt her head falling backward and a smile appeared on her face as memories from last night ran through her mind. She remembered how Munda had lifted her leg and kissed the insides. She reminisced about how he'd slowly entered her. Bre let out a low moan as she closed her eyes and held her breath for a couple of seconds.

"You said something, Breanna?"

"No, but I should get inside and settle down."

She wanted some settling down all right. Bre wanted to see that bare, black, shiny skin of Munda's next to hers. Munda made love to Bre again and again that night. As time raced by, they continued to see each other. Even while trying to keep her relationship with Charles intact, Bre had become emotionally involved with another man who wanted a deeper part of her. Things became more complicated. It was no longer about Munda wanting to be a father to Alex; it was a man who wanted forgiveness from a woman he was still in love with.

Chapter Ten

Even though Bre's workday was short, she was still eager to leave. She was excited about her long-planned visit with Charles.

"Girl, you're leaving here soon, huh?" Deb had a mischievous grin on her face.

"I sure am. When that clock hits twelve o'clock, I'm out of here." Bre took a short pause and then continued. "This is a trip I really need. Charles has been in Florida for weeks, and I miss him. With his dad being diagnosed with cancer and going through chemo, he had to be with him. Thank God he's a nurse and can work just about anywhere he goes."

There was a moment of silence before either one of them said anything. They both knew why the trip was important. Bre was running away from her growing feelings for Munda. With Charles being away and focused on his father's health, it gave Munda the opportunity to rebuild his relationship with Bre. Everything seemed cloudy for her; all she knew was that she loved one man but was falling back in love with another.

***

Bre drove for about an hour before calling Charles and letting him know she was on her way. She could hear how eager he was to see her. He missed her and was happy to have her away from Munda. Charles knew he was at a disadvantage by being far away and leaving room for Munda to get closer to Bre. With the crisis of his dad going on, he didn't have a choice. Charles didn't allow her to stay on the phone too long. He wanted to make sure she concentrated on driving, and so he could finish setting up the suite they'd be spending the weekend in. He made a path of fresh rose petals leading from the entrance of the doorway all the way to the bed and bathroom. Once the candles were lit, he stood back and took a long look at what he'd done to the room. Smiling from the approval of the romantic haven he'd created, Charles nodded his head and said, "My babe is in for a special treat."

Looking at his watch, he smiled. He knew it wouldn't be long before Bre's arrival. It was only moments after he started the music that he heard a faint knock on the door. Before going to the door, he looked around one last time to make sure everything was perfect. With a huge smile on his face, Charles opened the door, greeted Bre with a gentle kiss, and grabbed her bags.

"Come on in, babe."

Bre looked around in awe. The effort Charles had taken to prepare the suite for her was impressive.

"Now this is what I'm talking about."

Before she could say another word, Charles gave her a long and deep kiss. He finally let out a deep breath and stared deep into her eyes.

"Bre, you are what I need. I've missed you like crazy, babe."

"I know. Believe me, I know."

Cherishing the moment, they held each and slow danced to the soft music. It wasn't long before Charles was touching her all over her body as he swayed her over to the bed. He pulled her panties off, seductively kissed and slowly licked his way down to her pussy. The warmth of his tongue made her cool body shiver. She thought she would lose complete control, so she did everything she could to thwart an orgasm. The pressure was building, and she was enjoying every bit of the intense magical moments.

With moans of satisfaction, Bre called his name louder and

louder. She tried to push Charles back, but it only made him indulge in her pussy even more. She could feel the waterfall inside her release as she reached a full orgasm. He held onto her ass, still not allowing her to get away until she was too weak to move. While she held onto him and regrouped, his magical touches started all over again. Her energy level rose and responded to the calling. With the exchange of soft whispers and kisses, the sexual stimulation climbed to new heights.

Gazing at Bre's naked body, Charles rubbed it. Inch by inch, he noted her contours. Her breasts stood at full attention as they sat in perfect alignment. She could see the passion and desire building within him. He gently grabbed her wrist and held it as he aligned her body to his. Slowly, he inserted his thick, dark shaft into her pussy and made love to her with strong thrusting. His vein stood out, and Breanna felt every ounce of his strength. The harder he thrust, the louder she moaned. Charles watched as the beauty of her release unraveled. That alone was enough to make him let go.

***

Charles and Bre's weekend was one filled with passion and romance. Munda wasn't talked or thought about. Even on the drive back to Savannah, Bre didn't think about Munda once. All she could do was revisit the beautiful time she and Charles had shared.

***

"Long time since I heard from you," Munda said when he walked through Bre's front door.

"Well hello to you too. And what do you mean a long time? I was only gone for a couple of days." She followed him over to the couch. "You stayed away much longer that." Bre rolled her eyes.

"Where did you go?"

"I just got away for a little. Wait a minute, is this *Twenty Questions* or something?"

"No, it's not Twenty Questions. I only asked a simple question, but I see it made you uncomfortable. Well, I can see you're well rested. You look good."

Breanna looked at Munda with a half-smile on her face. She felt guilty.

"How have you been doing?" she said, trying to change the subject.

"I'm fine. I've been thinking about you and Alex a lot."

"Oh, really?"

"Why do you sound so surprised to hear this, Bre?" Now he was looking at her out the corner of his eye.

"No particular reason."

"Do you want to tell me about your little getaway?" he said.

Here we go again with all the questions, she thought. She started feeling uncomfortable in her own living room. Bre was trying not to let her thoughts show, but Munda was watching her every expression and gesture.

"Bre, what are you getting upset about?" He looked directly in her eye. "I'm only trying to make conversation with you. What's your problem? Why does this question bother you so much?"

Her problem was that she had experienced a wonderful weekend with Charles, which consisted of some good loving and awesome sex. Why was it she didn't want him to know? It seemed as if her emotions were pulling her apart. Things were getting increasingly complicated. Bre wanted to keep her personal life with Charles and Munda separate. She wasn't going to give Charles up at this point, but she didn't know what was going on between her and Munda.

"I don't have a problem with your question," she said.

"Are you sure?"

Munda had a look on his face as if he knew something, but she was not about to inquire.

"Yes, I'm sure. Is there something you have to say to me, because I'm tired of you taking me through all these questions?"

There was no smile on Munda's face; as a matter of fact, he

looked annoyed. Bre could tell he was pissed, but she wasn't about to discuss her emotions and the she'd spent with Charles. She knew Munda was upset and was trying not to let it show.

"I'll talk to you later, Breanna." Munda got up and walked out without a backward glance.

"Okay," Bre said just as the door closed.

Her attitude was passive. She didn't want there to be any type of animosity between the two of them, and there was no way she was going to have a guilt trip. Munda had messed up years ago–big time. Now was she supposed to give him her complete trust and forget about everything that had happened to her? No, she wasn't going to drop everything because he decided to *finally* return. The most important thing was that she wasn't about to feel wrong for loving someone else. It had taken years for her to look at a man seriously, and she truly believed Charles was one of the good ones.

***

A few days passed and she hadn't heard anything from Munda. She didn't receive a phone call or a visit, which made her wonder if he knew she'd gone away to see Charles. Although there was dysfunction between her and Munda, her main concern was not to damage the relationship he and Alex had formed. Alex had grown accustomed to Munda being around, and now he was starting to ask her for his dad.

Munda already knew she was involved with Charles, but that shouldn't keep him from his son. What right did he have to get angry? Though she knew there was some tension between him and her, she decided to call him anyway. She couldn't reach him over the phone. The closest she got to Munda was his answering machine, which he hardly ever checked. She wondered if something had happened to him.

In the early hours of the next morning, the phone rang. Before Bre got herself together to wake up and answer, the caller hung up. Frustrated and annoyed, Bre rolled over and looked at the clock: 1

o'clock in the morning. Who in the hell could that have been? Within a few minutes, the phone rang again.

"Hello?"

There was silence.

Bre repeated herself, "Hello?"

"Are you sleeping?"

It was Munda finally calling. Bre was speechless for a moment, but she eventually got herself together so she could talk to him.

"Yes, I was until you woke me up. Where have you been?"

"I've been around," he said faintly.

"You've been quiet for the past few days."

"I needed to do some thinking."

"Is something wrong?" she said with concern.

"I don't know, you tell me."

There was silence while Bre tried to sort out how to avoid an argument.

"Munda, is there something you need to talk about?"

"Bre, do you mind if I come over?"

"Now?" The only thing she could do was think about how late it was and how tired she'd be at work the next day.

"Yes, now, if you don't have someone there with you."

"What kind of comment is that, Munda?"

"I'll be there in a few minutes."

He hung up without waiting for a response from her. She took the phone from her ear and looked at it with surprise. She then got up, washed her face, brushed her teeth, and made sure she was presentable. It wasn't long before there was a gentle knock at the door.

She opened the door and he stood there in silence.

"What would bring you out this time of night, Munda?"

"Hi. Is Alex sleeping?"

"Of course, he is. Everyone is sleeping except you."

Munda proceeded to walk down the hall while asking her if Alex was in his room.

"Yes, he sleeps in his own room most of the time."

Munda peeped in Alex's room then quietly closed the door. Before Bre knew it, his arms were around her waist. The next thing she knew, he was kissing her deeply and pressing his body against hers so she could feel how hard his dick was. It wasn't long before they were tearing off each other's clothes.

"Wait! Just wait! I don't know if I should do this. There's too much going on."

"Bre, please don't fight what we share. We want each other, and we share something special."

"We don't share anything except for a child, and that's it."

Munda became very quiet and didn't bother to look into Breanna's eyes any longer. Remaining silent, he clung tight to her while pulling her closer into his chest. She could feel his heart pounding. Both of them were full of emotions. Even if Bre didn't admit it, she wanted Munda just as much as he wanted her. She tried to pull away, to look up at him, but he held her even tighter. Her heart pounded as she trembled. Munda lifted her and placed her in the middle of the bed. Soon, she was having multiple orgasms. The way his tongue wrapped around her clit in that gentle, sucking motion almost drove her crazy. It appeared as if Munda had come over with a plan in mind. She was at his tender mercy. The way he ate her pussy made her want him to never stop.

"You like that?" He stiffened his tongue and pushed it deep inside her.

A mere moan softly escaped Bre's mouth. Munda continued his mission.

"Oh, babe, put it in and let me feel you," she whispered.

"Babe, you can have whatever you want. This is your dick."

As Munda's thick dick filled her pussy, she opened her legs wider and pulled him closer into her body. With slow, hard, and steady pumps, he gave her ultimate satisfaction. Even after his climax, he continued making love to her; it was as if his dick never went down. He flipped her over and took her from behind. She placed her hand on the headboard to protect her head from pounding against it.

Holding onto her waist, Munda pumped and pulled her into his body. Suddenly, he released a loud moan. There was no more pumping in and out, but she could feel him trying to dig deeper and deeper into her, even though he couldn't get any farther. She felt a slight pain from the pressure he applied, but it was a sweet pain.

Once again, she could feel him erupt inside her. After he gave her everything he had, he lay on top of her and kissed her from her neck to her ass. She was exhausted and felt as if someone had run her over with a bulldozer. He gently turned her over on her back, and as he looked into her eyes, he shook his head. Suddenly, everything became quiet as a different tone overtook the atmosphere. Munda looked down in Bre's bright eyes with a serious look on his face.

"Bre, I'm crazy about you. I know there's someone else in your life, and it hit me hard just to think about you with another man."

Repositioning her body and clearing her throat, she responded to his comment in a low, but very firm and serious tone. "Is that why you tried to screw my brains out? Was this all about you trying to get something you think belongs to another man?" There was a puzzled look on her face as she waited for him to answer.

Munda jumped up into a sitting position as if he were startled. "No, babe, that's not it at all. Making love to you was an expression of what I feel. I love you."

Breanna could see and hear his sincerity.

He sat up on the bed and propped the pillows underneath her so he would have her full attention. "Bre, look at what we could have. Look at what we already have. Do you think two people who don't love each other can make love the way we do? You can't possibly think it's all about me getting my dick wet or being some meaningless fuck."

Rolling her eyes at him, Bre snapped, "I know this already!" She suddenly stopped and spoke in a lower tone. "Munda, don't you think this is hard for me, too? You chose the worst time to come back into my life."

Munda got out of the bed and walked to the side closest to her. "Bre, tell me what's wrong. Help me understand."

She started crying because she couldn't answer his questions. She knew in her heart she loved Munda, but she also cared deeply for Charles. Munda was silent for the remainder of the night, but he held Bre tightly until the light of daybreak pierced through the curtains. How could she deny that there was something special between the two of them?

Chapter Eleven

Betty and the kids finally arrived and everything was going smoothly. The kids were adjusting well, and they seemed to be relaxed and happy. Alex, Jamar, and Antwon were sharing a room together, while Betty and Angel shared one. Betty and the kids helped Bre just as much as she was helping them. In the beginning, Alex seemed to withdraw a little. Bre understood, especially considering it had only been the two of them for such a long time.

It didn't take long for Betty to become a favorite of Alex's. She had a way with him, and no matter what circumstances had brought her there, she was glad that she'd become a closer part of both his and Bre's lives. For the first time, Alex was able to identify with the meaning of having an extended family. He never knew his cousins. He wasn't too keen on the idea of their arrival at first, but he adjusted. He had always been the only one who required his mother's attention, but that changed when three other kids moved in.

Alex eventually became like another sibling to the three siblings. They would argue and fight, but they'd eventually work it out. The kids developed a very strong bond, and they were not going to let anything happen to each other.

***

It didn't take Betty long to get on her feet; it appeared as though she was destined to be there. Her attitude had changed completely, and even when Tony attempted to try to get back on her good side, she refused to have anything to do with him. Bre remembered when his sorry ass drove for hours and showed up at her door, demanding to see his wife. She never liked Tony, and now that she knew exactly what he'd put her sister through, she didn't have any respect for him. He'd been calling a lot, trying to talk Betty into moving back.

It was on a Saturday evening that he pulled into the driveway. Not only was he in someone else's car, there was a baby in the back seat. Bre couldn't imagine what was going through his mind.

"Hey. Is Betty here?"

Bre didn't bother to respond. She acted as though she neither heard nor saw him.

"Where are my kids, Bre?"

Bre still didn't respond. Out the corner of her eye, she could see the kids kneeling in front of the doorway, whispering to each other.

"Aunt Bre, I don't want to go," Bre heard Angel plead softly.

The kids were terrified of this man, and it broke her heart. The children were now living in her house. They were laughing, happy, and adjusting to the changes. The kids were relieved to be away from him. Bre got up and walked into the house.

"No one is taking you away from here. Do you understand me?"

"Yes, Auntie Bre," they said in unison.

"Go back in there and do whatever it was you were doing. Everything will be fine."

She gave Angel a hug and sent her on her way. Jamar looked at her as if to ask if she was sure she could handle things with his father, who was now standing at the bottom of her steps.

"Go on, Jamar. I'm fine."

Jamar gave her a hug and went on his way as well. As she watched him go to his room, she slowly walked back to the porch and took a seat in the rocker that faced the steps.

"What storm blew you this way, Tony?"

"I came to see my wife and kids."

"I wish you would have called before coming."

"When does a man have to give his family notice that he's coming to see them?"

"I guess that would be when a man really hasn't been a man. If that man had been a real man, then he wouldn't need to be going anywhere to see his family. If that man had been even a small fraction of a man, his family would be right there with him." Bre's was firm and cold.

"Don't start any shit with me, Bre. Nobody told you to stick your nose in my family's business. You talked her into moving here."

"It wasn't about me sticking my nose in your business. When you stuck your sorry-ass dick into another woman's pussy and got her pregnant, you invited everybody in your business."

"Fuck you, bitch."

"You must think you're talking to your baby's mother. I mean, the mother of the baby you have out there in the car. Let me tell you something, asshole: don't you ever think you can come to my house—that I pay a monthly mortgage on—and talk shit. You have me all fucked up, Tony."

"You don't want Betty to have a man because your white-acting ass doesn't have one."

Bre stood up, placed her hands on her hips, and walked closer to Tony. "Oh, so I guess you're attempting to call yourself a man. That's a joke. Get your ass away from my house before I call the police."

Just as she said that, Betty pulled up in the driveway. She immediately jumped out of her car to see what was going on.

"What are you doing here, Tony?" she said.

"I came to see you and the kids. We need to talk and get some things worked out, honey."

"What things?" Anger showed on her face.

"We have to work all this stuff out, girl."

"Really? Is this why you brought your baby? The one you fathered while married to me? Is it why you used me as a punching bag? Is it why you've always disrespected me and my kids? Get the hell away from here, boy! For the first time, I'm living without stress and drama, and it feels good." Betty took a brief pause and breathed deeply. "Tony, you almost destroyed me. The kids are afraid of you and emotionally withdrawing. They're happy and doing very well now."

"How are you gonna teach Jamar and Antwon how to be men? It takes a man to raise boys." He looked at her like he despised her.

Betty looked him up and down right back. "Whatever way I choose to teach them, it'll be better than anything they'll learn from your sorry ass."

"Bitch, who do you think you're talking to?"

"Your days are over, Tony. My life was a nightmare, and I finally woke up. I'm not going back to that hell and allow you to take the life out of my children."

Tony was sweating. His body motions were becoming more erratic. "Bitch! I...I'll take my kids, and you'll never see 'em again."

Betty slowly walked closer to him, laughing with each step. "You and what damn army?"

"You think you're all that now, bitch? You think you're white now, too, huh? Your sister is fucking your mind up."

Betty laughed and shook her head at Tony. He was pissed because he didn't get the greeting he was expecting. Jamar made his way back to the door. Tony looked up at his son.

"Jamar! Come give your old man a hug."

"Dad, leave us alone. Please, just go away."

"Boy, who the fuck you think you talking to?"

"That's it," Breanna said. "Get off my damn property. Get the fuck away and don't come back."

Breanna walked even closer to him than Betty had. She was making sure he could see her face and watch her lips as she spoke. She wasn't afraid of him, and she wanted to make sure he knew that.

She guessed this was the reason why Betty and the kids were always so jittery; it was as if they knew he was eventually going to show up at her house. Bre never imagined Tony bringing his ass down here, but Betty knew he would try something. That showed she knew him better than anyone. Tony was like a bomb ready to go off at any time.

Tony and Betty began to argue. Not one time did she back down from him, even through all of his screaming and name-calling. As a matter of fact, Betty was able to deal with him in a way that surprised Bre. Betty had already filed for child support, so Tony finally had to join the real world and get a job. Tony eventually left, but both Betty and Breanna were certain he'd show up again. For now, he was gone.

***

After arising the next morning, the past day seemed like a bad dream. That was okay because it was all behind them. Despite what had happened the prior day, they knew today would be a better one. Bre spoke to Munda, and they made plans to spend time together after work. It had been a while since the two of them had spent some quality time alone. She was longing for him, and he was probably longing just as much for her.

When she arrived at his house that evening, they embraced each other and kissed passionately. The affection Munda displayed was special; but most important of all, it was sincere. There was no mistaking what they felt for each other. She knew from the very moment she laid her eyes on him that this evening would be one of passion. She was right.

"This is nice, babe," Bre said as she looked around. The candle lights gave the room a romantic vibe. "I could come home to this every evening."

"Why don't you?"

Everything was quiet for a moment, then Munda gave her a long, smooth kiss and pulled her close to his body as his hard cock continued to grow. Her leg moved against *it* suggestively as they teased and tasted each other. Bre kissed him and pulled away. Looking back at him and smiling, she made her way to the dining room. Munda went back into the kitchen to slice fruit and prepare their plates.

***

They ate by the window that overlooked a beautiful landscape. While eating, they talked quietly and lusted for each other. When they were done, he took the dishes into the kitchen and sent Bre into the bathroom. Where she found a tub filled with warm water and bubbles seductively waiting for her.

Too consumed by Bre's sexy gesture, Munda could only look at her with a grin on his face when he came into the bathroom. He stepped into the bathtub with her, they relaxed, they conversed, and they kissed until the water was nearly cold. As the candles flames changed the room lighting from time to time, they both stood wet, admiring each other and lusting for a passionate session of lovemaking.

They dried their bodies and walked into the room. Munda prepared the bed for the two of them, and Bre made one last trip to the kitchen for the bedroom snack. A few minutes later, Munda laid back, and she took a piece of cool mango and rubbed it over his body.

"Umm, mango. Is it sweet?"

"Let me see." She took her tongue and licked the juice that was left on his body.

"It's very sweet."

Munda was mesmerized by Bre's actions. She proceeded to rub his body down with the fruit while licking, caressing, and kissing the juices away. Munda closed his eyes and turned his head from side to side while softly moaning. She could tell he was in heaven. His dick extended itself out to let her know that it, too, needed some special attention. She rubbed it down and slowly sucked it until all signs of the mango were gone.

Makayla Smyles

Munda joined in with the share of desserts. He took a slice of cantaloupe and placed it in Bre's pussy. She felt the soft fruit as he moved it about a little. When he pulled it out, he began to eat it slowly with his eyes closed. It was like he was savoring every bit of her that was on the fruit.

"Bre, I want you so bad."

"Show me how bad."

Without any delay, Munda's hand was all over her and her pussy. He was moaning, kissing, and calling her name. He lifted her ass in his hands and began to eat her pussy wildly. The moment became more intense as he sucked on her clit. Bre thrust her body back and forth with a gentle force as Munda continued his oral stimulation.

After Munda sucked Bre's pussy until she came, he put his dick inside her. She was ready for it. They made love and fucked each other with intense emotion. She was giving him just as much movement as he was giving her. They had to keep up with each other. Bre was at her best. Her body felt light. Her legs were wrapped around his waist and her arms around his neck. His dick was so good, it made her want to open up, completely allowing him to have all of her.

"Get on top of me, babe," he whispered.

Without any hesitation, Bre straddled Munda's thick body.

"Ah."

She heard him gasp, and then a long moan followed.

His hands rubbed slowly across her ass while she rode his well-endowed dick slow and steady. The sound of her wet juices pounding up and down on his dick was like music. Working his dick over turned her on. She could feel him trying to keep control as she carefully worked his cock over.

"Oh, babe," he mumbled as she began fucking him harder and harder.

"Come on, Munda...make me cum, baby...it feels so damn good."

Her body was sweaty. Her face had an intense look as she bit down on her bottom lip.

"Bre, Bre, Bre. Take this dick. C'mon, babe, this is yours. Damn, I love you, girl."

He clinched tighter to her ass, making sure he was getting everything she had to give. Bre was tired, but Munda wanted to make sure she was fulfilled. He wasn't only on a mission to soothe Bre sexually, he was trying to create new memories they would cherish for a long time.

They made love for what seemed like hours, but it was getting ready to end. Munda let it be known that he was about to climax, and Bre was tired and ready for him to do so. It was as though they'd both reached their limit. Once Munda reached his orgasm, he couldn't do anything more. When the moment came for Bre to leave, she immediately started missing Munda. After walking her to the car, they kissed and said their intimate goodbyes. The only thing Bre regretted was leaving Munda and going to her home. She dug in her purse, pulled out her cell phone.

"Hey, is Alex still up?" she asked Betty as she drove home.

"That boy is dead to the world. I just checked on him. He was snoring and had a drool stream a mile long."

Breanna had to laugh because she knew Betty was telling the truth.

"I'm on my way."

"Okay, but you don't have to rush home. C'mon, and we'll talk once you get here."

Munda lived less than ten miles away, so it didn't take her long to get home. It seemed as though Betty was waiting for her arrival; as soon as Bre got ready to put her key in the lock, Betty was opening the door for her. She looked at Bre with one of her hands on her hips and then looked at the clock. She started laughing.

"What's wrong with you, Bre?" Betty could tell there was something on Bre's mind.

"Nothing's wrong. Why do you ask?" Bre raised a brow.

"You seem preoccupied."

"I just have some things on my mind I need to sort out."

"I would say it's safe to say those things are Munda and Charles."

"Maybe." Bre looked up at her sister.

Betty led the way to the kitchen. They sat down and began talking.

"Girl, I thought I had problems, but I think you have me beat. Sis, you have a sweet little mess going on."

"What are you talking about?"

"Don't get all crazy with me, Bre. I know you and Munda are doing the nasty, and it's more than just screwing. I think it's safe to say there's something emotional going on, and it's something deep." Betty got up from the table and went to where Bre was sitting. She leaned over to her, almost with a full burst of laughter.

"And?"

"And nothing. You know what's going on. You talk all sweet and loving to Charles on the phone, and even when he came here you two were tight. You and Munda appear to be closer, and I don't think it's only because of Alex. Yeah, I know all your little secrets…most of them anyway."

"You think you know."

"Okay, then tell me you and Munda aren't into something strong and deep?" After a few moments of silence, Betty began talking again. "Girl, you'll handle it. Bre, you're strong, and you have a solid mind. Everything will work out the way it's supposed to."

Breanna stared at Betty and wondered if her problem was as transparent to others as it was for Betty. There was no way she could keep going this way, sneaking around with the man she truly loved and falling in love with another man who made her feel safe and secure.

"You don't have to look at me as if I'm stupid or something, Betty."

"I think that's your conscience talking. I didn't say or think anything of the sort." Betty paused and shook her head. "Bre, I found a good blend of coffee. Would you like me to make some for the two of us?

"Sure. Why not?" Bre said as she got up and walked over to look at what she had.

"Breanna, I know we haven't always been as close as sisters should be, and I'm the cause of that."

Bre was silent and alert, curious as to what Betty was going to say.

"Bre, I know you think I'm a real nutcase sometimes, but if you look close enough, you'll see I'm not."

"Betty, I never said that."

"I know you haven't, but I bet you've thought it. Bre, just because I made some screwed-up choices when it came to my husband, it doesn't mean I'm not capable of thinking clearly. You've been here for me and my kids, and I need to be here for you as well."

"I hear you, big sis."

"So, what's it gonna be, little sis?" She extended her arms.

Betty was right. Over the past few months, they'd become very close, developing a closeness that families share. Bre looked at Betty for a moment without saying one word.

After looking away, Bre said, "You say I'm involved with two men, huh?"

"That's right, and I know I'm not wrong."

"You're right." Bre sighed.

Betty only looked at her and smiled. "Who has the better sex?"

"You're not right at all!"

They both started laughing.

"Grab a cup of coffee and let's sit down to talk." Betty smiled with a twinkle in her eyes.

The mug warmed her cold hands. The coffee was Southern Butter Pecan, and for some reason, it seemed to fit the mood.

"Would you like to talk about what's going on? It's okay with me, Bre. You know I'm no stranger to drama."

As Betty spoke those words, Breanna could see her concern and love. Tears ran down her face, and she shrugged her shoulders.

"I don't want to hurt anyone. I've been thinking about this for weeks, and it doesn't get any easier. Betty, I can't keep going this way."

"Bre, you only have to answer one question."

Betty grabbed a nearby tissue and wiped her tears. She went back, got a couple more, and placed them in her sister's hand. Her sister had become her best friend once more.

"You have to ask yourself who you truly love? Allow me to spare you from going down the wrong road. What Munda did was wrong. You and I both know that. In order for you to see if he's true, you must give the man a second chance. Open yourself up to him and don't hold on to the past. We all make mistakes, but we can't keep dwelling on them or the person who caused the hurt. Forgiveness is the key."

"I know."

"Bre, yes, people are going to whisper and talk if it's Munda you are wanting to be with, especially when Momma finds out. She'll be talking, just like everyone else. Your friends will support and not judge you. Moreover, if they're your real friends, they'll be there to see you through the hard times. Yes, there will be those who'll be saying 'that boy left her when she was pregnant, and now she's taking him back'?"

They both chuckled because they knew those would be their mom's exact words.

"Bre, you know I'm right. You can't think about what others are gonna say and base your decision on that."

"You make it seem as if you've been through all this before."

"Hell, I lived with it every day of my life. People talked about me all the time. I knew how they were calling me stupid for staying with Tony all those years."

"Why didn't you ever leave him, Betty?"

"It's partly because of the same reason you can't let go of

Munda. I was really in love with him at one point. Once that part was finally gone, it was too late. I didn't think I could get out."

Betty seemed to be on a roll. She took a sip of her coffee and readjusted herself in the chair. "Don't think I'm through talking. I know you have to think about Charles. I also know you love him in your own way, but don't confuse love with being in love. There's a huge difference. Bre, he may be good with the little man, too, but…"

"But what?" Bre said without hesitation. There was a trembling in her voice she wasn't expecting. The questions that had been haunting her were finally facing her head on.

"You know what the *but* is for. The *but* is the fact that you still love Munda. Alex is his son, and those things will never change. If it weren't for the fact that Charles wanted you, he wouldn't try so hard to make Alex happy. Do you think Charles is gonna replace Munda as Alex's father? Do you think he can even replace the feelings you have in your heart for Munda?"

Bre remained very quiet as she continued to face each truth Betty spoke.

"Allow me to answer the question. Hell no, Munda isn't about to sit around and allow another man to take over his role. You're not gonna do it, either. You'd rather kill a man before you allow him to try to take over Munda's role. Perhaps, it wouldn't be the case if Munda hadn't shown up to claim his responsibilities and apologize for his mistakes. And, besides, you see how close those two are. You'd think Munda's been in Alex's life from day one."

Bre thought about how close they were and smiled. She knew Betty was right. It would only be trouble if Charles tried to come between the two of them.

"I'm glad you at least know that much. Bre, I even see how your face lights up when you're around Munda. You want your family back together, sweetie, and it's natural that you want that. In a sense, you're already a family. Bre, it's also natural to be scared, but don't be too scared to go after what you really want. Please, search your heart, mind, and soul before you make any decisions."

"Betty, I do want a full family so much, but I just don't know how."

"I know. And I do feel you, but you can't walk around worrying about what other people are gonna say or think or be too afraid of the possibility that Munda may hurt you again. This is about your happiness. This is your life."

"What about Charles, Betty?"

"Bre, only you know how you feel about Charles, and only you can decide who you're happier with. I don't have all the answers, but I'll be right here with you while you search for them."

"Thank you."

"Let me say this: I know you and your girls are tight, but make sure you work this out on your own. Do you understand me?"

Breanna was baffled by her suggestion to work this out without talking to her friends.

"Betty, is there something more you would like to say?"

"Since you asked, yes." Betty nodded. "Bre, friends are good to have and share things with, but sometimes a friend likes to see you make bad choices. Do you remember that saying mama would tell us about our friends when we were younger? 'Misery loves company'?" Betty got up and began moving around before she continued. "And that damn Renee…you shouldn't trust her with a penny jar."

"What makes you say that?"

"There's something that doesn't sit well with me when it comes to Renee. Yes, I've known her for years, but it doesn't mean I trust her. I've tolerated a lot of things, as well as people, because of Tony, but I kept hold of my morals. Don't forget those shifty eyes of hers. I think she and Charles are very much acquainted with each other."

Breanna was utterly shocked at what she was hearing.

"There's no way you can convince me you've never questioned her intentions. I've watched her look at you when you've been around Munda, and when you've been around Charles. Bre, it's the same damn look. Renee is one of those miserable women who wants everyone else to be miserable, too."

"But she has a man."

"Huh, are you sure? I see she didn't tell you she and that man broke up some months ago."

"What? She told me everything was going fine."

"She told you a stinky lie."

"You're serious about this, aren't you?"

"Yes, I am," Betty said as a matter of fact.

"Do you think something is going on between Renee and Munda?"

"Get real, sis! Do you think Munda would want someone like Renee? You and Munda need to stop all that fucking and start comparing notes. I have a strong suspicion she had something to do with Munda walking away. Shit like that just doesn't happen. Now, if you really wanna think about something, take a good look at her baby. It looks a lot like Charles to me. If I was a betting woman—"

Betty stopped in the middle of her sentence as she watched Bre's expressions change. Betty's words captured her full attention, and Bre began to think about many things that hadn't made much sense until now. Betty just nodded her head.

"I have to admit, this would explain a lot of things," Bre said as her eyes met Betty's.

For about an hour, the two sisters talked about all the strange things that had taken place, which all became clearer as they discussed them.

"What a bitch!" Bre mumbled.

"At least you know now. You really need to talk to Munda because you can see something really stinks here." Betty looked up at the clock. "Sis, sleep in a little later, and I'll drop Alex and Angel off at the daycare in the morning. I've gotten his morning clothes ready, so it won't be a problem. I know you've been a bit stressed and not sleeping too well."

Bre looked at Betty with her tired red eyes and smiled. "Thanks, Betty. That'll help out a lot."

"Go get a shower and go to bed." Giggling, Betty said, "I guess you just need to go to bed, seeing as how you've just come from Munda's house. You've probably had a bath already."

After she said that, they laughed, hugged each other, and said goodnight. It was nice having Betty around, and Bre was truly thankful for being able to talk to her about everything. The only thing she could think about now was the possibility of Renee having something to do with Munda walking away. This still wouldn't be any excuse for his actions, but it would explain a lot.

The only thing Bre had to look forward to was speaking to Munda and finding out if Renee had anything to do with him leaving. She thought about calling in, but she didn't want to waste a complete day dwelling on what may or may not have been. Her mind kept telling her to stay home, but she forced herself to get up and prepare for work.

***

"You look like hell."

"Good morning to you, too, Deb," Bre snapped.

"Whoa...are we in a bad mood or what?" Deb leaned back, looking at her.

"I'm just a little tired." Bre had a frown on her face.

Deb obviously could see Bre wasn't her normal self and was in a very strange mood. She walked closer to Bre. "Is everything okay?"

Bre wanted to cry, but she made sure to keep it together. "Hopefully, it will be." Bre smiled and dismissed herself from the conversation.

"When or if you need to talk, let me know, and I'll be here for you."

Bre smiled at Deb and acknowledged her by motioning her lips to say *thank you*. She was ready to vent, and she knew Deb would be willing to listen.

***

Later that day, Bre walked up to Deb and said, "Deb, do you

feel like taking a break?"

"Give me a couple of minutes," Deb said without hesitation.

It didn't take Deb long to free herself.

"Hey, what's going on, Bre?"

"Let's go outside and talk."

As they walked, Deb placed her arms around Bre and reassured her that whatever it was, it would be okay.

"Bre, what's going on? I haven't seen you like this before."

"Deb, I was talking to Betty last night, and Renee's name happened to come up."

"What's Renee done now?"

"What do you mean by *now*?" Bre had a frustrated look on her face.

"Maybe I should have said, what have you finally caught her doing? I told you I don't trust her. Hell, at one point I thought that she was involved with Charles."

"You, Betty, and Deloris are all saying the same thing. Am I missing something here?"

"Didn't you say she was friends with some of Betty's people or something?" Deb stood with her arms folded.

"Yes, Betty's known her for some time, but so have I. I never really got close or knew that much about her until she moved here and Betty got us connected. All I know is that she wasn't a favorite of a lot of people, but I've never been one to judge based on someone else's opinion."

"What's Betty's take on her?" Deb lifted an eyebrow.

"She thinks Renee had something to do with what happened to me and Munda. Betty also believes there's some sort of connection between Charles and Renee, like the baby. She made some comments last night that got me putting things together."

"Think things through and follow your mind, Bre. I believe Betty may be on to something."

"Absolutely. I'm gonna talk to Munda this evening so we can figure some of this shit out. Deb, I know it doesn't change what happened, or how Munda just decided to up and leave, but I can't afford to have someone like Renee in my life. Hell, when no one else would deal with her, I treated her like family. I thought I was helping, but it seems like I was being stupid."

"Don't say that, Bre. You were just being yourself. Don't let anyone take that from you. Renee is a jealous bitch. She doesn't have anyone and doesn't want anyone else to have anyone either. Personally, I say you need to beat the black off her ass if she fucked with your life like that. She not only screwed with your livelihood, she took away a father from his innocent child."

The more Bre talked things through, the angrier she became. Her head was pounding, and her throat felt as if it was covered in powder. It was dry from anger and venting.

"Bre, you have to be smart about this. Catch her in her own shit. Don't allow her to know you're figuring things out. If she does know, she's only gonna do things to protect herself and will continue her deceptive ways. Bitches like that, you have to catch them in the act and not give them the opportunity to lie."

Deb was right. It was a matter of coming up with a plan to catch Renee red-handed.

"Okay, girl, so how are we gonna catch this whore?" Deb was all in.

"I'm not sure yet, and I'm trying so hard to wait until I have all my facts in place. I don't wanna accuse her of something she didn't do. Let's get back to that hellhole and get some work done, Deb."

Bre was still upset, but she knew there was no way she'd allow Renee to get away with anything. If Renee started some shit, Bre was damn sure gonna finish it.

Chapter Twelve

It was 5 pm. and time to head home. During the day, it seemed as if Bre didn't have one ounce of energy. Now, however, that it was time for her to leave, she seemed to be rejuvenated. She didn't even wait to walk out with Deb. Instead, she waved good-bye on her way out the door. On her drive to pick up Alex and Angel from school, she called Munda and asked him if he'd meet her at the house in a couple of hours. She ran through everything she needed to get done to make sure she'd be finished by the time Munda arrived.

"Hey, Mommy. Aunt Betty took me and Angel to school this morning."

"I know, love. How was your day?"

"It was good. I didn't get in Time Out today, Momma." He was constantly moving and talking.

"Wow, that's the way to go, little man. Let's go get Angel so we can get home." She was waiting with her usual smile.

"Hi, Aunt Bre," Angel said as she ran to meet her and Alex.

They played while Bre was signing them out.

"Mommy, can we go to the store?"

"Honey, we should take Natches to the park for a long walk."

"Yeaaa!"

When they arrived at the house, Munda was already waiting outside. Alex was excited to see him. They greeted each other and carried on their small chat as Breanna took her things out of the car.

"How was your day, babe?" Munda sensed something wrong.

Bre sort of rolled her eyes and snapped, "It wasn't my best day."

She never stopped moving. Before she could get the door open, Natches flew out like the wind, trying to get to Alex and Angel. Even though he was bigger than his small master, he was gentle with him.

"That boy is always so happy." Munda was laughing and shaking his head as he observed Natches and the kids play.

Bre rolled her eyes and growled, "Most of the time, he is. You weren't around during the times he wasn't."

Shocked at her tone and attitude, Munda said, "What's wrong, Bre?"

"I've been trying to figure things out, Munda. I realize you thought I was cheating, and maybe I could have handled the situation better, but I tried to do what was best and protect my client. The one thing that puzzled me most is that someone was telling you lies about me seeing or being involved with someone else." Bre looked away and was silent for a moment before she continued. She stared directly into his eyes. "What did Renee have to do with you walking out on us, Munda? It seems everyone believes Renee may have had something to do with you leaving."

Munda became silent and gazed at her as if he was trying to read her mind. There was nothing but silence until Alex and Angel came rushing up, asking about the park.

"Okay, honey, let me change clothes, and I'll be ready. Alex, you and Angel come in and grab a juice and snack."

"Okay, Mommy."

"Well, come on so we can get going. And use the bathroom before we leave."

"I don't have to," Alex said.

"Get in there and use that bathroom, boy!" Bre said in a stern voice.

When he went to the bathroom, it seemed as if he was pissing for days.

"I thought you didn't have to use the bathroom, Alex?"

"I didn't feel it, Mommy."

"Get out here, boy, so we can get going."

Munda stood back laughing at Alex and enjoying every moment.

"You know him well, Bre."

"Yes, I do. Too bad I don't know you as well," she snapped.

"Apparently, you're really upset about something."

"Huh, that's putting it mildly," Bre said. "I want you to answer the question I just asked about Renee."

Munda hesitated while staring her in the eyes.

"Answer the damn question, Munda."

"Where is all this coming from Bre?"

"Answer the damn question. Did she have something to do with you walking out or not?"

Munda took a deep breath and pulled Bre closer to him. "She made it appear as if you'd been involved another man."

"And you believed her? I can't believe you! How could you take the word of someone else? And Renee, out of all people?" Her voice became loud, and her face expressed the look of anger and betrayal.

"Mommy, what's wrong? What did you do to my mommy, Daddy?"

This was the first time Bre had seen Alex become protective of her.

"Honey, it's okay. Daddy and I are just having a discussion."

Alex looked at the two of them deeply before eventually taking off again with Angel and Natches. She and Munda found a spot where they could sit and keep a watchful eye on the kids. It wasn't likely someone would harm them because Natches wouldn't allow the two of them out of his sight. He'd follow them everywhere they went and lay down until they moved to the next place. Everything became quiet between Bre and Munda for a long time, and a million and a half thoughts went both their heads. Munda finally got up the nerve to place his arms around her and hug her.

"Bre, I made some bad decisions and listened to some things I should've known to be untrue. I wasn't thinking clearly. By the time I'd figured everything out, we'd already began fighting bitterly. After I got over the fact that I'd hurt you for something you kept telling me wasn't true, I didn't know what to say to you. I was embarrassed and ashamed of myself."

Bre looked up and Munda placed his arms around her. Even though she was angry, she realized that they both had been victims of lies and deceit.

"Bre, I tried to find you and Alex, but you'd already moved. I looked everywhere. When I went to your mother's house, she was furious. She cussed and screamed at me and made me leave her house. She told me I could go to hell and that you never wanted to see me again."

"Munda, this woman is still in my life, laughing and talking to me every chance she gets. I must seem like a real fool to her. I defended her from everyone, and she intentionally set out to destroy my happiness."

"It's gonna be okay, babe."

"But it's not okay right now, Munda."

Munda went on to tell her what Renee had said about seeing another man she'd met on an outing. According to Renee, Bre "working overtime" meant she was making time to see the other man. As Munda spoke, Bre remembered a couple of late nights when Renee had called her and stated she was stranded and needed help. Now it made perfect sense because her helping Renee meant she had more unaccounted-for time, aside from overtime at work. This woman was dangerous.

"Have you spoken to her since you've been back?" Bre said.

"Yeah, she came by looking for you a few times. She said you told her you may come by."

"Bullshit."

Munda and Bre looked at each other in disbelief. He started laughing and shook his head.

"Babe, she was so drunk to the point of taking off her clothes," Munda said.

Breanna's mouth dropped open.

"Yeah, she was even rambling on about you and Charles and gave a lot of detailed information about the two of you. I guess there's something really special between the two of you that you've decided I don't need to know about."

Shocked by Munda's statement, Bre stared at him. She didn't say one word. When she finally gathered the gall to speak, she was on the defense. "This was never about me and Charles, so leave him out of this! All of this is about Renee and what you allowed her to destroy. She doesn't know anything about us. Munda, I only tried to be her friend because of Betty."

"It seems as if someone is always getting in our way; first Renee, now Charles."

Bre rolled her eyes then took a deep breath. With a firm tone, she turned to Munda and said, "Charles never kept us apart. He wasn't even in the picture at that time, so don't try to put any blame on him. Munda, you allowed someone to come in and fill your mind with bullshit. It was you and your stupidity that kept us apart. It was years before I could even think about trusting or being with another man."

The two of them became quiet and observed all the movements and activities going on. There was no way Breanna was going to allow Munda to shift any blame on Charles, a man she'd learned to love and trust. Neither of them said anything until it was time for them to leave the park.

Alex and Angel continued playing as if they had an endless supply of energy. It was almost springtime again, and it was visible all around. The days became longer, and the beauty of the season was coming into full blossom. There was nothing like seeing the pink azaleas sway as a gentle breeze passed over them. Sounds and scenes of joy were heard and seen as people moved about.

"Munda, we need to get the kids and Natches so we can go home. It's getting late."

Alex hated leaving the park, and he always gave Bre a hard time when it was time to go. When Munda told him it was time to leave, he didn't say one word. He ran along with Angel as Natches followed.

They continued their journey to the house where they found Betty and the other kids sitting outside in the backyard. Alex and Angel didn't hesitate in proceeding to play again. Natches followed as he barked and ran along with them.

"I guess I better get going, huh?"

Bre didn't respond to Munda's remark. Instead, she smiled and rubbed his arm.

"Bre, I could have been responsible enough to handled things better. Hell, I wish I'd had sense enough not to have listened to Renee; and I definitely wish there was no Charles in the picture...but since things are the way they are, I'll work hard to prove myself and my love in order to get my family back."

Munda didn't wait for Bre to respond. He gave her a kiss on the forehead and said goodnight to everyone else before getting in his car and leaving. Bre walked away from everyone as she stood in deep thoughts and sorrow.

***

Months had passed since Betty and the kids relocated to Savannah, and everyone was still doing well. Not only that, Betty and her kids had become much closer. Once all the drama was over, she discovered and treasured all those things that had been there the entire time. Bre didn't want to think about the hell her sister and children had been in for so long. One thing was for certain: she could see the positive changes in the kids. Angel was jittery when she first got there. Bre could tell she'd been yelled at a lot. Even when she didn't do anything wrong, she was apologizing with fear in her heart.

She hung on to Betty a lot, and Betty was just as protective of her. It was almost as if she could sense fear, maybe even danger.

Antwon was withdrawn and usually looked at each adult to confirm his every action. He was filled with insecurity. He was only a little boy and already appeared stressed and worn down by life. There was sadness within him. It was as though a part of him was dead, but he always made it through another day. It made Bre and Betty happy to see him blossom and find inner peace.

Jamar had grown to be a responsible young man. It was obvious he was part of the strength that had kept Betty going. With him being the oldest, Breanna was sure there had been plenty of times where he stepped up to the plate to help Betty out in ways Tony's sorry ass should have. He made sure his two younger siblings behaved. She watched him comfort his mother. Jamar never complained or fussed about anything. Bre thought he grew up way too fast. Since Betty arrived home earlier, she made sure dinner was ready by the time Breanna got off, allowing Bre to have some time to relax. She always teased Breanna about having to work such long hours for such little money. Betty was right in a sense because Bre's income as a social worker was modest, but making a difference in someone's life was a reward within itself for her.

The backyard was the place for them to hang out after dinner. The weather was pleasant during the day and would cool down at night. Bre and Betty would sit out back, talking about the old days and trying to figure out what happened to everyone. They would laugh about the things they did when growing up as children. The kids would look at them strangely, highly interested in hearing stories about people and the funny things they did.

"Those were the good old days," Bre said.

Betty nodded her head. "They really were. Things are so different now."

Bre could tell Betty had many thoughts going through her mind. She looked lost. Everything began to grow quiet, and the kids walked over to Betty.

"Babies, it's time to get ready for your baths," Betty said.

"Mommy, can we stay out just a little longer?" the soft innocent voice asked.

"Honey, you can come back out tomorrow."

Angel, a wonderful soul, was fine with that. Her little eyes lit up as if she'd received a great surprise.

"Mommy, I don't want to go back home," Angel said.

Betty lifted her up and sat her on her lap while the other two stopped what they were doing and walked over.

"We're never going back. This is home for a while. Soon we'll get our own place," Betty said with conviction.

"Is daddy gonna come?"

"No, daddy can't come."

Angel and her brothers seemed to be comforted in knowing they weren't going to have to deal with their father again. Breanna observed Betty and her kids with a watchful eye, being certain there was more to the story than they were willing to tell.

"Ma, do you want me to start Angel's bathwater?" Jamar said.

"That would be great, if you don't mind."

Jamar walked over to his mom and gave her a kiss on the cheek. He then called the other kids to follow him as he went inside.

"That boy will grow up to be a good man. I can't believe how much he's grown, Betty."

"Yes, he's gonna be one hell of a man. I don't think I have to worry about him being anything like Tony."

"I think it's safe to say that's the least of your worries."

The two sisters agreed on that. They continued to share stories about the kids, back home, and the good old times. Some stories were unbelievable. There was still a distant look in Betty's eyes, so Bre decided to find out what was troubling her so deeply.

"Betty, I've been around the kids for some months now, and I've been watching them carefully. I believe Tony has been beating those kids. I know he was verbally abusive. Hell, it's not like it makes a difference whether it was verbal, mental, or physical. Abuse is abuse, no matter which form it's inflicted in. I know he's the cause of their jitteriness and insecurities."

"The abuse was pretty bad. When you're trying to survive in an abusive relationship, you don't really know or understand how bad it really is until you're out of it and able to look back. There was screaming, yelling, and name-calling. At the time, yes, it even became physical. The abuse carried on almost daily. Me and these kids have scars, but the good thing is we're finally healing. We're healing really good." Betty was overcome with sadness and tears.

Bre became angry and hated that she was right about Tony being even more inhuman to his own family than she originally thought. Betty was right. She and the kids had come a long way and they were all finally happy and living a normal life. But the fact remained, she and the kids had gone through pure hell.

"Oh my, God," slowly came out of Bre's mouth with great sorrow.

The tears began to rush down Betty's face. Bre could see the evidence of hurt, sorrow, and pain. She could feel something deep from within her. Betty was hurting more than her sister ever imagined. Bre walked over to her and assured her that everything was going to be all right. Betty assured her that she would always be there for her and loved her and the kids dearly.

Even though Bre wanted to cry along with Betty, she refrained. She had to hold the tears back because Betty needed her strength. Bre had to hold back words of anger. By doing so, it was as though she were swallowing a rock in her throat. She embraced her sister and felt every bit of her pain and heartache. From the corner of her eye, she saw Jamar standing from a distance making sure his mother was okay. It must have given him some relief to know he wasn't alone in caring for his mother.

"It's gonna be okay, Betty."

"I know. It can only get better from here," she said with a slight smile on her face.

They hugged and headed back inside the house. Angel was in

the tub, waiting for Betty to come in and bathe her. She peeped in to check on her little girl, who was having a ball with the bubbles. She was in her own little world, laughing and talking to herself. Bre came up behind her and joined in, watching Angel silently with a heart full of love. Angel continued to toss her bubbles and water into the air.

She let out a loud giggle and said, "We don't have to go back." She was making herself a little jingle out of it. They were so tickled. Betty burst out laughing.

Angel was a little startled, but she was comforted in knowing she was safe and not in any trouble. She'd been there long enough to know there was no screaming, fighting, or yelling. She knew she could express herself openly and respectfully without being punished.

Betty went in to help her bathe and get dressed while Bre did the same with Alex. He was having a ball with his cousins around. They all got along like peas in a pod. Bre noticed Alex becoming less dependent on her. With all the peace and comfort, everyone had a chance to be themselves without fear and resentment lurking in the shadows. In essence, they learned the true meaning of the word *family*. After Angel and Alex finished their baths, they played around a few minutes longer. Neither of them liked going to bed early, and they both hated getting up in the morning.

"Come on, my Angel, it's time for you to go to bed."

"And, Alex, you come on so you can get some sleep as well." Breanna lifted him in her arms and gave him a quick kiss and hug.

It didn't take long for them to drift off to sleep. The two sisters found their way into the sitting area of Bre's room, where they reminisced again about their younger days. Even though Betty was laughing and talking, Bre felt as if she had something on her mind. She still saw the distant look on Betty's face from time to time.

"Betty, is there something bothering you? Is there something you'd like to talk about?"

Pausing and looking directly at Bre, Betty's mouth began to move. At the same time, the phone began to ring and broke the undivided attention they were giving each other. They both turned and looked at the phone.

"Go ahead and answer it. We'll talk later."

"Are you sure?"

"Yes, now get the phone before whoever it is hang up."

Before Bre could get the phone to her ear, she could hear Charles's voice.

"Hello?"

"Babe, are you there? I was about to hang up, but I could hear you answering. How was your day?"

"It was good."

Betty could tell by Bre's tone and smile that it was Charles. It had been several weeks since the two of them had spent any quality time together. With Betty moving in and getting settled, Bre's schedule had been much tighter, and that cut into a lot of her personal time. Charles was still in Florida helping care for his father, so Bre was always happy to hear from him and, whenever possible, spend time with him.

"What about your day?" Bre said.

"I found myself with this huge problem today."

"Is there anything I can do to help?"

"Well, you're part of the problem."

Breanna was caught off guard and distracted by Betty waving goodnight while she closed her bedroom door.

"Bre, why are you so quiet?"

"I guess I'm trying to figure out why I'm the problem, or what makes me the problem, Charles?"

"Bre, I'm missing you terribly. I get really lonely at times." Charles was speaking softly and from his heart. He exhaled and continued talking, "I've thought about our relationship over and over, and I want more. My dad is getting better, so I won't have to be here much longer."

Charles's words touched her deeply, and at that moment she wanted to be in his arms. The call didn't last long, for he only wanted to let her know the exact date he would be back. It was clearly his way of letting Bre know she had to get things in order with Munda. Charles might not know exactly what was going on between her and Munda, but he knew things needed to be sorted out if they were going to move forward.

They shared their goodbyes and hung up. Bre remained in the same spot for about ten minutes longer. She thought about Charles, and a smile came to her face. He was a special man, but it wasn't enough to make Munda disappear.

"Let me get up before I get too deep into that," she said out loud into the night. She didn't want to start trying to figure out what she was going to do about the two men in her life. She wanted things to continue the way they were for the time being.

From the other side of the door, Betty said, "Bre…are you still up in there?"

"Come on in, Betty."

Betty stepped in and looked down. "You're on the floor."

"I was laying down here while talking on the phone and was too lazy to move when I got off." Bre began pulling herself off the floor so she could converse with Betty.

"Bre, you want me to turn the lights off in the kitchen?"

"I'll turn them off. I'm a little hungry, so I'll get myself something to snack on."

She walked into the kitchen; Betty led the way. They chatted while having a few grapes and some deliciously pulpy orange juice. Bre thought back on their earlier conversation about the abuse Tony had inflicted on them. To keep from bringing the topic back up and having her to relieve such pain, she decided to wait until the opportunity presented itself again.

"Bre, I'm getting ready to go down for the night, so I'll be able to get up early in the morning."

"I'm right behind you."

Even though Bre was tired, she was also restless. She tossed and turned as the light from the moon peeped into her window. The words Charles spoke to her earlier clung to her thoughts. There was no way she could discard Charles and what he was feeling. In a way, it would be nice to have him closer. She knew the two of them connected. She made mistakes in her past, and she really didn't want to make any more. Charles was a special man. He was always consistent in everything he did. Breanna also realized there would be problems in having two men she cared about living close together. Bre trembled from all the thoughts going through her mind, eventually tiring herself out enough to get a little sleep before it was time to get up and face another workday.

***

Much of her daily routine repeated itself: getting up, preparing for work, and taking the dog out. These events were followed by cooking breakfast, driving the children to daycare, arriving at work, and eventually leaving work, all leading up to a much-anticipated bedtime. Energy became a lost friend of hers. On the bright side, Betty and her kids took care of some of the attention Alex required. God knows she appreciated the times when she could come home and not have to worry about preparing dinner. Betty kept a tight schedule within the home. With the responsibility of taking care of three kids on her own, she needed some sort of daily regimen.

Bre had one more day before her weekend started, and she was ready for it. She wanted to stay locked up in her room and sleep for a complete day. It seemed as if there was always something keeping her busy. Munda and Charles were never far from her thoughts. Each man still had his own role and distinct place in her mind and heart. Bre knew the whole thing was going to get more complicated as the days went by. She felt it was about time for her to take control, but she wasn't sure how. She knew she faced an incredible challenge. She wasn't about to make any hasty decisions. On the one hand, she wouldn't allow Munda to walk into her life and change everything on a whim. It wasn't like she'd forgotten about what happened between them. True enough, they'd lit a spark, one that turned into a fire she never saw coming; nonetheless, she decided not to rush. Soon after that conclusion, Bre slipped into a deep sleep, only to be awakened by her early morning alarm. She arose with extra energy; it being Friday surely had a lot to do with it.

"Girl, you're pretty perky this morning. If I didn't know any better, I'd think you got laid or something," Betty said in a devilish way.

"Well, we know that didn't happen…unfortunately."

"I hear you, sis."

They both laughed.

"I'm on a roll this morning, Betty. I even have the coffee ready. The kids have about another forty minutes before it's time to get up."

Betty said, "You know there's no school today, and I'm off."

"That's right! I won't have to worry about all that school traffic this morning. What a wonderful Friday!"

Bre got the coffee cups out of the cabinet and stepped outside the front door to retrieve the morning paper. For a moment, she stood and looked around to appreciate the simple things in nature God created. The fresh, cool, crisp air always rejuvenated her. It was like magic. Slowly, she closed her eyes and took a deep, long breath.

Betty opened the door and handed her a cup of coffee. "I know how hard it is to come back in after experiencing the early morning air. This time of morning at home, you would hear children crying, people yelling and screaming profanity and all kinds of traffic."

"I could never go back to the city, Betty. I have my own little paradise here."

"I sat out in the backyard a couple of days ago when everyone was away. Breanna, it is so soothing. I can't believe how much time passed with me just sitting there doing nothing, aside from relaxing. My problems swept away with the breeze. I observed the birds as they made their way to the feeders and birdhouses. The flowers and the greenery remind me of heaven on Earth."

"Come on, let's go inside. If I stay out here too long, I'll suddenly feel ill and call in sick to work. Is Angel going to daycare today?"

"I was thinking about letting her stay in with me and the other kids. Why don't you let Alex stay in with us, too?"

"Are you sure, Betty? That's a houseful of kids."

"If my kids are gonna be here, why should I mind him staying? We're at his house."

"Betty, that isn't how I'm looking at it."

"I know. What I'm saying is, if I can do anything to give either one of you any comfort, I want to. You've been wonderful to me and the kids, and I thank you from my heart."

"We're family, and no matter what's happening in this world, if there's anything I can do to make life better for you, I will. As we get older, we learn to better appreciate the value of family, sharing, loving, and understanding. You better take advantage of this because me and the kids will be in our own place in a couple of weeks."

"Betty, I can't believe you've already found your own place. I'm gonna miss you, but I know you need your own space."

"Well, it won't be like I'm far away. Matter of fact, I measured the distance. We'll be less than three miles away from each other." Betty hugged her sister.

***

As the days unfolded, their bond grew stronger, and nothing pleased either sister more. They discovered their mother had caused a lot of the fighting and animosity between them when they were growing up. She'd heard people with multiple children say they love them all equally, but she just couldn't believe that to be true for everyone. There was never a question in anyone's mind as to which one of them their mother loved the most. It was always as obvious as a picture on the wall that it was Betty.

"Bre, you'd better start moving so you're not late for work, honey."

Bre sighed. "Yes, I know. I need to get going. If I don't, I might end up staying here, and I can't afford that."

She already was dressed, so her hair and makeup were the only things left to do. She only needed fifteen minutes to get fabulous enough for work. She knelt down to give Alex a big kiss on the forehead before heading out. Half-asleep, Alex threw his little arms around Bre's neck as she kissed his forehead. She knew he would enjoy being home today.

Chapter Thirteen

Bre's day at work went smoothly. When it was quitting time, she promptly left. She was ready to get home, relax, and enjoy time with her family in the backyard. Bre could see smoke from the grill rising above her house as she pulled in the driveway. She watched the cloud of smoke as she proceeded to the backyard. The closer she got, the more laughter and play she heard. Betty and the kids were getting down in the backyard with the grill.

"Happy Friday!" Betty yelled as she walked toward Bre with a very cold drink.

"Girl, it's Friday! TGIF!"

Bre started snapping her fingers and moving her body to the beat of the music as she looked around at everyone enjoying themselves. Betty handed her a drink.

"Um, girl, this is slamming! This is a bad-ass margarita."

Bre continued to sip her drink while looking around for her little man. Once they made eye contact with each other, Alex ran over and wrapped his little body around her legs. He hung on long enough for a quick kiss and hug, and then he was gone again. Bre kicked off her shoes and placed her feet on the cool grass that lined her yard so pristinely. This was the way to come home, and a great way to begin a weekend. There was nice music, good food, and good company.

"I invited Dee and Deb. They should be here soon. I thought

you might need to let your hair down. It's Friday, and there's plenty of food."

Bre didn't know it, but Betty had planned the gathering some days ago. She knew Bre needed to exhale and enjoy some time with friends and family.

"Mommy, can we get something to eat now? I'm hungry."

"Are you sure you're really hungry, Angel? You've already eaten like a lion."

She couldn't blame the kids for wanting to eat, because Betty had a real feast going on, not to mention the fact she cooked like Rachael Ray. They weren't about to wait for everyone's arrival before getting down on the grub.

"Come on! Hot dogs! Let's eat!" she shouted to the kids.

Natches was wandering around with his tail wagging, a sign of his happiness. Bre was certain he'd had a few bones to chew. Even with his tongue hanging, she could still see a smile proudly presented on his face.

"Hello, everyone," Munda said as he entered the backyard.

"Hey, Munda, what's going on?" Betty said, giving him a hug.

Bre could feel him looking at her, even though Betty was the one talking to him.

"Hey, Daddy," Alex said as he ran into his father's arms.

"What's up, little man? What's going on?"

"I'm eating ribs and potato salad."

While Alex was speaking, he wiggled his way out of Munda's arms and ended his conversation quickly, running away to join the other kids.

"Damn, that boy can play hard!" Munda said, watching Bre and shaking his head good-naturedly.

Betty yelled, "That's why you shouldn't allow him to be the only child! He's capable of getting lonely, like everyone else."

"Who asked you for your opinion, Oprah?" Breanna balled up a napkin, threw it across the picnic table at Betty, and giggled.

"Now he has cousins close by, and he has Natches, too. He

couldn't ask for a more faithful friend and companion. Plus, he doesn't have to go through the hitting and yelling crap siblings go through."

"So, are you comparing the company of a dog to that of a sibling?"

"Damn right, I am."

Munda was sitting back, laughing at the two of them going back and forth. He knew when to keep his mouth closed.

"Hey, everybody, are we too late?" Deloris yelled.

"Come on back. It's Friday night, so there's no such thing as too late."

Bre and Dee greeted each other with hugs and kissed each other on the cheek. Those who didn't know each other were introduced. Deloris had brought Zack and a long-time male friend of hers, Don.

Betty debated about inviting Renee since she knew Deloris wasn't too keen on her. It was also a problem because she and Bre knew what Renee had done. Despite all the downfalls Renee possessed, Betty invited her anyway. Renee and Betty hadn't seen each other for a long time, so she thought they might at least enjoy catching up on some of the things going on in New York.

"Bre, Munda is looking good! I see he's part of the friends-and-family functions now. What's going on with that?" Deloris said as she put her arms around Bre's neck.

"Not what you think. He happened to stop by. I wasn't expecting him, but when he showed up, Betty offered him a place at the table."

"Well, I'll tell you one thing, girlfriend, he has his eyes on you."

"Don't come over here starting any shit, Dee," Bre demanded.

"I'm calling it like I see it. Don't think I haven't noticed you looking at him as well."

"Whatever," Bre said as she threw up the "W" hand gesture.

"You don't have to hide it from me. I don't blame a girl for admiring her baby's daddy. Now tell me it's not true. Bre, on a serious note, if you know you still love Munda, follow your heart, girl. You're my friend, and I'll support whatever makes you happy."

"Thanks, but I think Charles and I will be okay." The tone in Bre's voice wasn't very convincing.

Dee lowered her head and peeped over the top of her sunglasses. "All right, I see Renee isn't here."

Breanna watched as the expression on Deloris' face changed.

"What's wrong, Dee?"

"I spoke too damn soon. I see Renee has made it here after all."

"Don't start anything with her, Dee."

"I believe in following what I feel. That girl makes my skin itch every time I'm around her. Renee has a bad spirit, Bre. I don't trust the bitch at all. I've tried to do right and be nice to her because of you."

"Okay, Dee, she has her issues, as we all do. Hers just seem to be a little more prevalent than ours."

Before she could finish talking, Deloris stood up. "Oh, hell no! Don't tell me that's the man she's dating."

Deloris rolled her eyes as she looked down at Breanna for a response; Bre could see the anger all over her face.

"Yes, that's him. Why do you ask?"

"Girl, do you know who that is?"

"Am I supposed to?" Bre had a confused look of on her face.

"Bre, think back. He didn't have a full beard the last time you saw him. Remember the bridal party we went to when you first got here?"

"Yes, I remember now. Oh hell! That's your co-worker's husband, isn't it?"

"Hell, yeah, and not only is she my co-worker, but she's also a friend. Not only that, she's about to have that son of a bitch's baby any day now."

"Get the hell out of here!" Bre exclaimed.

Deloris watched the two of them with tangible anger.

"How could he leave Rosa at home and be with that piece of trash? I should go and kick both their asses right now."

"No, please don't start a scene. That'll ruin the evening for everyone."

"Oh, I want him to know I know his shit is stinking, Bre."

"Let me distract Renee for a moment, and you can get his attention and send his ass back home to his pregnant wife. That's where his ass needs to be."

Betty walked over to them, trying to figure out what was going on. "The two of you are looking guilty in this little corner. What's going on?"

A bit puzzled, Betty still recognized that something was wrong; it was just a matter of time before she'd find out exactly what was going on.

"Nothing," Bre responded quickly.

"Bre, don't you say *nothing* when that bitch is standing over there with my friend's husband," Dee growled.

Betty turned towards the direction they were staring, trying to figure out who they were talking about. "I guess Renee is with someone else's husband again."

At the same time, Deloris and Bre shouted, "Again?"

"Shh," Betty said while indicating with her hand to lower their voices. "This is why her trifling ass left New York. She was messing around with a married man and his wife kicked her ass."

"No way, girl!" Deloris said as she let out a short laughed.

Betty proceeded. "She was sitting up in that woman's car, riding around in it like it was hers. That same woman was waiting on her one day, and when she got into the car, the woman snatched her ass straight out by the hair. They were fighting in the street, and that woman kicked her ass all over the pavement."

"Get out of here, Betty. You've got to be kidding!"

Before she said anything else, Deloris began walking in the direction of Renee and her date. Betty was watching the whole thing unfold. They could only imagine what was going to happen. Deloris directed them, Renee and the man, to an area of the backyard that was away from the kids. They could see her head moving as one of her hands was on her hips and the other was used as a scolding stick. They saw the man walk out, but Deloris was still talking to Renee. It seemed as if Deloris was doing all the talking, which they knew wasn't good. Betty and Bre began walking over to make sure things wouldn't get out of hand.

"Maybe we should let Dee go ahead and kick her ass," Bre said to Betty.

"She's not worth it. She still wouldn't understand why her ass was getting beat."

When they were close to them, Betty said, "Is everything okay over here?"

"Everything's fine," Renee said with an unconvincing smile.

"It's fine? How in the hell is it fine when you're fucking my friend's husband? You know he's married, but being the nasty bitch you are, you don't give a damn."

"I think it's time for me to leave. I don't have to take no shit from you!" Renee yelled to Deloris.

"I think so, too. You shouldn't have brought your ugly ass here anyway. You should be home with your child instead of always running around with someone's husband. Where in the hell did you leave your baby, anyway? It's bad enough you have a child, but it's even worse your child doesn't know who his mother is. You shouldn't be here, especially when Bre found out you lied to Munda about her seeing someone else and told him it was possible Alex wasn't his. You trifling bitch!"

Before Bre could intervene, Deloris slapped the hell out of Renee. Betty and Bre got between the two of them before things could escalate. Standing there without saying anything, Renee looked at her. She was now aware they all knew what she'd done to Bre and Munda.

"How are you gonna get home, Renee? Your friend's already left," Betty said.

"Her stinking ass can walk home. She has a lot to think about!" Deloris shouted.

For a brief moment, Bre felt sorry for Renee, but Deloris wasn't letting up.

"I'll call a cab," Renee snapped.

"No! You don't have to do that. Finish your evening, and I'll take you home when you're ready to go. I don't want this evening to be rained on any more than it already has been." Bre felt bad about what happened, but she knew Renee probably deserved it.

Deloris walked away mumbling, and Bre knew she wasn't about to let this go. Dee found her way over to the kids as they were running around playing. Zack got her to blow bubbles with him. Just as Alex was Bre's heart, Zack was Dee's. It didn't take long for her to start smiling after being around the kids for a few minutes.

Betty had a few words with Renee and walked away in another direction. Bre could tell it wasn't what Renee wanted to hear.

"Is everything all right?" Munda said.

"Everything's fine," she said while trying not to let him see her facial expression.

"Okay, I hear you, but something just went on between you women. I heard some heated words. You know how you women get with one hand on your hip and the other pointing and shaking all over. You know what I'm talking about, Bre." He stood there imitating the way Deloris was pointing and shaking her finger at Renee.

"Come on here, with your sick self," she said as she laughed and shook her head at him.

"Bre, didn't I hear Deloris telling Renee something about her kid?"

"Yes, you sure did."

"Babe, I didn't know she had a kid."

"Most people don't. That poor child doesn't see her too often because she's always out fucking or trying to fuck around instead of loving her son and allowing him to love her. It's really a sad situation.

I understand the father doesn't want anything to do with him. Oh, Jesus…enough of that talk. What made you drop by this evening, anyway?"

"I hadn't seen or spoken to you in a couple of days, and I wanted to check on you and Alex…and everyone else."

"We're doing fine. Alex is having lots of fun with his cousins. Life's been pretty good, Munda."

"I can see that."

He looked back to see if anyone could see them as he moved closer and closer to her. It was dark in the corner of the yard where they were standing. They could see everyone and everything, but they were invisible to the group. He finally got to the point where he could touch her and steal a kiss. Everyone was busy doing their own thing. Deb, Deloris, and Betty were sitting at the table laughing, talking, and eating away. The few other people present were busy becoming acquainted with each other. It was obvious they were all having a good time. Renee looked out of place and miserable. Though they had tried to keep things down, it was obvious other people were discovering the latest happening. Renee had made a reputation for herself as the town whore. One couldn't help feeling sorry for a person like her.

"I need to take Renee home," Bre turned and said to Munda.

"Didn't she just get here?"

"Yeah, but she's ready to leave."

"Why didn't she just leave with the guy she came here with? If she was ready to go, she should've had the man she came with take her."

"I'm taking her, so it's not a problem."

She didn't offer any explanation as to why Renee hadn't gone home the same way she came.

"Would you like me to tag along?" Munda said.

"Nope, but you can hang out here with everyone until I get back if you'd like."

"What if I said I'd rather hang out with you?"

"I would say that's fine if you're gonna drive."

"I'll drive you anywhere you wanna go."

"Let me tell Renee we're ready to take her home."

Munda grabbed her arm and pulled her back. "I've missed you, Bre."

Bre pulled away before anyone could see them. "Come on, if you're coming."

She excused herself from everyone so she could take Renee home. Renee said her goodbyes before ending her night.

In a nice, calm manner Deloris said, "Renee, I'll be seeing you later."

Renee didn't acknowledge Deloris at all.

The drive to Renee's house was quiet, aside from the small talk she and Munda were making as she gave instructions to her house.

"Thanks," was the only thing she said.

"It's nothing, Renee. Try to get some rest."

"I will."

When Renee was almost at her door, Bre called out to her. "Renee, wait a minute."

Renee turned and waited as Breanna ran up to her.

"Deloris was right about my knowing about what you did. That was wrong, but I blame Munda just as much as I do you. But if you ever try to cause any problems with my family and loved ones again, I will fuck you up personally, and that's a promise."

With a mean frown, Renee rolled her eyes at Bre and began walking away. Abruptly, she stopped in her tracks and turned back toward Bre. "Whore, you're screwing two men and don't even realize one of them has a child and isn't all that you think he is. Who are you to judge anyone? Figure that out, bitch!"

Renee's day had been rough, and she'd had enough. She gave Bre the finger, turned and walked away. Before she was able to get inside her house Bre grabbed her by the arm and told her she wasn't through talking. Renee tried to snatch her arm away, but Bre yanked her even tighter.

"I saved you from Deloris earlier, but there's no one who will save you from me. What you did was unthinkable and cruel."

"Fuck you and your self-righteous ass, Breanna"

Before she knew it, Bre slapped her and the fight began. Anger took over, and Bre wanted to hurt her badly.

"Breanna!" Munda yelled from inside the car. He jumped out of the car, ran over, and pried Bre's hands off Renee. It took all his strength to keep her from getting back to Renee and causing more damage. "Renee, get in your house now!"

***

Munda was riddled with shock and disbelief while forcing Breanna to the car. After he got in the car and sat for a moment without saying anything, Munda finally spoke. "What in the hell just happened, Bre? What were you thinking?"

"Things were building up and enough was enough. She pushed all my wrong buttons, and I lost it."

"It was pretty damn obvious you lost your temper." Munda glared at her as he started the car.

"It was supposed to be one of those woman-to-woman conversations and she started verbally attacking and cussing at me."

"Apparently, a lot's going on. What happened at the house between her and Deloris?"

She knew at this point she had to tell Munda what had taken place. There was no avoiding his questions.

"Renee showed up at the party with Deloris's friend's husband."

"Ouch! What was she thinking?"

"She wasn't, that's the problem. Renee didn't realize Deloris knew him until things started going down."

"Did Renee know he was married?"

"I don't know, but if she's been fooling around with him for some time, she has to know. Munda, how could she not? I'm sure she wasn't invited or allowed to his house. That should've been the first clue. Even if she wasn't aware in the beginning, she should have seen some obvious signs and put two and two together."

The whole time Bre was speaking, her arms and hands were constantly moving. When she finished speaking, she placed the palm of her hand on her forehead as she shook her head.

The drive back to the house was quiet. By the time they got back, the kids had already gone in and Deloris and Betty were outside wrapping things up.

"Bre, it's so nice out here," Deloris said.

Bre shot Dee an unconvincing smile. It was clear something had happened. Confused, Betty walked closer to Bre and Munda.

"What the hell happened? Munda, did you do something to my sister?" she said in a snappy voice, keeping her eyes on Bre.

Quickly defending himself, Munda lifted his hands and claimed his innocence. "Betty, I didn't do anything to her. She and Renee got into it."

"What?"

Breanna made a sudden gesture so Munda would stop talking, but he continued.

"I didn't do anything to your sister. She and Renee had a physical altercation."

Still, in disbelief himself, Munda shook his head and then let out a short laugh.

Deloris and Betty were both looking at Bre. Their mouths slightly open with shock. Within the next moment, they were all laughing. Bre was so upset, she could've exploded with anger.

"My sister was fighting? She was the one who kept Deloris from beating Renee's ass earlier."

"Huh, I guess she was saving Renee for herself. I must say, she has one hell of a swing." Munda laughed and walked off.

Betty burst out laughing. "Bre, you and Renee were fighting? What in the hell happened?"

"I let her know not to interfere with my family again, and things got nasty. It shouldn't have gone that bad. It was as if she had hatred for me. That whore told me I was sleeping with two men. Not only that, she also indirectly told me Charles has a son."

"Wait one damn minute, Bre! Charles really is Renee's baby's father?"

"Betty, I'm not sure what's going on. Thinking back, I knew something was odd between Charles and Renee, but I never thought they shared a kid. They were uneasy when we ran into each other. How's he gonna be so hard on Munda when his ass is worse? He's judging Munda about how he left me and Alex, and I'll be damned if he's not doing the same goddamn thing!"

"Sis, I knew there was a reason I wasn't too particular about Mr. Charlie. He has his nose so high in the air, he can't smell his own shit."

"Betty, I can't judge him without hearing the whole story. I only know what Renee said."

"Well, she's right about one thing: you are screwing two men," Betty and Deloris said at the same time while laughing.

"You two shut up. Just shut the hell up. I didn't ask for this shit. I didn't ask Munda to come back in my life. I didn't ask Charles not to care for his child. Hell, I didn't know he had a child. You all know I'm battling with everything going on. It's complicated."

Everyone became quiet. All of a sudden, Deloris reached out and gave Bre a much-needed hug. They all knew Bre had fallen back in love with Munda, but things were complicated.

"I can see Munda got a real kick out of that," Betty said. "I bet he got an even bigger kick out of knowing Charles has a child he isn't doing right by."

Bre quietly said, "He doesn't know yet."

"Come on, girl, you don't think he deserves to know Charles' shit stinks?"

Bre didn't bother to answer Betty because she knew Munda would only place more pressure on her for more of a commitment.

"Is Alex asleep?" Bre said.

"They went inside to watch a movie. Go sit down and relax.

Betty and I will finish putting things away," Deloris said.

Breanna walked over to the lounge chair and took a seat. It wasn't too long before Munda found his way over to her. He patted her leg, signaling for her to scoot over so he could sit next to her. Munda lifted her hand, squeezed it, and then gave her a gentle kiss on the back of it.

"Why are you so hard sometimes, Bre?"

"I'm not hard, Munda. You've always had this problem with me saying exactly what's on my mind. This is how I am. This is who I am."

"Babe, there's a way to go about doing things. The right way."

"Excuse me?"

"Calm down, Bre. You're too defensive. Do you see what I'm saying? Just like tonight, you wanted to put me in the same category with the guy who was cheating on his wife. That's not fair. We make mistakes. We do things we may live to regret later. I've never said I was perfect, and I'll never say I won't make mistakes again; however, Bre, I do know not to repeat the same ones."

Munda was now directly in her face. The only light was the nearby candle. Just as Munda began to kiss her, Bre noticed the quietness in the air. She knew Betty and Deloris had been nearby a few minutes ago. After stepping away from Munda, Bre noticed that they'd captured an audience. She couldn't do anything besides attempt to play everything off. Betty and Deloris weren't fooled and didn't waste any time letting her know. Before those two women could say anything to Munda, he politely walked away.

"You aren't that slick. I don't think it's only Munda who still has some deep emotions. If I had to call a spade a spade, I'd say you two are still very much in love."

"Get away, Deloris."

"Okay, you tell me if I'm wrong."

Betty wasn't saying anything, but the conversation between Deloris and Bre definitely captured her attention.

"Yes, you are, Dee."

Deloris chuckled. "Bre, you're gonna sit there and tell that lie? I can't believe you. You should claim him if he's who you want. Not only is he fine as hell, he's a good man."

"It's time for you to take your tired ass home, Deloris."

"I'm going so you don't kick me out. Hell, if I had a man like Munda standing in my backyard, I'd kick everybody out, too."

They all started laughing.

"You know you can stay as long as you want."

"I know I can, Bre, but it's late." Deloris gathered her family and said her goodbyes to Munda.

"Bre, you're working both him and Charles. Damn! I don't blame you one bit. Munda gets my vote."

"I don't know, Dee. I'm confused about everything right now."

"Charles knows Munda is trying to regain what he lost. You and Munda have a small child. Don't you know Charles is looking at that bond? He isn't stupid."

"Girl, go inside, get your belongings, and I'll wait out here for you."

Bre let out a soft laugh and shook her head as Dee walked away. She then headed back to find Munda, who was heading to the front of the house.

"I'm getting ready to leave," he said.

"You don't have to leave yet."

"Do you have a reason for me to stay?"

She looked deep into Munda's eyes and said, "What reason would make you stay?"

"How are you gonna answer a question with a question? You're supposed to answer my question first."

Bre watched the movements of his lips as if she were reading them. Before getting her words out, Munda gave her a long, passionate kiss. It was broken up suddenly when they heard someone clearing their throat. Deloris was standing there with her arms folded and a smirk on her face.

"You and Munda are too old for that shit. Y'all around the side of the house like two teenagers. You're busted."

"Go home, Deloris."

"Don't worry, I am. Bre, come walk me to the car."

"Munda, will you make sure all the candles are out?"

"Sure, babe."

Dee stopped, looked at Bre, and smiled. "Huh? What up with that *babe* stuff?"

Bre stood close to Dee and pinched her. They walked to the car like two kids, giggling and talking. Deloris gave people a lot of shit, but she was a good person.

"Bre, I bet Munda's dick was all hard, wasn't it? I bet your hairy scary down below was boiling like hot water on the stove. I'll be damned if I let you get some tonight and I don't get any. I think Zack is on to me when I'm thinking about steaming up the sheets. Don said his little ass is always cock blocking."

Laughing hysterically, they were enjoying each other's comical hearts when the porch light from across the street came on.

"Bre, is that Bernice's nosy ass?"

"Who else would it be?" Bre said as she looked around.

"I guess she's still in everybody's business."

"Yeah, but Betty had her quiet for a couple of weeks."

"Naw, Bre!"

"She caught Betty on a bad day. Bernice was just being her nosy self, and when Betty wouldn't play into her game, she tried to get the dirt from Antwon. Betty caught her and told her some ugly shit that would have made you cry. When Betty started going off, Bernice stood there shaking with fear and embarrassment. Then Betty told her, 'Now take that old fucked up body of yours inside your damn house and figure out how to get a damn life. Try me again and see what happens'."

Dee could barely talk from laughing so hard. "She caught Betty on a really bad day, Bre."

"She did. Betty had just got off the phone with that crazy ass Tony, too."

"Oh shit. You didn't tell me all this stuff was going on."

"Girl, it doesn't seem as if I'll get to tell you now either." Bre pointed in the direction of Dee's car where her son was becoming restless. It was only a few seconds before Zack was yelling for his mom.

"I bet that was a welcome sound for Munda," Dee said as she giggled and made a quick dash for the car.

Bre walked inside and made sure everyone was settled. The kids had fallen asleep in front of the television. The house was quiet, and there were no movements from anyone aside from Betty.

"Did Munda come in?"

"Isn't he still in the backyard? The way you've been tonight, perhaps he's still outside waiting to finish something you two started," Betty said.

Bre stopped all movement, then said, "I'm not going there with you."

"That's fine. Oh, and Charles called while you were gone, but he said he'll talk to you tomorrow."

"What did you tell him?"

"I told him you went to take your girlfriend home who was stranded. I didn't tell him Munda was assisting you."

"Does this mean I'm supposed to be forever grateful?"

"Take it however you want. I'm not mad at you."

Betty burst out laughing and quickly dashed into her room. Breanna walked to the back patio and looked around. In the darkest corner of the yard, she saw the flickering of a candle flame; she knew she'd find Munda there. As she walked toward him, she could see the blanket he'd placed on the grass. As she got closer, she could see his hand reaching out, as if to ask her to join him.

"I thought you disappeared."

"Well, here I am. I started putting out the candles and found myself sitting and thinking."

Munda looked down at the spot next to him and beckoned for her to join him. She sat down next to him, not really knowing what to say or do.

"Earth to Breanna! What are you thinking about, beautiful?" he said.

"My life is messy. I see myself coming to a crossroad and having to make decisions."

"Let's not worry about anything tonight. Whatever you wanna do, let's just enjoy the evening. I wanna make sure you're okay."

"I'm okay."

Munda pulled another blanket off the chair and threw it over them. Their conversation was soothing. He had a way of looking deep into her eyes and making every emotion surface. She wanted desperately to tell him how she was feeling about him.

"Munda."

"Yes, babe."

"Make love to me under the stars."

Munda raised no objections. He kissed her lips and then pulled away slowly. He gazed at her once again "Bre, I don't know where your head is sometimes. Sometimes it seems like all you want from me is my good loving."

She didn't have a quick response, but eventually, she was able to come up with something to say. "Haven't you been enjoying the sweet loving you've been getting too?"

"That's not the point, Bre. I think the last problem we have is our sexual relationship. Don't you think it's time we build this into something bigger?"

"Why are you so serious all of a sudden? Munda, why can't we just take one day at a time? Why worry about tomorrow right now? You want me to just open my mouth and tell you something. I don't know where we're headed, and I don't want to think about that right now. I just can't."

"Eventually, you're gonna have to. I don't like waiting here in limbo for a decision that should be right in front of your face."

Bre began to get tense and restless. It seemed as if Munda was putting her on the spot. She knew what she wanted. After everything she'd been through in the past with Munda, at this point she could only focus on her own selfish desires. Her desire was to make love to Munda, not worry about what to do or how to go about doing it. The chemistry between the two of them was volcanic.

It didn't take a psychic to know Breanna wasn't the only one having thoughts of desire. Munda looked down at his rock-hard dick, which was showing through the soft linen of his casual shorts. She got up on her knees and gripped her hands around his neck, entwining her fingers together, creating a loose lock. The night wasn't going to pass without her appetite being fully satisfied. As Bre kissed and rubbed his body, he slowly gave in. The intensity had risen. She guided his arms up so she could help him take off his shirt. Once it was off, he proceeded to stand and unfasten his belt and loosen his shorts.

Bre watched with deep desire in her eyes as his succulent cock stood strong and proud. Assisting her to her feet, he reached under her dress, only to find her bare ass. Looking up at her, he let out a soft laugh. He liked her kinky ways. With one hand in the front and the other in the back, he rubbed all over her sweet spots. She wanted to tell him to eat her like a sweet potato pie with a scoop of vanilla ice cream. She imagined the many ways his tongue did what it did best, giving her nothing but pure sensual adrenaline.

On his knees, he allowed his dick to find a direct path to her juicy pussy. The head of his cock entered inside her with a gentle force. Feeling her soft warmth gave him insurmountable relief as he grabbed her ass and began thrusting harder and harder.

She held tight to him as her body pled for more. Without missing a movement, Munda lifted her dress over her head in a quick motion, bearing their glistening naked bodies to the dim light. Their kissing was intense. They were holding, feeling, rubbing, and sucking. Time and space slowed. Bre wanted to remember every action that transpired.

The sharing of genuine emotional-felt affection was indefinable. The feeling caused her to tremble. Breanna knew the moment was one of deep emotion. Munda was giving his undivided attention to her mind, body, and soul.

"Breanna! This is what we live for...this is why we keep going."

Although he was unable to express his feelings and emotions with words, Breanna already knew. There were no words to express the deep love they had for each other. Really, no words were needed because everything was within their hearts and souls. Munda took a deep breath and squeezed her tightly.

"Go ahead, Munda. Make love to me and let me feel your heart."

Never losing eye contact, he laid her down on the blanket. She was longing for him. She wanted everything he had and more. He continued to make love to her, and she could feel every inch of his cock burrowing along the way, sliding past her G-spot and creating uncontrollable ecstasy. The force behind every powerful push gave way to nuances unexplored or unconquered.

"You like it, babe?"

"Yes, Munda."

Holding on and appreciating every touch and movement was putting her in a trance. Even with the slight pain from the hard thrusting and the oversized horse-like cock Munda had, it was too good to think about stopping. From position to position, Munda was leading her on an in-depth journey.

The expression on Munda's face was intense; it was as if he were calling her soul to answer his. He pulled back a little while, lifting her legs over his shoulders. She braced herself because she already knew Munda was about to give her the down-to-earth fucking her body was calling for. He adjusted her body so his dick would touch the very core of her.

Munda spoke words she was unable to hear, but Breanna was sure they were an expression of what he was feeling as his dick pounded against the slippery walls of her warm pussy. Even though she tried to keep up with him, the power of his thrusting restricted her movements. Munda was full of strength, so she knew she'd end up at his mercy.

He didn't care if it was too much for her to handle. He understood Bre. He was in his own world. As the thrusting became even more powerful, it seemed as if he would have to take a pause while fully inside her, but he didn't. He softened the impact for a moment, only to return to the force he'd given for what seemed like an eternity now.

"I'm gonna take your pussy to places it's never been before," he said in a low, sexy voice.

Not even seconds after those words were spoken, Bre felt her exorbitant wetness overflow like a waterfall. Munda knew her pussy all too well. She moaned as he hit the perfect spot.

"Does it feel good to you, Bre?"

"Yes, Munda, make me cum good. Keep giving it to my pussy."

"I'm gonna keep giving it to you for us, babe."

Munda kissed her and proceeded to make her call his name over and over again. It felt so good. Clenching tight to his body, she prepared herself for the ultimate collision of their souls. As she tried to push away gently, he held her tighter. She was at his complete mercy. Emotions were exploding. Their bodies were speaking to each other in their own language. Sweat trickled down their bodies.

"Let yourself go, Bre. I'm here to catch you. I'm not gonna let anything hurt you."

"Please, don't stop. I want it all, Munda. I can feel your heartbeat. I feel our souls entwining, embracing each other. I'm feeling emotions overpowering my heart. You feel so damn good in me. It's just so right. This is our love."

The overpowering emotions heavily touched her heart, making her forget about yesterday. Their hearts didn't care what was going on outside of themselves. Things were happening that they couldn't control. It was no longer a physical thing; it was all about their hearts and souls.

"I'm not stopping. I know you can feel what's going on. It's real, Bre. It's alive in us.

"Munda," she said.

Looking in his eyes, she knew that he understood their emotions were the same. Munda was holding to his word. She knew it wasn't going to be long before she'd cum, but she wanted to enjoy every second of his pleasures. Their emotions for each other were high and ready to explode. Embracing each other, their souls collided like a comet crashing into Earth. Bre didn't want the moments of their passion to end. Their lovemaking was phenomenal. His attentiveness presented itself with strength and boldness.

"Come on, babe, let's cum together," Munda whispered. "Give it all to me. It's the right time now."

"Oh…oh…oh, Munda" was all Bre could manage to say.

No other words followed. As her eyes slowly opened, she saw the moonlight encapsulating their entangled bodies, protecting them from anything wrong. That was it: she couldn't hold back any longer. She pressed her fingers into Munda's back and held on as if she were holding on for dear life. She could feel Munda's dick grow even more as he released inside of her. He continued until they were both lifeless, limp, and soaked in sweat.

There was nothing but silence all around them as they lay with their naked bodies under the dark sky. The sounds of their voices no longer existed, but their souls were surely communicating. Something always pulled them together. Even when she was angry, Bre still loved him. It took time for her to come to that realization, but eventually, she did. There was something about their connection that was an utter mystery she couldn't seem to solve.

"Are you cold?"

"A little," she whispered.

Before now, they hadn't paid any attention to the coolness that had entered the air. Munda pulled the blanket over their bodies and cuddled her. They both remained quiet while dreams ran through their minds like a great movie. Without any warning, Munda squeezed her tightly and allowed his leg to rub up and down the side of hers.

"We're a danger to each other." Bre burrowed her face in Munda's shoulder.

"How so?" he said.

"We're going to kill each other making love in the backyard."

"Bre, it's a beautiful thing we just shared. Is it not what you truly wanted?"

He was right. It was what she wanted.

They laughed. She teased him about how he'd acted as if he didn't want to give in at the beginning. She was his weakness; just as he was hers. Time passed as they watched the moon and enjoyed the night. The stars were twinkling as if they were smiling upon them.

"I hope your sister didn't see you out here exposing yourself."

"Oh, please, as if you weren't involved. But if she did, I know we didn't bore her."

As they enjoyed each other, Bre felt a sense of belonging with Munda.

"We better get some clothes on and get moving. I wish we could stay out here all night."

"Yeah, you're right. I don't want the mosquitoes to catch us out here sleeping naked."

"Do you wanna come home with me?"

Breanna paused to think about it but decided she would take him up on the offer at a later date. For a moment, she stood and looked deeply at Munda. She felt that special something again and couldn't make it go away. She wanted to hold tight to him and not let go.

"Babe, what's wrong? You're shaking."

She couldn't explain it, but it was powerful.

"I don't know. I was overcome by something."

"Tell me about it, Bre. I wanna know."

"I can't explain it. I've never felt anything like it before."

"I bet I can tell you what you're feeling."

She wasn't expecting those words from him, but she was curious to hear what he had to say. "Tell me, then."

"What you felt was a sense of belonging. It made you feel as if you were a part of me."

She couldn't say anything, but she was certain her facial expression was enough to validate her agreement.

"Am I not right, Bre?"

"How did you know?"

"Babe, every time I make love to you, I feel the same way. We've been sharing the same feeling all night. It took me a minute to understand what I was feeling, but now I'm able to understand exactly what it is. I'm falling in love with you all over again."

Still, no words would come from Bre's mouth. Munda pulled her into his chest and held her tightly while tears made their way down her face.

"Babe, we'll be okay. Our love is strong. Just give it a chance to breathe."

She nodded her head and wiped the tears from her eyes. "I'm scared, Munda. I'm just scared."

"Don't be scared, Breanna. You don't have to be. I'm here now."

His body language and expression were solid and serious. "I love you, Breanna."

"I love you, too, Munda."

"I already know you do, Bre. You just needed to accept that and let go of the past."

He gleamed at her with a smile of contentment on his face. Munda patted her on the ass and proceeded to lead her through the dimly lit backyard. She almost changed her mind about going home with him.

"We'll talk later."

"Okay."

"Go inside and lock up before I leave."

They waved goodbye, then Bre made her way inside the house.

As she turned to lock the door, Betty startled her as she stood there smiling.

"I thought the two of you were gonna camp out."

"No, we sat outside talking and time got away."

Betty burst out laughing and shook her head. "I guess that was some kind of talking. Deloris forgot to leave your bag, so she brought it back. She was gonna give it to you, but you and Munda were pretty busy, to put it mildly."

They both started smiling.

"Yeah, the two of you were busted. We only watched to the point of him unfastening his belt. We thought we were watching a love scene by Mandingo."

Still smiling, Bre pushed Betty aside and went into the bathroom.

"Want some coffee to warm you up a little?"

"I guess I'll take a cup."

***

By the time Bre finished showering, Betty had the coffee ready. They sat and talked. Despite Bre's altercation with Renee, it had been an exceptionally good evening. Sharing such special time with her friends and family made her realize how much she'd been missing.

"Bre, don't think you're gonna avoid talking about that hot action that went on in the backyard."

"It was nothing" Bre waved her off.

"Bullshit! We could feel all the energy just from watching the two of you. Even Deloris said there were deep vibes coming from you. Bre, we could see fireworks going off!"

"It probably was the liquor talking in both of you," she said.

"Okay, call it what you want, Bre, but time will tell. You know that old saying, 'What's done in darkness will come to light'."

"You have an old saying for every damn thing. Leave me alone."

Bre poked her tongue at Betty like a spoiled kid and headed to her bedroom, but Betty wasted no time following her. They sat on the edge of the bed, reflecting over the complete evening. They even laughed about the incident between Deloris and Renee. After talking for a while, Bre lay down and relaxed. After having laid there for some time, she finally drifted off to sleep. Her day had been long, but it ended very well. She'd even found out something about Charles that made her decision much easier, or so she wanted to believe.

***

It didn't take long for morning to come, and eventually for the weekend to come to an end. Time seemed to have zoomed by without any delays. Even with it being a dreaded Monday morning, Bre was full of energy. Nothing or no one could do anything to bother her.

"So, I finally got to meet Munda," Deb said.

"Yep, you met Munda," Bre said.

"Alex looks just like his dad. Did he carve a picture of himself on his sperm, then sent it up? Charles had better be careful."

"Yes, Mr. Charles better," Bre said with attitude in her voice.

What was that all about? Has Charles gotten on your bad side?"

Before answering, Bre remembered what Renee told her earlier.

"Deb, I think he might be Renee's baby's dad."

"What! I'm not sure about that one, Bre. I've heard some crazy stuff, but that's way out there."

Deb remained quiet and pondered with that thought. She didn't have an immediate response, but she was attempting to put the puzzle together. "You really think he's the father? Damn, is that why she intercepted his phone number so quick? If he is the father, it would make sense why she wouldn't want him to have your number. She was trying to keep him for herself. It all makes sense!"

Bre stood there waiting for her to finish her analysis of the situation. It didn't seem likely that Renee would have been a choice of Charles's. Without all the facts, though, it was hard to conclude anything.

"Bre, I know his ass ain't trying to put Munda down because of what happened between the two of you. Yeah, Munda really fucked up by leaving and believing some bullshit told to him, but if Charles isn't taking care of his child, what gives him the right to judge anyone? You're talking about a real hypocrite there. And what did he have to say?"

"He's not aware that Renee told me unless she told him that she told me. I don't feel one way or another. I'm numb when it comes to all that."

"It really doesn't matter, Bre. Everyone thinks Munda's your man anyway. I know you two went through some tough spots, but I guess it's all about forgiving."

"But there are some things you can't forget, no matter how hard you try," Bre said with a tangible sadness in her voice.

"That's true, but there are things we learn to get past. Maybe I just believe in second chances. I think you need to search your heart."

Deb winked as she smiled and walked away. Her words lingered in Bre's mind. Deb had even caught her during some of her deepest and most intimate thoughts. She assumed Munda was on Bre's mind.

Chapter Fourteen

Time went by quickly and smoothly. Almost suddenly, Charles would be home the next day. Breanna never mentioned what Renee had disclosed. She decided she'd wait and question him face to face. Things were changing for Breanna. She thought her relationship with Charles had been built on trust, but then she discovered he'd been lying. She wasn't going to enjoy their future conversation at all. She was sure he was anticipating a disagreement involving Munda, but he couldn't possibly anticipate that he was going to have to deal with explaining himself to Bre.

Bre felt like Munda's presence was with her all the time. They shared a ravenous, wild side that was gentle, yet so indulgently satisfying. There was a sense of closeness that appeared out of nowhere. She couldn't help picking up the phone and dialing his number. After Munda answered the phone and heard Bre's voice, they delved directly into an effortless and continuous conversation. Munda sat in silence as he held the phone tight to his ear.

"Babe, do you ever find yourself thinking about me?" he said out of the blue.

"Yes, I sure do." Bre sounded very sentimental. "I've been thinking about you all day."

"I miss you, girl. I know it's gonna get worse before it gets better."

Puzzled. Bre said, "What do you mean?"

"Chuckie boy," he said sarcastically. "He's not gone forever, you know?"

She kind of laughed. "He'll be here soon."

"Sorry to hear that."

"Munda, don't start…please. I didn't mean to disturb you, so I'll let you get back to what you were doing."

"You can't hold me up. I can't do what I was thinking about doing."

"Why not?" she asked him.

"Because you aren't here," Munda said sadly.

"Oh, really?"

In a soft, deep, sensual voice, he said, "That's right. I was thinking about sexing you up slowly while telling you how much I love you without saying one word." Munda let out a slow moan like the one he made while making love to Bre. "Babe, doesn't it make you wanna open your legs and rub that sweet kitty of yours? I want you bad, Breanna."

He kept going on. It was as though he had set out on a mission to make her want to run over and fuck him to death.

"Munda, we can't do this."

"Bre, just close your eyes for a moment and think about us making love. Feel how alive it is. Please come over this one last time, babe."

"I can't do that."

"Sure, you can. Where is everyone? Is Betty staying at her place this weekend?"

"Yeah, they're getting things put away and organized."

"I guess it gets pretty lonely there now since she has her own place," Munda said.

He was right about her missing Betty, but at this moment she bet he was glad Betty had her own place and Alex happened to be visiting his cousins, leaving Bre alone in her home.

"Go pull off those wet panties and get that velvet kitty ready for me."

There were no more words spoken. He hung up soon afterwards.

Without thinking, Bre grabbed a quick shower. Before she was done, Munda was at the door, ready to come in. He didn't say a word as he scooped her wet body into his arms and made his way to her bed. He sat her down softly and then peeled off his shorts and T-shirt. He removed the towel from her dripping wet body and kissed her all over. She could feel his finger go inside her and stimulate her G-spot. She couldn't help giving in to all his desires. Munda's stiff tongue went all in and around her pussy. Her body became limp, and the soothing, sexual pleasures took all tension away.

Munda gorged himself on her pussy to the point of almost making her scream. The pleasure was overwhelmingly good. He then pounded away in her pussy as if it had no bottom. She'd been flipped, spanked, sucked, and fucked in every way the body could be.

When Munda was about to cum, he took his dick out and came on her stomach. Munda was able to put his dick back into her pussy and continue fucking her after that. He made love to her so long, her pussy became dry and swollen.

Finally, he was getting ready to have another orgasm, and she could tell he was exhausted. Munda lay on top of her as they held on to each other tightly. Again, there were no words, but they could feel strong emotions that were capturing each of their hearts. Munda knew this had caught Bre off guard, and by no means was she planning for this to happen. Here it was, days before Charles's return, and she was making love to Munda. Bre turned to Munda to say something, but he stopped her.

"Don't say anything, Bre. Please let us have this moment."

He kissed her and smiled.

"Bre, when something's meant to be, it will be. If we are to be, Charles or no one else can stop it. You do what you need to do, and I'm gonna be patient. C'mon, let's get some sleep."

They snuggled up together and slept in between their lovemaking sessions. Bre could already tell that trying to let go of

Munda was going to be more of a challenge than she anticipated.

***

The sun rays that made their way through the partially closed blinds awakened them. Bre looked down at Munda as he slept. Just as she was about to mess with his lips, he grabbed her. He scared the crap out of her, but he found it very amusing.

"I don't know why you find it so funny," she snapped at him.

"You thought I was asleep, didn't you? I've told you about that." He smiled and kissed her on the nose. "Breanna, I was watching you sleep."

Within moments, Munda was wrapping his mouth around her breast. His gentle sucking felt so good. Her words came out slower and slower. She wrapped her arms around his neck and pulled her upper body even closer to his. He slowly ran his hand over her body and down to her wet pussy. She lifted her legs and opened them wider so Munda could be free to roam. It felt so sensational, she nearly lost her breath.

"We better stop while we're able to. I'm gonna let you save some for later."

"You're gonna stop just like that?" Bre was disappointment.

"Yes, I am. When you start missing me come back and get some more. There's plenty left." Munda stood up and walked up to her face. He grabbed his dick and pulled on it. It began to grow bigger and bigger. He began speaking to her without losing eye contact. "This is all yours, Breanna. All yours, babe."

His dick looked good hanging from his sexy chocolate body. Munda knew exactly what he was doing, and he also knew that he had something Bre wanted. No sooner than he finished putting on his clothes, Bre heard a car drive up. It was Betty and the kids.

"Dang, I forgot we were supposed to go shopping this morning." Jumping out of bed quickly, she said, "What time is it?"

"It's almost ten o'clock."

Bre could only hope Betty wouldn't figure out Munda had

spent the night. She somewhat managed to get herself together before they came in. Betty watched both Munda and Breanna as they stood, trying not to make eye contact with her. Betty couldn't say what she wanted to because the kids weren't too far away. You could see the relief on Munda's face as he made his exit.

"I know there's been some foul play over here," Betty said while looking around for evidence.

"Don't come in here with any assumptions."

"You know I can blackmail you and Munda. You two have been doing the nasty, and Charlie doesn't know it yet. Um hum."

Bre hit her on the head and walked away while Betty stood laughing. Munda was outside fooling around with the kids. Jamar was always following him around. It did some good to Betty and the kids having a man near them that genuinely cared about family.

"I'm going home to do some work in the yard. Do you'll mind if the kids hang out at the house with me?" Munda said.

"I don't mind you taking Alex at all."

Betty yelled, "And you can keep mine."

Munda was good about making work seem like fun to the children.

"Bre, he's so good and so patient with the kids. How many men are gonna take a carload of kids and a dog home with them? I bet I know who won't. Hell, how can he make time with someone else's kid and don't take care of his own? Bre, you have to deal with the possibility that Charles and Renee may share a child. It doesn't seem like Charles has been completely honest."

Bre rolled her eyes and gave Betty a nasty stare, but didn't bother to defend Charles in any way.

"Betty, I'm not getting into that today. Let me bathe so we can leave."

"I know you're right because I don't want to smell you and Munda's funk while walking in the mall." Betty made a nasty face and laughed.

Chapter Fifteen

Charles was finally back, and Bre had mixed emotions. Despite Munda's and Betty's feelings, Bre welcomed Charles home and spent plenty of time with him. She lied and told him her period came early to avoid anything physical since she'd recently been with Munda. Their time was spent talking and catching up on all the new happenings and rekindling. She waited to see if he would mention Renee, but he never bothered. Bre believed it was safe to assume Renee hadn't spoken to him.

Not only was Charles getting closer with Bre, he was attempting to gain her family favor as well. Bre thought it may have been a bit much for him at times, but he was slowly adjusting. He and Alex got along very well; they, too, were developing their own relationship. Alex knew Munda was his dad, and there was no replacing him. Munda wasn't thrilled with the thought of Charles being around Alex. So, to control that, he spent more time with Alex and kept him overnight a lot. Munda also reminded Charles that Alex was his son and he would be the influence in his son's life. Munda's role in Alex's life was clear.

Bre heard the door of a car closing. It was Charles.

"Hi, honey." He had a huge smile on his face as he walked towards her and gave her a long kiss. "Let's go to the creek for a minute."

She looked around to see if Betty was standing near.

"I need to see if Betty will watch Alex for me."

"He can come if you wanna bring him."

"Let me check first. It'll be late soon, and it's hard enough getting him up in the mornings."

Just as Bre was headed in to ask her sister, Betty walked outside. She greeted Charles and made small talk.

"Betty, do you mind if I leave Alex with you for a little?"

"Girl, get out of here."

"Thanks," Bre responded warmly.

***

Charles and Bre made their way to the creek. No matter how many times she went there, its beauty always amazed her. Charles spread the blanket on the bank close to the water, and they began to cherish the peace.

"I remember the first time we came here," Bre said. "Who would have imagined something so beautiful could be so close by? It's been my getaway from stress. It's my haven. I guess I need to thank you for inviting me and showing me such a peaceful place."

"The first time we came here was nice." Charles looked at Bre and gave her a slight smile. "I discovered this spot when I was going through a lot of stress. It was the only place that offered me the peace I needed to think things through."

Charles became quiet and distant. She knew there was more, something much deeper. A strange expression appeared on his face for a moment.

"Is there something you'd like to talk about, Charles?"

He placed his arms around her and gazed deep into her eyes with a smile on his face.

"What are you looking at?" she said.

"I'm looking at you. You don't like me looking at you?"

"I didn't say that."

"Anyway, I like looking at you. You're beautiful. I see you and desire so much."

"What do you desire, Charles?"

"Let me show you." He kissed her wildly and passionately.

She looked at him. "Is that what you desire?"

"No, I desire a lot more. That was just a tiny bit of what I want."

"Show me what else."

"Do you wanna know my complete desire, Bre?"

She nodded. "Yeah, I'm interested in knowing it all."

"I can't tell you everything right now, but I want us to have bright and happy future. Come and lay back in my arms and let me show and tell you a little."

She rested her back on his body, and he began to massage her neck. Charles had the magic touch. After he'd gotten her to loosen up, he kissed her neck as his hands filled themselves with her breasts. Her body sank more and more into his. His hands began to claim all parts of her body. Their temperatures were rising higher and higher. He slid his hand into her pants and began to feel her. He situated her body on the blanket and proceeded to undress her. The sun was beginning to go down, but he was prepared with the two candles he'd carried from the car.

"I'm gonna eat your pussy the way you like, and then we're gonna make love under the stars and listen to the sounds of the flowing waters."

The attention he was showering her with was captivating. Charles kept his word. He proceeded to eat her pussy. He almost made her cum instantly.

"Don't try to get away from me. This is just the start."

Charles knew he could set her on fire when eating her. It was enough to make her pull her own hair. He surfaced from between her legs just to make love and speak sweet words to her. It wasn't long before he was back down between her legs, working his tongue.

"Talk to me, babe."

"Charles, it's so good. Whatever you do, please, don't stop. Make me cum."

"Yes, sweetness. I'm gonna make those juices flow."

All she could remember was Charles holding onto her.

"Come on, babe, you can handle this."

Charles found his way back on top and placed his dick inside her. Slowly, but with strength behind it, he made passionate love to her.

"I want you to let go and give it all to me." As he pounded away, she watched his body movements and facial expressions.

The closer he came to reaching his orgasm, the faster he fucked. The friction of his movement was taking her to the edge of having another orgasm. The harder he pounded, the more she opened her legs. At the same time, they moaned out from the pleasure they were sharing.

While kissing Bre's body all over, Charles held her close. For the moment, it was their world. They remained there only a short time longer before walking to the car, holding hands, and taking little kisses along the way.

"Do you wanna go to my place and take a shower?" he said. "You can freshen up a bit."

"I don't think I have any clothes over there."

"You can grab a pair of my sweats and a T-shirt. They may be a bit big and long, but you'll still be sexy."

He looked back at her ass and smiled.

"You seem to like this ass a lot."

"No doubt. I love that nice, round, plump ass."

He kept his hand on it the whole time they walked to the car. They went to his house to shower, but she knew it wouldn't be anything quick by any means. As they both undressed, she watched Charles's dick. It was nice, firm, and hung well.

"That's a nice dick you got there, mister."

"Yeah, and I'm more than willing to let you play with it. Come on over here and touch it. Matter of fact, you can have it."

Bre couldn't help laughing at him and his silliness. They eventually made it in the shower and freshened up so she wouldn't have to listen to any smart remarks from Betty. There was no way she wanted that, especially since Betty was taking close notes of everything and everyone.

"Come on, Charles, I have to get going. Did you forget you have to take me home?"

It wasn't that Charles forgot; he was just trying to get as much one-on-one time with Bre as he could.

***

The entire gang greeted them and then questioned Charles as he walked Bre to the door. She observed as he stumbled his way through, trying to avoid the many questions the kids were asking. After watching his uneasiness, Betty came out and rescued him. An instant sign of relief was on his face. Even with Charles being around a great deal, Betty never conversed with him much. There were times when he would come over and Betty would get her kids and leave, even if it had been her intention to spend the night. Jamar was also somewhat quiet when it came to Charles. Bre had noticed that on several occasions. She wasn't certain if it was something she should be concerned about, but she would definitely keep observing the situation. As Charles stood up, she watched his discomfort.

"Bre, I need to get going."

She walked over to him, and they walked outside together.

"Thanks for the wonderful evening, Bre."

"You're welcome, and the pleasure was mine, love."

He leaned over, kissed her, and said, "I'm sure we'll meet up again later."

"I'm sure we will," she said in a sarcastic way.

"Oh, give me a break. You know I have this crazy schedule. I promise you're definitely on it, though."

He kissed her again and left. There she remained, reflecting over the evening they'd shared with an irrepressible smile displayed on her face. She thought about how much he worked and how little she got to see him at times. It was okay, for it gave her a little time to figure things out. She also knew it was time to find out about him being the father of Renee's baby.

"Damn, he must have put it on you."

Bre couldn't respond to Betty. She had caught her in deep thought. There was no need to try to get out of it. Bre's thoughts weren't about what Betty thought they were.

"Yeah, it was that good," she said as she lifted her head in the air and took a few steps away.

"You have some wild stuff up your ass, don't you, little sis?"

"Nah, I just got it like that."

They started laughing. Bre did let her know she and Charles had gone down to the creek and gave the little animals something to look at. Betty didn't think Charles had it in him. She was amazed at how romantic he was.

"I guess every girl wants a little romance," Betty said as she looked at Bre.

"It's not all about romance, Betty."

"I guess not, especially when you've stopped fucking Munda."

"What do you mean?"

"Well, Munda had this very romantic side to him, and it was pretty heavy between the two of you. You can look at him and tell he can fuck a woman to death. You can also see that affectionate side to him on a consistent basis."

"That was the past, and I'm trying to build a future with Charles."

"You remember that old song 'If It Don't Fit, Don't Force It,' don't you?"

"That has nothing to do with me."

"That's what you think. We've been around each other for almost a year now, and you think I don't know you?"

It's only been eight months, and that doesn't mean you have the right to tell me what I'm doing."

"Let me do this since I know you're battling with a problem. When you're ready for some time to think things through, let me know, and I'll keep Alex for a week at my place. You can do all the thinking you need to without any interruptions."

For Betty to say she was going to stay at her own place for a complete week was very serious. Anyone could find Betty at Breanna's house more than her own. Breanna couldn't deny she was torn between two men, so she believed a time might come when she would have to take Betty's offer.

"I'm gonna get ready for bed now."

Bre knew where the conversation was going, so she was making a quick getaway from Betty. Charles was claiming his territory and he wasn't giving Munda time to get in it. Betty had anticipated *that* before Charles's return.

Bre knew it was going to be tough, but she didn't know she would be in such an emotional war. Charles's presence didn't take away the memories and thoughts of Munda. There was no way she could tell anyone, but she was longing for Munda. There were nights when she would fall asleep sad after thinking about him.

Chapter Sixteen

As the days passed, the time came for Charles to make good on his word. He knew Bre always teased him about not having time because of his hectic schedule. Oftentimes, she told him his job was his woman. No matter how hectic it seemed, they always seemed to find time along the way.

"Hello, babe, are you asleep?" Charles said.

The words came through the phone slowly as she came to life. The sound of his voice was welcoming.

"I was sleeping, but I'm wide awake now," she said.

Bre listened to Charles' sultry voice, and at the same time she was captured by the sound of the falling rain. "Where are you?"

"I'm still at work but preparing to leave. Is Betty at your place tonight?"

"No, she didn't stay over. Why? Are you coming over?"

"I was hoping I could."

"Hmm, are you coming now?"

"No, I'll cum when I get there, and it'll be inside of you."

She smiled and flirtatiously reminded him of the dirty man he was.

"I'll see you in about half an hour or so. Will you still be awake?"

"Maybe, but if I'm not, I'm sure you'll wake me."

She told Charles she would unlock the door so he could let

himself inside. He became used to her doing this from time to time.

It was after one in the morning and the rain was falling harder and faster. While waiting, Bre drifted away with the calming sound of the rain. Soon, she was awakened again, but not by the ringing of the telephone or the sound of rain. It was from the soft, gentle caressing and nibbling on her neck and shoulders. As a smile came across her face, she rolled over on her back and placed her arms around Charles. As he pulled the covers away from her, Bre's naked body was exposed. Her breasts were perky and ready for action.

He sucked each one as if he were making gently love to them. He stopped just as her body began to fall into deep thrusting and erotic movements. Backing away slowly, he gave her a slight smile. Without speaking any words, he parted the lips of her pussy and sucked. Bre's breath was taken away.

"Are you still sleeping, love?"

"No, not anymore," she said with her eyes closed and a smile on her face.

"Babe, I'm gonna jump into the shower and freshen up a bit."

She simply nodded her head. She knew she'd be getting something really special after he was done.

"Bre, can you come here for a quick minute?"

Entering the bathroom and pulling back the shower curtain, there he stood stroking his fully erected dick. She immediately melted from the sight of him standing naked, completely wet and with a very hard dick. Their eyes met. He beckoned for her to come closer. She climbed in the shower with Charles and forgot all about the fresh hairdo she'd just gotten. Now, they were both wet and admiring the sweetness of each other.

"When it first started raining this morning, the only thing I could think about was your sweet, sexy voice and making love to you."

After Charles spoke those words, he placed his hand between her legs and began massaging her pussy. It wasn't long before Bre's hands were on the walls supporting her as Charles banged her wet pussy from the back. As he fucked and squeezed her breasts, Bre closed her eyes and moaned. She was lost in the moment. The longer he fucked her, the better it felt to him. His eyes rolled up and then closed as he mumbled how good she felt. Charles positioned himself in a squatting position, pulling Bre's body down and then lifting her up again and again. Every muscle in his body was at work. Just as Bre thought he was about to lift her body up once again, he held it down tight as his cum shot into her.

While drying off, Bre and Charles played like kids: touching, feeling, grabbing, and just enjoying the moment. While continuing to help her dry off, he guided her to the bed. Stopping without notice, he looked at her as if he were seeing her for the first time. It was easy to assume he liked what he was seeing. The silence was quickly broken.

"How's the little man?" he said.

"He's fine."

"Let me go check on him and make sure he's sound asleep. I don't want him waking up and catching me doing the nasty with his mommy." He giggled and gave her a kiss, then he went to check on Alex. Soon he came back in the room and teased her about the sounds Alex was making while he slept. "What did the two of you do today? He's snoring as if he's been out doing hard labor. Even the dog is snoring."

While laughing, Bre told Charles about spending time at the petting zoo and park with Alex and the dog. She'd taken half the day off to spend some special time with her little man. She knew they needed the time together. The zoo and the park were her and Alex's favorite two places. As she chatted on, Charles kept moving closer and closer to her. He had a very serious look on his face.

"Do you know how much I love you, Bre?"

While attempting to open her mouth and answer his question, he slowly began to kiss her. It was one small kiss after another. He lifted her up and placed her on the bed properly. The only visible light was from the flashes of lightning. He softly kissed her lips and rubbed the soft brown skin of her face. Slowly, he worked his way to her neck then her breasts. He was sucking and clinging to her breasts like a hungry bear. Lifting her legs, he positioned them to have full access to her pussy. A wet pussy that was calling his name. "Tonight is all about you," he whispered. "I'm gonna remind you what it is to have an unselfish lover."

Bre's heart was melting, and she was beginning an emotional roller coaster ride. As he took proper care of her breasts, she gently rubbed his head and allowed her nails to go gently across his back. She was horny, and all she wanted to do was feel his dick enter her in slow motion. Charles believed in taking care of every part of her. As he stroked her pussy with his fingers, she closed her eyes and accepted every second of pleasurable stimulation. He knew how bad she wanted to feel his hard dick inside of her. As he continued his journey farther down, kissing and caressing her all over, she spoke soft words of love. Even before his tongue touched her pussy, she moaned aloud because she knew what was coming. Her pussy became a puddle of sensual juices Charles used to quench his thirst. As he moaned and mumbled about its sweetness, he separated her legs and the lips of her juicy pussy. Her body became limp. She was at his mercy. She could only call his name in a weakened, helpless voice, and she'd completely surrendered to him.

Charles navigated Bre's body as if he'd created every inch of it himself. Her pussy became like an opening for an overflowing river, and he took every ounce as if it were the sweetest thing he'd ever tasted. She felt exhausted and unable to move.

"Don't let me lose you, babe. I told you this was going to be your night, and I'm gonna make sure you know what it's really like for someone to make love to you."

He rubbed her pussy up and down with his dick. Instantly her pussy was wet and ready. Gradually, he entered her. Inside her, his strokes were long and strong. As her body began to move in unison with his, they began to get lost in their own world. What pleasures and emotions! She was on a natural high. She returned the pleasure by fucking him with more force. Bre wanted to take everything he had. Charles turned her in a different position without missing a beat. He slid his dick inside of her from the rear and pulled her closer to his body. She could feel his dick pulsating inside of her, but he was determined to hold on until Bre's juices were flowing onto the sheets. She was tired, but it was too good to stop.

"Oh, damn, babe, give me all that sweetness between your legs. Take all you want" were the words he could get out.

Bre could see that neither one of them would last much longer, so they both worked and came at the same time. She could feel the hard pulsating of his dick inside of her. As he released himself into her, it seemed endless. Emotions and passion were everywhere. It was intense.

"We're gonna send each other into cardiac arrest," Charles said.

He was right. The way the two of them made love left no room for boredom. Following their imaginations, sexual gratification was always theirs. As they held each other during their remaining awakening moments, they shared small talk. She placed one of her small hands on top of his to acknowledge and reply to the gentle stroking he was giving her. She always felt comfortable and even safer when he was around. It seemed they were placed on a path whereas they were destined to meet.

"Babe, I love you."

"I know, honey," she said. "Charles, I know neither of us is perfect, and God knows we have our faults, but somehow we've managed to keep things going strong."

"Babe, I know."

"No, let me finish, Charles. There are days when it seems I struggle to keep things balanced. I don't know what the future holds, but I do know I love you."

"Bre, I know a lot is going on, and it's more than you've told me, and I also think you have to figure things out for yourself. I also know it's been hard with Alex's father in your life, and I know he wants his family back. Babe, I can't just hand you over."

There was silence for a moment, but she could feel him rubbing her arm. The silence was still present. She didn't know what to say. She finally had to admit Charles was aware something might have taken place between her and Munda. As she turned to face him, he began to speak and hold on tight to her.

"What's wrong, Charles?"

"I need to talk to you about something. It should have been before now, but I didn't know how to begin or where to start the conversation."

"Just start and let me hear what you have to say. Please, you're scaring me."

"Don't be scared," Charles said reassuringly. After taking a deep breath and slowly releasing it, he began talking. "Breanna, I know Renee told you I'm the father of her child. Believe me, I'm not trying to get out of my responsibility as a father if the child is mine. Renee never said one word to me until a few months ago."

"Charles, why did I have to find out from her and not you? Why did you continue to judge Munda so harshly when you have your own set of problems? Yes, Renee was happy to tell me you're her child's father. I sat back patiently waiting to see when, or even if, you would mention this."

Bre rolled over and propped her head in her hand so she could face Charles and look in his eyes. Her face displayed no emotions, but many thoughts were rushing through her mind.

"Of course I'd tell you." Charles's face had a look of shock. He momentarily gazed into Bre's eyes. "What you have to understand is I don't even remember how Renee ended up in my bed. When I woke up, I felt as if I had the worst hangover in the world. It was really weird. I wasn't always a good guy, but I'd never forgotten how a woman ended up in my bed before."

"I was gonna bring this up soon, but I decided to wait and see if you would tell me. Now that you have, we need to figure out what's going on," Bre said. "I don't know what went on between you and Renee, but I do know there's an innocent child involved who deserves to have both his mom and dad in his life. Being a woman and a mom, I'm not taking either yours or Renee's side in this matter. What type of person would I be if I were to just sit back and encourage you to avoid the issue?" Bre was now sitting up in the bed, and her voice became a bit firmer. It was apparent she was becoming disturbed. "Charles, right is right and wrong is wrong."

Before she could continue, Charles stopped her.

"Wait a minute, Bre. I think you're beginning to draw the wrong conclusion. I'll accept responsibility for the kid if he's mine. I've been constantly thinking about this. If he is mine, I don't want Renee raising my child. Look at her lifestyle, Bre."

"Nevertheless, she's the baby's mom. Why haven't you spoken to her about this?"

"I have. Well, I at least tried. The conversation was more about you than the kid. I asked for a paternity test, and she's dragging her feet."

"Just tell her you're paying for the whole thing."

"Bre, you know the cost wouldn't have stopped me. She knew I was paying for the testing. You have to believe me when I say none of this is making any sense. I didn't want to tell you right away because I didn't want to risk losing you."

"This happened before we ever got together. Who am I to judge you for your past when we all have one? Is that not what you told me some time ago? Didn't you tell me no one is perfect? You have to do what's right and hold to it, no matter what obstacle you may have to face. We have to be calm and mature about the issue and figure things out."

"Bre, you can make me so angry at times, but it's moments like this that make it all seem worthwhile. I didn't know how you'd react, and I definitely don't want to lose you. I promise you I'll take responsibility and do what's right if the child is mine."

"I know you will." Breanna was going to make sure she monitored the situation carefully. Even if she didn't let on to Charles, she was going to do some of her own investigating.

He gently began to kiss her. Moving to her breasts, he began to nibble and caress them. Suddenly, there was a pause.

"I guess you're worth holding on to," she said in a soft tone.

From those words, they began their lovemaking session all over again. It was even deeper and more passionate than the previous time. They both understood they were two people who shared a great deal of love for each other.

The next thing Bre knew daylight was coming through. She jumped up thinking Charles needed to get to work. "Honey, what time do you have to be at work?"

Still half asleep, he said, "Babe, I belong to you and Alex today. Come back to bed and get some sleep."

She was exhausted and needed the rest. Climbing back into bed, she looked over at the clock: 6:27 a.m. It was a Saturday morning, so she knew Alex would be up in about another hour, wanting to see the Power Rangers, which he faithfully watched. "Charles, you need to put on some clothes before Alex comes hopping in the bed and asking questions as to why you're naked."

He quickly got up and started laughing. It seemed as soon as they lay back down and drifted off, it was over.

"Good morning, Mommy," Alex said, climbing in the bed to get his kiss and hug.

When he took note that Charles was in the bed, he immediately rubbed his head with his little fist. She guessed it was their little thing.

"Good morning, little man. What's up?"

Alex began talking up a storm as he jumped down and stood by the bed smiling.

"Go brush your teeth, Alex."

She didn't know what it was about kids and morning breath. They all had it, but damn, it was like they punished parents by getting directly in their face and talking. It was almost as if they thought parents heard them with their noses instead of their ears. Bre was tired and could barely function. She had less than two hours of sleep and was up already. Her eyes were barely able to stay open, and every word being directed to her sounded as if it were coming from under water.

"Babe, go back to sleep. I'll take care of Alex."

Breanna didn't turn down the offer.

Charles got up and made sure Alex brushed his teeth. She could even hear him asking the little man what he wanted for breakfast. She knew the answer to that without even having to hear it. Of course, he wanted blueberry pancakes, bacon, and orange juice. His favorite breakfast foods.

"We have to take Natches out to pee," she heard him telling Charles.

"Okay, get his leash so he can go," Charles said.

The next time she awoke, it was a few hours later. Opening her eyes, she could see her little boy's bright eyes and the big smile on his face.

"Good morning, sleepyhead. You must've had a very tiring night," Charles said, standing in the doorway of the room.

"Something like that." She smiled.

They both smiled mischievously.

"I can't believe Alex and Natches are still inside."

"Bre, it's still raining outside. It's been pouring off and on since last night. I have a pot of coffee waiting for you."

"Is it really still raining?"

"Yes, it's supposed to rain all weekend. At least that's what the news report says."

"There goes my weekend."

"I'm gonna go home and freshened up a bit. That way, you can have some time to spend with Alex. I'll be back in a few hours. You need to figure out what you want to do on this rainy day, so when I come back, we'll know where we're headed."

"Can we go to my dad's house?"

Alex's little voice shocked her, and she didn't even realize he was paying the conversation such close attention.

"Honey, you can't go to your dad's house today."

"But he said I could come anytime I want."

"I'm afraid not today, Alex."

"Why not?" he said with a look of confusion on his little face.

"Alex, it's too messy outside." Bre was firm.

Alex's lips were stuck out, and she could tell he had a serious attitude.

She and Charles looked at each other and finally went on with their conversation. She walked Charles to the door. As she passed by Alex, he was sitting on the floor in front of the TV. Pouting. She didn't say much. Instead, she gave him a kiss on the forehead then went into the kitchen to pour a hot cup of coffee. Breanna sat by the window, looking out at the falling rain and thinking. It was gloomy and dark outside, and there were no signs of sunshine.

"Mommy."

"What is it, Alex?"

While a commercial was on, Alex went over and talked about his show. He gave her a hug. He was a good kid, and she had every right as a mother to be proud of him. He stood next to her and watched the falling rain.

"No going outside today, right?"

"That's right, sweetie. It's too messy out there."

As she looked at him, she could see every bit of Munda. Alex was his little clone, and the two of them were close. He was a constant reminder of his father. The commercials were over, and his cartoons were back on. He gave her a quick hug and took off running into the family room where he continued watching his cartoons.

Even though Bre wouldn't admit it to anyone, she'd never stopped missing Munda. For a moment, she battled with the thought of calling him. Eventually, she convinced herself not to. The two of them had created many memories. There was no doubt she cared for him a great deal. The reality was a part of him was always with her. They shared Alex. The phone rang, interrupting her thoughts. She knew it had to be calling.

"Hey, girl, you're late making your calls, aren't you?" Bre said when she picked up the phone.

"I guess I'm not who you were expecting," Munda said.

There was silence until Munda called her name. Even then, Bre spoke very slowly, as if she were in a state of shock.

"I thought you were Betty."

"I figured as much. How are you?"

"I've been good. What about yourself?"

"I'm hanging in there, but you know I miss you. I was thinking about you earlier."

"Really?" she said, surprised.

"Yes, I was, but I'm sure it doesn't mean anything to you."

"Why would you say that? Anyway, it's not true. I was thinking about you this morning as well."

Bre had thought about him, and she missed him as much as he missed her. Her heart was beating fast, and her palms became sweaty. Breanna quickly changed the subject. She knew Munda would try to figure out what kind of thoughts she may have had about him.

"Alex was desperately trying to get to your house this morning."

"Why didn't you bring him over or call me to come get him?"

"It was too nasty outside, and it's still pouring as we speak."

"Bre, it wasn't like he was gonna be outside. Do you not remember I have a roof on the top of my house? Even if you didn't want to come out in the rain, you should have called me, and I would have come and gotten my son. Don't ever keep him from seeing me. Nothing will stop me from getting to him, not even hell or high water. He didn't have to get wet at all. If he did, it would have been minimal."

Bre could tell Munda was angry, but with the weather being so horrible, she didn't want to run the risk of Alex getting cold, wet, and then becoming ill.

By this time, Alex had figured out she was talking to his dad, and he made his way over to her quickly.

"Is that my daddy? I wanna talk to my daddy," he said,

reaching for the phone.

"Honey, just wait a minute."

"Okay, babe," Munda said.

"Not you, Munda."

"I know, but I figured it was a good try anyway."

She passed the phone to Alex so he could begin his conversation with his dad. He and Munda talked for some time. Whatever Munda was saying to Alex, it seemed to please him. As they talked, Bre sat back down at the table and continued watching the falling rain. Even though she missed Munda a great deal, she wanted to do right by Charles. She was trying to give them a fair chance at making their relationship work.

"But mommy and Charles said I can't come to your house," she heard Alex say and knew she would have to deal with that soon. "Mommy, my daddy wants to talk to you."

She knew this wasn't going to be good. She got on the phone and walked in her room. "Yes, Munda?" She braced herself.

"As long as you live, you better not let that motherfucker tell my son he can't come to my house! I mean it, damn it! He doesn't have the right to play daddy with my son. Better yet, he needs to be at Renee's house taking care of his own child. Yeah, I heard what Renee said that night, but I really didn't put it together until later. Tell his ass to man up while he's trying to keep me away from my blood. I'll be by to get my boy!"

Bre didn't get a chance to say anything before he slammed the phone down. She felt bad, and she knew he was angry and hurting. What he didn't realize, Charles had nothing to do with her decision of not letting Alex go. It wasn't done to be mean, but to keep Alex safe from getting sick.

"Alex, your dad is on his way to get you. Go put on your shoes."

Alex took off shouting for joy.

It wasn't long before Munda was pulling up. Bre saw him getting out of his car with a big black umbrella. By the time he got to the door, she had it open. He didn't say one word to her before scooping Alex up in his arms and making sure he was completely under the umbrella. Just as he started to pull off, he came back on the porch. He opened the door and called for Natches. When Natches came out running, he jumped in the car and they took off. She'd never seen him so angry before. She was glad Charles wasn't there because Munda probably would have kicked his ass. It would have been all-out mayhem.

Charles kept his word and returned as promised, but the rain was still falling. It wasn't as bad as it was earlier, but it was still falling fairly hard.

"Where's Alex?" he said.

"His dad came by and got him."

There was a puzzled look on his face. "In all this rain?"

"Yes. Alex told him he wanted to be with him, so he came and got him."

Charles didn't say too much. He just shook his head and laughed as if he were in disbelief. They watched movies, laying together on the couch. It turned out to be a good day with them staying in. Betty had called earlier to let Bre know she was coming by, but when she found out Charles was there, she didn't bother. Bre only wished Betty and Charles could work out whatever problem they had.

Charles left around eleven in the evening to prepare for his early morning. It wasn't too long after he left that Bre got back into bed. The rain was still falling, but this time she wasn't able to fall asleep so easily. Munda had entered her mind, and as always, it wasn't easy getting rid of the thoughts of him.

Bre woke up to a new morning without the rain, but there were plenty of soggy signs reminding her of it. The bathroom was her first stop. Afterwards, she started her morning coffee. While she waited for it to brew, she phoned Betty to make sure she and the kids got up on time for Sunday morning services. Betty was already up and doing the same thing Bre was. They chatted plenty about nothing, then discussed what they'd have for their Sunday meal, which they had prepared together ever since Betty arrived in Savannah.

"It's pretty quiet there. Where's Alex's little talking butt?"

"He's with his dad."

"He got out early this morning."

"No, Munda picked him up yesterday, and he spent the night."

"When is he coming home?"

"I don't know. Munda is so pissed with me right now, so I'm not even gonna call and find out."

"Am I missing something, Bre?"

"He thought me and Charles tried to keep Alex from him."

"What happened, Bre?"

"Alex wanted to go over yesterday when it was pouring down raining, and I told Alex it was too messy to go out. When his dad called, he told him Charles and I wouldn't let him come."

"Oh, shit!"

"Yep, that's what went down. He told me he was coming to get Alex, and when he came, he didn't say a thing. When they were about to leave, he called for Natches and left."

Betty burst out laughing uncontrollably and said, "Charles had better stay out of Munda's way!"

"I was so glad Charles had gone home. It would have been a big mess."

"That would have been ugly. Girl, you should've known not to try to keep Alex from his dad. That man is crazy about that little boy. He would have gone through anything to be with his son. This is a very sensitive issue. You know he and Charles can't stand each other to start with."

"I know, Betty, but it was nothing like that."

"Maybe not to you, but I bet it was that way with Charles."

She became very quiet and began to think about what Betty was saying.

"Girl, we need to get moving so we can get to church on time," Bre said.

"I'll see you at service. You should call Munda and see if they're coming."

Breanna started laughing and told Betty goodbye. She let go of the whole situation and enjoyed her coffee in peace. She managed to shower and get out on time. Before leaving, she phoned Munda, but no one answered.

After the sermon was over, Betty and the kids headed to Bre's. No matter how wet it was outside, everyone eventually made it to the backyard. It was what they now called *The Gathering Place*. There was something special and magical about it; perhaps, it was from all the love she poured into it, trying to make it a part of her home.

Charles never bothered to come by after work on Sundays. Instead, he made it a point to call and check on her. Betty always said it was because of her and the kids, but Bre tried to assure her that wasn't the case. Betty could never convince Bre that, perhaps, her point was valid. It was obvious Betty and Charles weren't the best of friends, but they seemed to tolerate each other for Bre's sake. There were times when the situations seemed awkward, but they managed to remain civil.

"I guess Charles isn't coming over again."

"No, he's just getting in from work and needs to get some rest."

"Bre, you're always making up some excuse for him, but I already know what the deal is." Betty didn't bother to hide the contempt and anger she held for Charles.

"Betty, why do the two of you have a problem with each other?"

"Perhaps, it's because he thinks he's so much better than me."

"That's not true at all."

Betty began to speak loud and firm as she looked directly at Bre. "You ever notice how he tries to talk down to me and my kids? You should really think about it and begin to take note of the situation."

"Betty, give him the benefit of the doubt."

"I have, but it doesn't change the fact that we have a problem with each other. How can he claim to want to be with you so much when he can't stand your family? Maybe the kids and I should stop coming over every Sunday. That way, you'll be able to see him more."

"No way, Betty! Sundays are a special time for us. This is a tradition we're creating, and it's a good one. Something will give, I promise."

"Bre, there are some things none of us can promise and make good on. Sure, Charles may have gone to school for many years to obtain his profession, but it doesn't mean he's better. Munda has a wonderful education as well, but he doesn't walk around here with arrogance. Matter of fact, you wouldn't even know his education level if you didn't see him in that expensive car. He doesn't just care about you. He cares for all of us."

"Betty, leave Munda out of this. It's not about comparing the two."

"I bet you've compared them in more ways than one."

She changed that subject quickly knowing Betty was right.

"We need to feed those kids so we can get this kitchen taken care of."

They did just that. The kids were fed, and Betty and Bre cleaned the kitchen while they laughed and talked about different people and things. When it was time for them to leave, the kids fussed a little. It was a great feeling knowing they loved being there. She loved having them around and wouldn't want it any other way.

"Bre, I wanna keep Alex on Friday night so he can hang out with me and the kids."

"That'll be fine."

"It'll also give you some down time to do some thinking without being interrupted."

Betty was looking directly at her, waiting for a response or reaction to what she'd said.

"We'll talk later. Drive home safely, Betty."

They said goodbye to each other as Betty backed out of the driveway. Just as they pulled off, Munda pulled up with Alex, who jumped out of the car with Natches behind him and ran over to her. He gave her a big hug and began telling her about the time he'd spent with his dad. Munda still wasn't talking to her.

"He had his bath and has also eaten." He didn't look at her. Munda called Alex over and gave him a hug. "I'll see you later, son," he said to Alex.

After that, he got in his car and drove away as she looked on. She was hurt by Munda's behavior, but when she looked at it closely, she understood his anger. Once he cooled off, she would let him know about the misunderstanding. She loved him and Alex too much to try to tear them apart. After she and Alex had settled down, she tucked him into bed and read him a story. As she read, he curled his little body as close to her as he could. When she looked down at him, all she could see was Munda. In the midst of her reading, she stopped and looked at Alex in silence. She sensed the feeling of him missing his dad. The emotions were about to pour out, but she regained her composure. Breanna continued reading until she'd reached the end of the story. She remained with Alex until he drifted off to sleep.

She rubbed his face and said in a low voice, "I can't keep doing this. I have to do something about all of this soon."

She had to give what Betty said serious thought. The more she thought, the more she realized Betty was right. Charles was a good man, but she knew there was a bit of arrogance within him. Breanna decided she would call him, see what was going on, and to try to feel him out. Maybe ask him a question or two about her sister and her kids. During the conversation with Charles, she asked him why was it he never came by on Sundays when her family was around.

"Where is this coming from, Bre? You know I work and I'm tired when I get in."

"What about the Sundays you don't work?"

"Bre, do you want me to come over now?"

"What would be the point when you know my sister and the

kids are gone? I guess it would be convenient for you to come now."

"What is this all about? I try to give you space to be with your family, and you take it the wrong way."

"I don't think it's taken the wrong way at all."

"We shouldn't get into this now because, apparently, you're disturbed by something."

"You're right. Maybe this is a bad time for me to be speaking to you, so have a good night."

She didn't wait for him to respond before ending the call. From the tone of her voice, Charles knew she wasn't happy at all. The phone rang, and she knew it was him even before answering.

"What's wrong with you, Bre?"

"Charles, let's talk later. Wait. I will say this: my family is the most important part of my life, and they always will be. They will not come second to anyone."

Charles couldn't say one word. He knew this was now an issue, and he knew where she stood. When she said goodbye this time, she waited for him to acknowledge her declaration before hanging up. The acknowledgment never came.

Chapter Seventeen

Weeks passed since Bre had distanced herself from Munda. Even though she'd limited her time being around Munda, she didn't interfere with his time with Alex. Breanna purposefully avoided any extended interaction with Munda so she wouldn't have to deal with the longing that she had in her heart for him. It was difficult most of the time, particularly in the moments when she would watch him leave with Alex and their eyes met when he looked back. She loved him deeply and Munda was well aware. His feelings weren't any different from hers.

Bre hadn't seen Betty for a few days. Tony showed up at her door a couple of days ago. He tried to get her to let him in, but she refused, asked him to leave, and threatened to call the cops. He didn't put up much of a fuss and soon left. She knew that wasn't enough for Tony. He left too easily. She insisted to herself he was the reason for the uneasy feeling that had settled within her in the previous weeks, but she refused to let that get her down.

Betty and the kids were happy and finally had some peace in their lives. She remembered the day she'd closed on her house. That purchase was a huge accomplishment for her. There was much joy and celebration. She and the kids were finding their way and feeling safe. Since those days of being insecure (due to Tony) were over, everything Betty aimed for resulted in success.

"Good morning, Betty," Bre said into the phone.

"Good morning, Bre. What's going on with you?"

"Too much of nothing. I was just sitting back having my coffee and thinking."

"About Munda?" she said with laughter.

"Don't go there, girl. That's a whole other story."

Breanna was trying to wait on the perfect time to bring Tony up again. She knew he was really angry about the divorce papers that were served to him. Their mother had already called multiple times and told both of them he wasn't taking it well. Breanna knew Tony blamed her for Betty leaving him, but she couldn't take such credit. Their mother said he'd been acting crazier as time went on.

The girl who had the baby by him left town with another man. That young girl had given him a great lesson in life. Not only that, it came out that the baby wasn't even his. Betty and Bre laughed about it when they first heard; not just laughed a little, but that gut-wrenching laugh that always makes one cry.

"Betty, I woke up with the strangest feeling this morning. I felt like you and the kids should come over here."

"What kind of feeling, Bre?"

"It was a very eerie feeling, and Tony was the first thing that came into my head."

"You know, I've been getting these strange calls for the past few days, but the person doesn't say anything. I was thinking it was someone with the wrong number."

"Mama told me he's been acting stranger than normal. I'd feel safer right now with all of you over here with me and Alex."

"I don't think he'd be crazy enough to try to hurt me."

"Betty, what makes you so certain about that? Did you forget what he put you through?"

"I can't run from my own home every time I think he may show up. This is my home. This is my children's home. I'm not scared of him anymore. I'm supposed to feel safe here, Bre."

"I know, but there are times when we have to avoid situations. I'm not telling you to always run away. I'm telling you to be safe and take whatever measures you need to for the safety of you and the kids."

"Bre, I'm a much stronger person than I used to be. There have been those days when I've reflected back and realized I was the one to allow Tony to take away my self-esteem. He made me feel like I was nothing and would never be anything. He made me feel like no one else in the world would want me because I have three kids. Forget Tony! All those wasted years I stayed with him. Yeah, I loved him at one time, but it was about pride at the end. I didn't want to fail. I didn't want to be without a man. I didn't know how to walk away."

"Betty, you did it, and look at you now. You've taken full control of your life, and you did it all by yourself."

"No, I did it with you and Munda being there for me and the kids. You gave me something more than just positive words. You gave me something worth living for: family."

"We're family, girl, and I love you. All we have is each other."

"I love you, too, little sister."

"Girl, let me get up and get prepared so when Alex gets up I'll be all set for him. Betty, get up and come on over. We haven't fired up the grill in a while, and it's a beautiful day to do so. We can hang out and have a good time in the backyard."

"Actually, that sounds good. We should also invite a few people over. Just make sure Renee isn't on the list."

After ending the conversation, Bre made a list of the things they were going to need for the cookout while preparing Alex's breakfast. Breanna could hear him in the bathroom taking a piss that would make a camel envious.

"Don't you pee on the toilet now, Alex," she yelled out. "And brush your teeth and wash your face so you can eat."

Alex knew the routine, but he still needed reminding from time to time. He fiddled around in there for about ten minutes before dragging himself into the kitchen where Breanna was standing over a home-cooked meal.

"Good morning, Mommy."

"Good morning, tiger. How was your sleep?"

"It was good."

"Get to the table and eat your breakfast. And say your grace before you start eating."

His little eyes lit up every time he saw his blueberry pancakes, bacon, and orange juice. His legs swung back and forth as he devoured his breakfast.

"Your Aunt Betty and I are gonna go to the store, so you make sure you listen to Jamar."

"I will."

By the time Alex was finished with his breakfast, his dad was at the door. Bre had forgotten Munda was going to take Alex and Natches to the park this morning.

"Munda, I completely forgot. He's not ready yet, but he will be in a few minutes."

"I'm in no hurry, Bre. It's fine."

Even though she'd told Munda she needed time and distance, he really didn't seem to be bothered. There were nights when she longed to be in Munda's arms, but it seemed Charles was always the one who was there. Trying to forget about Munda was like trying to forget about Alex. It was impossible.

While Breanna moved about, cleaning and putting things away in the cabinets, she could feel Munda's eyes on her. She became jittery and a lump formed in her throat. She wasn't ready to make eye contact with him. While her mind was somewhere else, a plate she was trying to place in the cabinet fell. Without thinking, she looked directly at Munda. There they were, each of them expressing their emotions in complete silence. Once the contact was made, it couldn't be broken. Breanna felt as if she'd been hypnotized. Munda walked towards her, knowing his actions were in good faith.

"Are you okay, Bre?"

"Yeah, I'm just a bit clumsy."

"Here, let me help you with that."

They both bent down at the same time, only to find themselves looking deeply into each other's eyes. The words were there, but she just couldn't say them. Her heart was aching for his touch.

"I—" Bre couldn't get the words out.

He nodded his head and waited patiently for her words.

"Nothing."

"Say it, Bre. Go on and say it."

She jumped up and walked away. She grabbed the broom and started cleaning the broken glass. Whatever was going on was deep. Bre was afraid that if she started, she might not be able to stop.

With a look of desperation in his eyes, he finally said, "I'll say it then, Bre." He locked eyes with Bre then spoke his mind: "I miss you. I miss you like crazy. I miss making love to you. Bre, I miss loving you. How can you not follow your heart? There's no way you can tell me you truly need space to figure things out. You already know the answer; it's looking at you right now. You felt the very same thing I did every time we made love. Are you gonna stand here and tell me you didn't pour all yourself out when we made love?"

"Munda, please don't do this now." Tears were forming in her eyes.

"Do you make love to Charles like you make love to me? Does he make love to you the same as me?" There was a brief pause. He gently stroked her hair and began speaking once again. "Let me tell you this: We have a bond, babe, and it's real. You have my boy, and he has a part of each one of us. I love him for the same reasons you do. Sure, I fucked up. I fucked up really bad, but I'm not giving up on my family. If you want some space, you'll have to move far from me; and let me tell you, as long as you have my son, no place will be far enough."

Munda stopped talking but his frustration was clear. Now she knew both of them were feeling the same thing.

"I've missed you, too, Munda. I told you already I don't know what to do. I don't wanna go on another roller coaster ride."

"Bre, if you don't listen to your heart, how do you expect to be happy? You must be honest with yourself. Don't settle for someone because you think they're more secure or dependable. Help me. For God's sake, help yourself. Trust me to do the right thing, Bre. Damn it, babe! I want my family back. You have to let go of the past. We have a future."

She tried to turn and walk away, but Munda pulled her back. The next thing she knew, the two of them were kissing. It felt so good and so right. Breanna wanted to eat him up right where he stood. Munda's hands touched every part of her body. She could feel his manhood growing at a rapid rate.

"No…we can't do this."

"Why not, Bre? Are you gonna tell me you didn't feel my soul? Well, guess what? I felt yours, and I know it's longing for mine."

Munda had her backed up to the counter. There was nowhere for her to go, so she was forced to hear and face everything he was saying. Alex came back out of his room, still half-asleep. Munda settled him back in bed. It wasn't long before Alex drifted back off to his world of dreams. Bre peeped in to see Munda tucking the covers around his small body. Just as Bre began to back away from the bedroom door, Munda looked up.

"I guess he had a long night or very early morning," Munda said as he smiled.

"Yeah, he was up late with Betty's kids, and then he was up early for breakfast. So, he's probably still a bit tired. If you'd like, I can call you when he's up and dressed or…" Bre stopped before she could complete her sentence.

Munda smiled and said, "Or stay here until he wakes up?"

Bre stared without responding.

"Do you reflect back on the wonderful memories of me, of us?"

She nodded her head.

"You ever think about how we used to make love and the way we embraced each other? How close we felt? You don't have to answer if you don't want to, but if you decide to answer, be honest with yourself."

"I've thought about you a couple of times."

"Making love?"

"That, too."

Munda walked over to her and began kissing her again. He rubbed his body up and down on her so the friction would give them some stimulation. Her panties were getting wet, and she wanted to lie down and open wide. Breanna was overcome by the urge to ride out on Munda.

"Let's go in your room for a little."

"My sister is coming over soon."

"Call her and tell her you're running behind."

"I can't do that. Plus, Alex might wake up."

"Bre, he's not gonna wake up within the next thirty minutes. If he does, I'll get to him before he knows what's going on." Munda continued kissing on her neck as he gently rubbed her breasts. "Let me lick your pussy, Bre. Let me make you feel good."

Munda's hands made their way into her pants, and when he touched her down south, she felt the heat and lost control. Breanna was ready for Munda to push his entire dick inside her. He slowly pushed two fingers inside her and slowly pulled them out. He didn't stop until she was completely outside of her panties and stark naked.

He put the drenched fingers inside his mouth as he looked directly into her eyes and gave them a long suck. He turned her in the direction of the bedroom and told her he was coming in after her. She walked quickly and went into the bedroom first, closing the door behind her. When he walked in he found her laying on her bed, on her back, with her legs up.

Munda locked the door and pulled her to the edge of the bed. He didn't say one word. The next thing she felt was heavenly. Munda wasted no time making her feel good. With his tongue, he found spots she'd forgotten existed. Breanna wanted to scream from the pleasure. She twisted and turned, but Munda didn't let her go. She was at Munda's mercy. The only thing she could keep telling him was how good she felt. Munda was working her pussy over. She braced herself. There was nothing going to stop the orgasm she was about to have. She lost all control of her body and fluids gushed out.

Munda didn't hesitate with continuing his journey. As his dick entered her pussy, she held tight and wrapped her legs around his body. It had been some weeks since the two of them had made love, so she knew there was a lot of build up going on. As his dick moved in and out of her body, he supported his weight with his arms, which stood as solid as steel beams. Munda was fucking her harder and harder, not questioning his own strength.

"Bre... we're here," came from somewhere in the house.

She heard Betty and the kids, but Munda had blocked out everything. The moment she was about to push Munda away, he exploded everywhere. He let out a long, strong sound. Betty and the kids' arrival had awakened Alex. He was at the bedroom knocking and telling his mom his Aunt Betty was outside. Breanna hopped up, threw on a pair of lounge pants and a T-shirt then rushed to the door. She left Munda in the room, closing the door behind her.

"What are you doing in there? For a moment, we thought you all had gone out," Betty said.

Alex was standing at the door, jumping around because he was very happy to see his cousins and playmates. "HI, Aunt Betty. My daddy's in my mom's room."

Breanna couldn't say anything as Betty looked at her with a grin.

She was busted.

"Hi, kids. Come on in. Betty, you can come in, too, but you better be nice."

***

The kids, Betty, and Bre settled into the family room with the TV and video games at their disposal. It wasn't long before Munda was dragging himself out.

"Good morning, Munda."

"Good morning, Betty."

She was giving Munda the same look she'd just given Bre. The two of them had become good friends again. Munda had also found his place in each of her kids' hearts.

"You two surely must have been cleaning house. You look exhausted."

They purposely ignored Betty and spoke quietly to each other. They both knew she was waiting for the perfect time to bust them properly.

"Alex, are you ready?"

"I'm coming, Dad," he yelled.

"Don't forget your pal."

"Betty, I'm taking Alex to the park, and if Angel wants to come, she's welcome to do so."

"I'm sure that would suit her."

"I have to go shopping with Bre, so if you get back before I do, she'll be fine with Antwon and Jamar."

"Okay. We'll be gone for a couple of hours."

Munda, Alex, Angel, and Natches took off for the beautiful park nearby. Jamal and Antwon would be fine with the video games they always got deep into. Betty couldn't wait to start asking questions. She started before they got to the car.

"I guess I broke up something this morning, huh? Bre, why is it the two of you keep hiding and going through changes when you could just get back together? It's obvious there's something there keeping you two together. I've been telling you this for the longest. What's wrong with you, girl?"

"I need time to figure things out. I don't wanna hurt anyone."

"You see how Alex just told me his dad was in your room? One day, he's gonna tell Charles the same thing. Come on and let's get going. We can talk in the car."

Bre and Betty talked for a long time. She was still convinced she hadn't been honest with herself. The more she listened and talked, the more she had to think about.

***

They'd finally finished shopping and wrapping up a few things before heading back home. She was tired and dragging, but the day was still early. Breanna didn't have any intention of inviting many people over. It would be the usual family and friends they'd already called while out shopping.

"Bre, we should have gotten some blue crabs."

"Ooh, that sounds good. Let's get these things home and prep them, then we can run back out."

When they arrived, they washed and seasoned meat, peeled potatoes, and prepped the grill. Everything was pretty much set.

"Jamar and Antwon, we're heading out again. Don't let anyone in except Munda and the kids."

"Okay, Ma," they both replied.

Jamar and Antwon stood at the door and watched as they drove away.

"Jamar's turning out to be a really good man, Betty."

"Yeah, as long as his father stays out of the picture and doesn't try to take away his identity or self-esteem."

"Who did you invite to the cookout, Charles or Munda?"

"I guess you wanna be a comedian now. You know Charles isn't coming, especially if he has to deal with you for too long."

"I just asked a simple question. And I meant no harm by it, but I guess when you have a guilty conscience, you're always on the defensive."

"Don't even try selling me that bullshit, because I'm not buying it." Bre knew Betty was just teasing her, but she also knew she was Munda's greatest fan. She didn't mind her teasing at all. "What's that noise?" Bre said, noticing the buzzing.

"That's my cell phone." Betty dug in her purse and pulled it out. "Hello?" She listened intently, and it was obvious by the look on her face something was wrong. "What's wrong, Jamar?"

Bre couldn't hear what the boy answered, but she suspected the worst: Tony had returned.

"Stay inside and don't open the door for him. Does he know you and Antwon are there alone?"

Bre found a spot to turn her car around and hurriedly headed back home.

"Whatever you do, don't open that door! Go make sure all the other doors are closed. Stay calm. We're on the way."

"What's going on, Betty?"

"We need to get back to the house now. Tony is there, and I could hear him in the background screaming."

Bre immediately thought about her gut-instinct from that morning. Somehow, she knew Tony was somewhere close by. She didn't have a good feeling about this. She knew the deep concern on Betty's mind. She knew Tony was a time bomb who was ready to explode at any minute.

As they approached the house, they could see Tony acting crazy and out of control. Before the car could even stop, Betty grabbed her purse and jumped out of the car.

Tony went straight at Betty. "Bitch, who the fuck do you think you are?"

"Why are you here, Tony? Why can't you just leave us alone?"

Bre's neighbors were looking at the unfolding scene.

"You need to leave my house right now," Bre told Tony.

"Fuck you, bitch. I'll leave when I'm fucking ready. Who the fuck do you think you are telling me to leave?"

"Fuck you too, negro. Is this your way of showing your manhood? Why don't you be a real man and walk away? Life has gone on for everyone except for you. So why don't you get the hint?"

"Bitch, I will fuck all of you up. I will fuck you up, your sister, and those damn kids."

"Let me tell you something, motherfucker. If you ever threaten me and my family again, you will rest in peace. Don't you ever threaten us again!" Betty screamed.

Tony finally started walking away from the house in anger.

Betty went to the door and called for the boys. As soon as Jamar unlocked the door, Tony made a run for them. Everything seemed to go in slow motion. Bre could hear Betty's scream as if it were a faraway echo. The boys were also screaming. Tony knocked Betty down and proceeded to drag her back out onto the porch. The boys wasted no time trying to help their mother.

"Get the fuck back! Get back now!" Tony screamed.

He pulled a gun from his pocket and threatened to use it on Betty. The moment became silent. The air filled with stillness. Bre was shaking. Tears were pouring from her eyes. Fear for her family had taken over.

"Here I am, Dad." His voice trembled with terror, but Jamar was ready to protect his mom. "Go ahead and shoot me." Jamar was shedding no tears, and his face didn't display any emotions whatsoever. "Shoot me if you wanna be a big man. Go ahead and just shoot me, Dad."

Jamar's hand was out as he pleaded with his father to spare his mother's life. His facial expression finally changed. He began to look at his father like the piece of crap he was. His voice became calmer and softer as he continued to speak to Tony, but his body gestures became more intense.

"My brother and sister need Mom, so take my life. I'm tired of you hurting us. You broke up this family. You messed everything up. You can't blame Mom for this. She took care of us all. You didn't do anything except hurt her. You hurt all of us."

"Shut up! Just shut the fuck up!" Tony yelled to Jamar.

Though Tony would never admit it, he knew his son was right. His bottom lip was trembling. He turned from Betty to Jamar, then back to Betty again. Tony pointed the gun at Betty as she lay there helplessly. Jamar took his stance as a man and didn't back down from his father. He was going to be there with his mom until the end. Suddenly, a clicking noise came from the pistol, and it was no longer pointing at Betty's head. Tony turned back to Jamar once again and began to shout.

"If your punk ass wants to die in the place of your mother, come on!"

Tony kicked Betty as hard as he could a few times. The expression on her face after each kick was pure agony. Breanna wanted to help her, but he wouldn't allow her to get close. The tears poured down her face from the deep sorrow she felt for her sister.

"Here I am. Be the big man you are and shoot me. Do you know what you did to us? Shoot me! Go ahead and kill me if you want to! Let my mom go!"

Jamar made it next to his mother, and they both held tight to each other. Terror showed across both of their faces. Suddenly, they could hear Tony cocking the pistol and from out of nowhere appeared Munda. When he ran up to hold Breanna, she almost jumped out of her skin.

"Where are Alex and Angel?" she asked frantically as she looked around.

He pointed to his car. "They're safe, Bre. I called the police, and they should be here any minute." He gave her his keys and pointed to his car. "Go with the kids and make sure they stay inside of that car."

"Where are you going?"

"That's my family, too, Bre. I'm gonna do what I can to make sure they're safe."

She could see Munda had great concern with what was taking place, but she wasn't certain there was anything anyone could do. Tony had lost complete control of himself.

"Is this your way of proving you're a man? You want to kill the mother of your kids and your own son?"

Tony looked around to see who was speaking to him.

Munda said, "Why don't you put your gun down and let's talk?"

"Who the fuck is you?"

"That's my family, man. I don't have any intentions of letting anything happen to any of them. If you're ready to beat up on someone, come on."

"Fuck you, man!"

Little by little, Munda moved closer to Tony.

"Is this what you want? Is this what you want your kids to remember about you, Tony?"

Tony turned and focused his attention on Munda. "I'll kill your ass, too. You think I give a damn about what you think or say? You don't know who the fuck you talking to."

"Obviously, I'm talking to a coward, trying to keep him from making a grave mistake."

Betty and Jamar were still sitting and holding each other tight, too afraid to move.

"Kick his sorry ass!" someone shouted out.

"Yeah, kick his bitch ass!" someone else shouted.

By this time, the street was lined with cop cars, and an ambulance had arrived as well. Munda was now within arm's length of Tony. Betty could see he was pissed beyond any level she could ever imagine. The two men began arguing, and without warning, Tony placed the pistol to Munda's head.

"Tell your fucking family goodbye, boy!"

Bre jumped out of the car, trying to get to Munda, but she was held back. Suddenly, there were two shots.

"Munda!" Breanna shouted as tears raced down her face. She was devastated and didn't know what to do. She was trembling and crying uncontrollably. All she could think was that she'd lost the one man she truly loved. She fell to her knees and cried out. "Why, God?" Her fists were clinched and pulled into her chest as tears kept pouring.

"Mommy, Mommy, I want my daddy!" Alex screamed.

As she came up to reach for Alex, there was Charles. He was standing there watching her cry out for Munda. The crowd was noisy, but she couldn't see anything because the cops were keeping everyone back. The crowd opened, and she could hear her name being called. It was Betty searching for her. Jamar was holding on to his younger brother as Betty was trying to hold on to both of them. They were crying. Jamar's face was wet from tears. He had a peaceful but distant look on his face.

Breanna hugged Betty and the boys as they ran to meet her. She couldn't thank God enough for sparing the lives of the people she loved so much. They all looked at each other and held tight for a moment without saying anything.

"Bre, go to Munda," Betty said as she wiped away her tears and looked in the direction of the front porch, where everything had unfolded. Tony shot Munda before he was killed by a member of the S.W.A.T. team.

Breanna walked slowly to the porch where paramedics were frantically working on Munda. He wasn't moving, and he was barely breathing. "My dear God, don't take him away from us," Bre cried as she looked to the sky.

Munda began to moan and mumble Breanna's name.

"I'm here, Munda. I'm not gonna leave you, but you have to hold on, please. I love you, Munda. Don't leave us. You have to fight." Sobbing uncontrollably, Bre feared she'd lost him until she heard him call her name. She stopped crying and looked over at him as his weak eyes focused on her.

"Betty and the boys," he mumbled.

"They're fine. Don't worry. We have to get you better now."

The paramedics loaded Munda into the ambulance and headed for the hospital. As Bre turned to look for Betty and the kids, Charles was standing there watching her. He heard her as she told Munda she loved him. There was nothing either one of them could say as their eyes met. The same thing Bre had been denying to Charles was now out. He knew there was no way he could hold on to her any longer. After witnessing the intense emotions she and Munda shared, he knew it wasn't about the son they shared. It was about the love they shared for each other.

The End

www.ingramcontent.com/pod-product-compliance
Lightning Source LLC
Chambersburg PA
CBHW071331250626
47159CB00004B/1562